MW01165112

Praise for Carolan Ivey's *A Ghost of a Chance*

"A GHOST OF A CHANCE is imaginative in its originality, and the dynamic characters are absolutely memorable."

~ *Amelia Richard, ecataromance.com*

"Well written and always gripping, this one had me turning the pages eagerly just to see where Ms. Ivey will take me next."

~ *MrsGiggles.com*

Look for these titles by

Carolan Ivey

Now Available:

In the Gloaming: Abhainn's Kiss

Love and Lore: Wildish Things

Legends Series

Beaudry's Ghost (Book 1)

A Ghost of a Chance (Book 2)

Print Anthologies

Love and Lore

In the Gloaming

A Ghost of a Chance

Carolan Ivey

A Samhain Publishing, Ltd. publication.

Samhain Publishing, Ltd.
577 Mulberry Street, Suite 1520
Macon, GA 31201
www.samhainpublishing.com

A Ghost of a Chance
Copyright © 2009 by Ivey, Carolan
Print ISBN: 978-1-60504-412-5
Digital ISBN: 978-1-60504-261-9

Editing by Lindsey McGurk
Cover by Tuesday Dube

This book is a work of fiction. The names, characters, places, and incidents are products of the writer's imagination or have been used fictitiously and are not to be construed as real. Any resemblance to persons, living or dead, actual events, locale or organizations is entirely coincidental.

All Rights Are Reserved. No part of this book may be used or reproduced in any manner whatsoever without written permission, except in the case of brief quotations embodied in critical articles and reviews.

First Samhain Publishing, Ltd. electronic publication: December 2008
First Samhain Publishing, Ltd. print publication: October 2009

Dedication

For B.J.

We miss you, Mom.

Acknowledgements

Rick. As always, for always.

J.C. Wilder. Who knows where all the bodies are buried.

Liz Craven, Anya Delvay, Patricia A.B. King and Beth Williamson. The devil is, indeed, in the details. You are all goddesses.

Kemberlee Shortland, for insight into How Things Work in Ireland.

Again, the Civil War re-enactors of CompuServe's History Forum, particularly Duchess, Gene, and Pappy. Any mistakes are mine alone.

To everyone who kept after me to bring Troy's story to life: Thank you!

Chapter One

Gráinne Cottage, Dingle Peninsula, Ireland

"I cannot complete this reading."

The older woman's hands moved quickly to gather the Tarot cards spread on the kitchen table, the movement causing the flame of the single white candle at its center to flicker.

Carey Magennis leaned back in the creaky wooden chair, trying to decide if she should be amused or alarmed. For now, she chose the former. After all, Genola's informal Tarot reading was only for fun.

She sipped her tea, admiring the vase of freshly picked heather on the table. The moist breath of an afternoon breeze felt unusually cool on her cheek as it puffed in through the open window. But then again, an Irish July felt downright arctic to any North Carolina native. The morning rain had passed, and through the storm door she saw the rich, green hillside below the cottage. Beyond, the sea glittered like muted pewter. Great Blaskett Island lay a few miles offshore like a sleeping giant, half covered by a fluffy blanket of mist.

She had left Kyle poring over maps and guidebooks while she had gone in search of a cup of tea to settle her still-queasy stomach, the aftermath of getting food poisoning from a Killarney restaurant. Thanks to her twenty-four-hour stint on her knees before the porcelain god, they were now a full day behind schedule. They were darned lucky Genola McCarthy had a vacancy in her little cottage B&B at the height of tourist season. Carey had been too ill to make it to their original destination.

Kyle had been less than thrilled with the comparatively rustic accommodations, but Carey, now that she was well enough to have a look around, loved the old stone cottage with its thick, whitewashed walls and cozy thatched roof. Traces of the morning peat fire still tanged the air inside the little dwelling, blending with the aroma of fresh bread baking in the Aga.

Genola had welcomed her warmly into the homey, low-ceilinged kitchen, and cheerfully joined her for a cup of strong Irish tea with plenty of fresh milk and sugar. Spying the new engagement ring on Carey's left hand, Genola had reached into her apron pocket and withdrawn a set of Tarot cards, saying with a wink that she was going to see how long it would be before Carey and Kyle began adding to their respective family trees.

Carey glanced down now at the sparkling diamond solitaire on her left ring finger as Genola continued to gather the spread-out cards. She'd thought they'd only be spending a few days in Dublin, he making contacts for his fledgling, international real-estate development firm, while she wandered in and out of old churches and museums, feeding her insatiable appetite for all things historic. But he'd presented her a ring at dinner one night—in between taking business calls on his mobile phone—and swept her off on a surprise whirlwind tour of Ireland, attempting to see the entire country in five scant days.

She idly turned her hand and wondered why the sight of the glittering stone didn't set her heart to glittering in return. She ought to be deliriously happy. She should. After all, her life was turning out exactly as she'd planned.

"Are the spirits carrying around erasers these days?" She tore her gaze from the ring and, propping her chin in her palm, winked to let the woman know she was only kidding.

Genola smiled and winked in return. "Oh, 'tis nothing, darlin'. Simply a mistake, that's all."

"What kind of mistake?" Carey was relieved to see the Death card disappear back into the deck.

"This blank card—" Genola held it up, "—shouldn't have been in the deck. It's included only to replace a lost card." She put the card back into a small wooden box and firmly shut the lid, then shuffled the deck three times. "Now, let's be after tryin' this again. Please cut the deck into three piles."

Carey did as she was told, and watched Genola restack and spread the cards across the table with one smooth motion.

"And choose three cards, please."

Again, Carey pulled three cards at random and placed them facedown in front of her.

Genola turned over the first card, and Carey swallowed a gasp. It stuck in a painful knot at the base of her throat before she forced herself to relax.

"Now that's interesting," said Genola, unconcerned. "You drew the Death card again. This card represents your past, and at some point..."

"I'm going to die?" Carey croaked, only half joking.

Genola chuckled. "Not at all, dear. You simply underwent a time of great change. Or you will. Sometimes the timeline is a bit vague."

Carey relaxed, leaned her elbows on the table again, and allowed a small smile. "Well, I got engaged recently. Maybe that's it. And I lost my parents at a very young age..." She quickly shut her mouth. This wasn't something she normally shared with relative strangers.

Genola stilled, her expression distressed. "I'm so sorry, child."

Carey reached out and patted one of Genola's hands. "It's all right. It was a long time ago and my aunt raised me."

Genola relaxed, then looked her up and down, eyes slightly unfocused. "Your aura is very strong, particularly around you heart. It's bright green." Her eyes focused again and she smiled gently. "I thought when I first saw you, that you had the look of a faerie child."

Carey found herself toying with one of her wild black curls. Chemical processing had tamed the unruly mass that was her hair, but Ireland's damp weather had brought back its tendency to kink. All she had managed to learn about this gift from her father's side of the family were four tight-lipped words, "Black Irish and Indian." At which point her aunt's lips would compress into a tight, thin line.

"Faerie. Yes, well, I don't much resemble Tinker Bell," she said ruefully, remembering her own mother's petite, fair beauty, lost to her now except in photographs.

"Oh, the other crowd are nothing like you see in the movies. The Magennis people in Ireland are mostly fair in coloring, but once in a while they throw a dark one, and it's said such people are touched by the good folk. You may be several generations removed from Ireland, my dear, but the magic still lingers about you, that I can see."

Oh, this was getting good. Carey dismissed the uncomfortable notion that Genola McCarthy could somehow know exactly how she'd been feeling these past months. As if she were poised on some great precipice of change. She'd chalked it up to the ticking of her biological clock.

The Irishwoman flipped the next card. "This card

represents your present. Oh...dear..."

Carey stared in amazement. She'd drawn the exact same card as last time.

"My, my! The oracle certainly is speaking strongly this afternoon." Genola's voice quavered a little, despite her efforts to sound cheerful. "I can't remember any other time someone has drawn the exact same cards in this way, in spite of the deck having been shuffled. Very...odd."

"What do you think it means?" Carey watched Genola's face. This was only a Tarot reading, for heaven's sake.

"This card represents your present situation. It's the suit of Wands, which is the suit of change, restlessness, possibly upheaval. And this is the Knight. There's a man involved. Quite possibly a blond man."

Curious, Carey leaned in for a closer look at the card in question. The card depicted a warrior in battered Athenian armor standing on a hilltop overlooking an ancient city. The soldier held a heavy sword, and a helmet adorned with a horse-tail plume covered his head. Lion-colored hair flowed out from under the helmet. But it was his direct stare that snagged her attention. His vivid green eyes—all she could see of his face—glowed like living things in the stillness of the picture.

She had the absurd notion that she wished she could step into the picture and straight into his protective arms. With a hard mental shake, she tore her gaze away from the warrior and noticed a banner flying over the city in the background. It was clearly labled *Troy*.

Her scalp prickled.

"Interesting." She tried to sound offhand. "My middle name is Helen."

Genola's eyebrow went north. "Is that so? You should see the queen of this suit. It is, indeed, Helen of Troy."

A woman who brought disaster down on an entire kingdom for loving the wrong man. Carey's stomach started to feel funny again, and she forced herself to relax. "But I don't know any blond men. At least not well enough to consider them part of my personal life."

Genola smiled, serenely confident again. "If there isn't one now, there will be. And I daresay his entrance won't be subtle."

"Hm. If you say so." Maybe Kyle was going to bleach his dark hair or something. Then she laughed to herself. Not bloody likely.

"I certainly do say so." Genola nodded and reached for the third card. "Well, then let's see what all these changes and this mysterious blond man will mean for your future. At least we know the card won't be..." she flipped the card, "...blank."

Now Carey's heart really did turn over. What the...?

Genola's calm demeanor vanished, and she turned white.

The card was blank. Again.

"Impossible," Genola whispered. "I just put that card back in the box. You saw me put it there, didn't you?"

"Don't be silly," said Carey, reaching for the box and popping off the lid. "Maybe it stuck to your hand."

But the first blank card still lay inside. She looked up at Genola. "Is there more than one blank card in this deck?"

Genola shook her head. "Only one."

"Do it again."

"What?"

"Shuffle the cards and let me draw again."

Genola seemed to come back to herself. "Of course, of course." She gathered the cards and began to shuffle them, then her fingers slowed. "Let's try a different deck. This one's new—I haven't worked with it much." She leaned back in her chair, reached into a half-open kitchen drawer, and extracted a small, battered wooden box. Sweeping the offending deck off the table and back into its own box, she spread the well-used deck face up on the table so they could both see that no blank cards lurked. Then she quickly shuffled, humming softly to herself as she worked.

"Now," she said confidently, her face relaxing into another smile. "This deck has never failed me."

Again Carey went through the ritual of drawing three cards, wondering why she was doing this when she ought to be telling Genola "t'anks, but no t'anks".

"Here we go." Genola turned over the first card.

Carey gave a bark of surprised laughter and nearly fell out of her chair.

The Death card grinned mockingly up at her.

"Ehm..." Genola turned the middle card. Knight of Wands. Again. "I, ah, don't know what to say, Miss Magennis. I truly don't. This has never, ever happened before. To draw the exact same cards repeatedly? From different decks..." She reached for the third card, her hand visibly trembling.

Carey reached out and gripped her wrist. "Let me." If the woman was indeed doing a sleight of hand, she was going to make darned sure it didn't happen again. Not that she believed in this stuff, not at all. But she'd rather sleep without nightmares, thank you very much.

She turned the card. Blank. She let it drop from her numb fingers.

Get a hold of yourself, girl. It's a trick. Just a trick.

She forced a laugh and quickly gulped the rest of her tea. "You're very good. Ever thought of going on the road?" Her laugh trailed off when the other woman said nothing.

Genola didn't look at her, but down at the cards, her face pale and still. Then she looked up at Carey, her eyes seeing something beyond the here and now.

"I tell you, miss, these cards have never lied."

Carey gave the woman what she hoped was a bright smile that hid how rattled she was. "Thanks, Mrs. McCarthy. I…think I'll take a little walk down to the headland. Kyle should be finished re-planning our schedule, thanks to me and my rebellious tummy."

Genola nodded and began picking up the cards, one by one, examining each one as if she'd never seen it before. Carey rose from the chair, uneasy and unsure what to say next. Genola touched her arm as she passed, eyes troubled.

"Just be careful, miss. Be very, very careful."

Carey chuckled again, trying to put the poor woman—and herself?—at ease. "Oh, don't worry. My fiancé plans everything down to the last detail. I won't have time to get myself into trouble. Trust me."

Cape Hatteras Beach, North Carolina

Where the hell are you, John?

Troy Brannon gave in to frustration and roared out loud, the release of energy kicking up a half-dozen whirlwinds that scattered Outer Banks sand in every direction.

A nearby fisherman yelped in surprise, hunched his shoulders against the onslaught and dropped his gear into the knee-deep Atlantic surf.

"Ah, hell." Troy muttered an unheard apology as the startled man gathered up his gear and warily scanned the skies, undoubtedly wondering if an errant nor'easter was on the way.

Troy turned his face toward the late-morning sun he could not feel in any normal way, except perhaps how a battery feels when it's in recharge mode. He pivoted in a slow circle, trying to focus his scattered thoughts, trying to hone in on the familiar energy pattern of John Garrison's missing spirit. A spirit Troy himself was responsible for losing.

Most people, he mused as he watched the frightened fisherman make his way over the dunes, thought ghosts were just protoplasmic mist floating around in some nether world. Scary on a dark night, but basically harmless.

He indulged in a grim smile. If only they knew how much havoc one determined spirit could wreak on the tangible world.

He ought to know. He'd wreaked enough of it all by himself to affect the lives of dozens of people. One in particular. The one he'd meddled with and lost.

He knew John's energy fingerprint. He'd felt it when he'd wrested the man's spirit from his body so another desperate spirit, that of a Union soldier named Jared Beaudry, could use it to regain honor lost during the Civil War. He'd felt it again when he'd tried to guide John back to where he belonged. But he'd failed. In some misguided attempt to be noble, John had let Jared's spirit remain in his body while he took his chances elsewhere.

The trouble was, Troy had no idea where that *elsewhere* was. In the blink of an eye, John had disappeared into the void of space and time. Troy'd had the devil's own time learning to drill down through time as well as he could move himself through space. But with his inborn bulldoggedness, he'd figured out how to focus his thoughts and energies in just the right way. It was a tremendous drain, and after each jump it took him hours, if not days, to recover.

The process was tedious and more time-consuming than he'd anticipated, penetrating down through layers of time and sweeping the area he'd last seen John on the Outer Banks. Day by day. Hour by hour. Hell, minute by minute. He'd come up empty, time after time. He'd gone as far into the past as he dared—he wasn't sure how far his ability extended—and back again until he'd bumped up against an unexpected ceiling. What he could only surmise was his twin sister Taylor's current time. He could sense her nearby. She must not have moved far from where she'd last seen him.

Good girl. Stay right there, Tee. I'll find you after I'm done here.

Troy scratched his head—an old habit left over from when he'd possessed a body of his own—and dredged up from his memory what he'd learned about the real Jared Beaudry. Where he'd been born, what battles he'd fought in. Maybe John would end up there. If not... Troy closed his eyes against the daunting task before him.

A task with a ticking clock. For a long time now, he'd sensed he was being tailed. Probably by forces that were none too pleased that a lowly human spirit such as himself had learned to mess with people's souls, to skip through time and space at will. Staying one step ahead of those who would force him to be a good boy and get along to heaven.

Troy had no use for heaven. He had things to do, rights to wrong. A family to protect.

He groaned, his formidable powers of concentration failing him, exhaustion threatening to send his energy sinking into the sand at his feet, where it would lay until he found the strength to gather himself up again. He couldn't let that happen. It left him too vulnerable.

One more time, he promised himself. One more sweep and

he'd take a break. Touch base with Taylor—she was bound to be worried sick. And if she was still in the same expectant condition as when he'd left her, she didn't need any extra burdens right now. Focusing his energy like a beam from the nearby Hatteras lighthouse, he swept the area, his back to the sea. Too tired to care where he aimed, he swept wider, letting the momentum turn him around.

Whoa.

He froze in a twisted position, torqued somewhat to the northeast. He felt something stir in his chest and he gasped at the unexpected contact. What was that? Who?

Not John, he told himself. He must have forgotten to tune out all other energies in his quest for John's unique pattern. This one was nothing like he'd felt before. It seemed to reach out and touch him from head to toe, side to side, humming and singing along his energy meridians like warm water turned to music. His weary soul, acutely aware all of a sudden how long he'd been without a living body, drank it in, begged for more.

He tilted his head and let the vibrations form a vision. Green hills. A white, thatched-roof house with a scarlet door. Fields enclosed in seemingly random stone walls. A vertical, black cliff with cold, crashing waves at the base. Ireland.

Troy clenched his jaw and reluctantly turned away, intending to break contact. But something brought him back, making him turn all the way around to face northeast. He narrowed his eyes as this new energy wavered and flickered, like a candle caught in a high wind. In danger of going out.

She's in trouble.

He had no idea how he knew this energy was a she, but he'd learned not to question his instincts. No matter how often they'd gotten him in trouble. Forgetting John for the moment, Troy focused on this new target.

It was too far. Across open water. And he had no time for this.

He narrowed his energy with laser precision to the northeast and prepared to make the jump.

Powell Beach House, near Cape Hatteras Lighthouse

Taylor would deny it, but with each passing day—and each additional inch to her expanding belly—Jared Beaudry thought she grew more beautiful.

He'd glanced up from his task of sanding the beach house's porch railing as Taylor's blue pickup crunched on the driveway gravel. Frowned mentally at the long, lean lines of her body, still a bit too thin despite her wolfish prenatal appetite. He dropped the sandpaper and hit the bottom step before she finished gathering an armload of grocery sacks from behind the front seat.

She squeaked in surprise as she turned into him. In one smooth motion he neatly relieved her of her burden and tucked her under the other arm. He lifted his chin an inch to tuck the top of her head under it. She relaxed and settled there like she was made to fit in the space.

"How did your session with Daira go?"

Her sigh was hollow. "Rough. But I managed a whole minute bare-handed without any visions this time."

"And after a minute?"

"Daira's dead grandmother told me in no uncertain terms to get my paws off her string of pearls."

He squeezed his eyes shut and held her closer. This was all his fault.

"This was a long time coming," she said into his neck. "It

would have had to happen sooner or later."

"Will you stop reading my mind?"

"I don't have to. Besides, I've been in your mind. Cobwebs. Yeesh." She gave a mock shudder of revulsion.

Jared laughed, and caught Lily Brannon's gaze over the top of her daughter's head as she ambled around from the truck's passenger side. Her eyes, exactly like Taylor's, sparkled with a knowing that made him blush and set Taylor a few inches away from him.

Public displays of affection were something he was still getting used to in this century. Particularly in front of a woman who wasn't quite sure what to make of the man who had come out of nowhere to tell her—not ask her, *insist*—that he was marrying her daughter.

Lily grinned and took the grocery bags off his other arm. "I'll take these and get dinner started... Who's that?"

The dinging chime of an open car-door alarm reached his ears. He turned his head in the direction of her raised eyebrow as Taylor muttered, "Uh oh," and pulled her big overshirt closed around her body.

A tall, middle-aged man strode toward them, apparently too agitated to remember to remove his car keys and close the door of his nondescript rental car. He wore an older version of the face Jared had almost gotten used to seeing in the mirror.

"Ross," Jared muttered.

In the next second Taylor was behind him. Whether he'd moved first or she had, he didn't know. His instinct to shield her was automatic. *Stupid*, he thought. *This is John's father. He's no threat to us.* Not physically, anyway. But to Taylor's emotional stability, Ross Garrison was the worst kind of threat.

He opened his mouth. Closed it. Stuttered a little before

Taylor's subtle poke in the back helped him get the word out. "Dad." He had seen Ross only once before, a few days after the re-enactment that had irrevocably changed his, Taylor's and John's lives. Jared had put in a brief, awkward appearance at the family law office in Columbus, Ohio to raid John's files for information vital to his survival in this modern, unfamiliar world. Thanks to Taylor's friend Stephen, who had accompanied him and knew which strange pieces of equipment to take, Jared had managed to get in and out of the office with a minimum of fuss. It also helped that everyone there had been too stunned by the bandages and purple bruises on his face to respond when he'd shown up to announce he—rather, John—would be taking an extended leave of absence.

Apparently, Ross hadn't been satisfied and had come looking for him. Not an easy task, as Jared had found it fairly simple to stay, as Taylor put it, "off the grid". In his time, the telegraph had been brand-new technology.

Ross stopped a few paces away and settled into a deceptively relaxed pose. "Son. We didn't get much of a chance to talk. Before."

"Yes. Um, no." Jared could feel Taylor's eyes boring holes in his back.

An awkward silence, in which the Outer Banks wind rustled the plastic grocery bags still dangling from Lily's arms. A seagull wheeled overhead in the late-morning sun, its yodeling *scree* punctuating the tension.

"Aren't you going to introduce me?"

Jared started guiltily. Manners were something his own parents had drilled into him back in the nineteenth century, and apparently John Garrison's had been no different. That Ross bore more than a passing resemblance to Jared's own father made his throat kink in painful knots. He took a half step to one side, enough so Taylor could see around him but not enough that Ross could get a clear view of her.

"Ah...yes. D-Dad, this is Mrs. Lily Brannon and her daughter Taylor. Taylor, Mrs. Brannon—"

"Lily," she put in.

Damn it. "Lily, this is Ross Garrison. My father." John's father, he reminded himself. And for John's sake, he would make an effort at normalcy.

Ross stepped around him and extended a hand toward Taylor. She reflexively let go of her overshirt and returned the gesture. His gaze flicked down at the thick gloves she wore, and up. Then back down to stare at her rounded belly, which had only recently started showing enough to leave no doubt.

Ross's dark eyebrows went north and his mouth looked like it wanted to form words, but had forgotten how. "Ah," he finally managed. "Now I'm beginning to see—"

Before Jared could respond, a golden flash of blonde hair zipped past his peripheral vision and Lily Brannon planted her diminutive self under Ross's nose.

"I know what you're thinking, and it's not what it looks like," she snapped, fists planted on hips.

Ross looked down and backed up a step, as if a snake had unexpectedly reared its head out of the sandy yard. Startled...and maybe just a little scared. Jared crossed his arms and prepared himself to enjoy the show.

"Mom..." Taylor began.

"You have *no* idea what these children have been through in the past few months. The last thing they need—"

"*Mom!*"

Ross's gaze snapped back and forth between the sputtering mother hen in front of him, and the taller, younger version over her shoulder. His brow furrowed deeper with each shift.

"—is judgment passed on them by some...some *trial lawyer* who—"

"Ma'am..." Ross wasn't looking at Lily now. His gaze was locked on Taylor.

Bad move, Jared thought. Lily Brannon, once wound up, would not be ignored. Much like her daughter. No, *exactly* like her daughter.

"—sits in a cushy, leather-bound office deciding who's guilty or not guilty—"

Without a lick of warning, Ross put both hands on Lily's waist, picked her up and swung her to one side, setting her down as swiftly and gently as he'd lifted her. In the next second he'd lunged past her to catch Taylor just as her knees buckled.

Muttering a curse for allowing himself to get distracted, Jared managed to catch one of her arms. He placed it around his shoulders, pulling her away from Ross as he bent and picked her up with his other arm under her shaking knees. He got one look at Ross's stricken face as he swept her toward the front door.

The expression on it was not unlike the one on John's before he'd slipped out of Jared's grasp and vanished into the void of space and time. Determination...and sheer terror.

"Jared." Taylor's whisper rasped in his ear. "Troy was here. I felt him. Then he was gone."

He headed up the steps and into the house, throwing over his shoulder, "Make yourself at home, Dad."

Behind him, he heard two sets of feet hit the wooden steps at a run.

"Now look what you've done," hissed Lily.

"Me?" barked Ross.

Jared half turned to get at the doorknob with one free hand.

"Your door's open," Lily remarked, and curled a lip in satisfaction when Ross's gaze automatically dropped to his own fly. "Your *car* door, genius."

Ross spun on his heel, muttering under his breath.

"God help us all," Jared breathed to himself.

Hours later, their stomachs comfortably full of Lily's cooking, Taylor made contented nesting sounds deep in her throat as Jared slipped into bed to spoon himself behind her.

"Mmmm. You're naked."

"These days, I think it's best to follow your lead." He smoothed his hand over her warm, bare belly then up to cup one of her breasts.

"Smart man." She covered his hand with hers, still gloved, and let a few moments of silence pass. Then, "I think he took it well, don't you?"

He remembered Ross's look of total concentration as he and Taylor had carefully laid out all the details of how his son's spirit had gone missing during that April re-enactment of the Battle of Roanoke Island.

And how all hope for his recovery lay in the hands of her dearly departed brother, Troy.

Ross had sat for a long time leaning forward in the kitchen chair, elbows on knees, staring at his loosely clasped hands before nodding curtly, getting up and going out for a long walk. In an hour he had returned and, without a word, picked up a piece of sandpaper and helped Jared finish the porch railing.

After dinner Ross had set up his laptop and was on his cell

phone, barking orders to some unfortunate underling to ship a variety of office equipment from his Columbus, Ohio law firm to the Outer Banks beach house.

"I think he's probably dialing that cellar phone of his to cart us both off to an asylum," Jared said into her hair.

"That would be a *cellular* phone, dearest."

"Cellar, cellular...it's still the most evil contraption ever invented."

"No argument from me on that point."

"I think Ross is more concerned that I haven't married you yet." He felt her body shift as her defenses went up.

"I did make it clear that you asked."

"I'm still asking. And if you don't make a decision soon I'm not going to give you the luxury of a choice."

She rolled over in place and faced him, her eyes flashing in the gathering darkness. "We've already had this discussion, Jared." Then she sighed quietly. "It's been months. At some point we're going to be finished renovating this house for Stephen, and we'll have to decide what's next for us. I...can't go back to my job at the museum. Technically you have a license to practice law in Ohio..."

"Thanks to John's investments, when the time is right I will find my place in this century. That's the least of my worries." Jared smoothed her shaggy, chin-length hair behind her ear. "When Troy's found something, he'll come to you no matter where we are. I have no doubt."

"That's what I'm afraid of. That he's found *something*. Otherwise, why was he here and gone so fast?"

He reached across her body to open the drawer on the bedside table, extracting a brass Civil War infantry uniform button. "Then summon him." Knowing her damnable sense of honor precisely matched her brother's, Jared knew what her answer would be. But it was the only way to break her out of her downward spiral of worry. It wasn't good for her. Or the baby.

She took the button and turned it over and over in her gloved fingers. "I could."

"But you won't."

"No." Her voice was small. She dropped the button back into the drawer, slid it shut and turned into his arms.

"Don't worry, Miss Taylor. If it comes down to it..."

She drew back, expression tortured. "You'll what? Tell John sorry, he can't have his body back after all? What if you don't have a choice, Jared? What if I marry you now, but wind up legally married to a virtual stranger? What if..."

He placed a hand on either side of her head and made her look into his eyes. "Our child. Will have. A name. And a family on both sides that will love and protect him."

She blinked. Then a half smile played at one corner of her mouth. "You've been waiting a long time to play that card, haven't you?"

There. Distraction mission accomplished. "Once I saw my...the way Ross looked at you, I knew it was safe to lay my last one down."

Taylor rolled back over and pulled his arm around her. Her next words were muffled.

"What was that?"

"I said..." and she muttered something into the pillow.

He felt a grin spread wide across his face. "I didn't quite catch that."

She lifted her head and tossed over her shoulder, "I said *okay. You win.*" She flopped back down and muttered another word into the pillow that sounded distinctly like *bastard.*

Jared laughed, pulled her closer and closed his eyes.

Damn it, Troy, where the hell are you?

Chapter Two

It's true, Genola. Tarot cards don't lie.

Carey pressed her face to the rock, fighting with the last of her survival instinct against the sucking current. Fighting to keep from being swept farther back into the dark, deep crevices of the sea cave where no one would ever find...

...my body.

The tide hadn't finished rising yet, and she had only a scant inch of breathing space remaining. She wasn't strong enough to overcome the rushing water, so cold it stole what little breath she had left.

She'd only meant to be a few minutes. But a moment's curiosity about the cave mouth beckoning in the seaside cliff had turned into over an hour of exploration. Her ignorance of how swiftly the tide could come in had cost her.

Icy salt water washed over her face. She coughed and sobbed, feet treading water and fingers scrabbling in a futile search for a fresh handhold. The slippery, unforgiving rock yielded none. No light, long ago blocked out by the dark water rising above the cave mouth. By feel, she found a knob in the rock and tried to hook her camera-bag strap over it. At least after she drowned, she thought distantly, maybe she would be lucky enough to have her body found and taken back home to North Carolina to bury. Odd how her thoughts boiled down to practical matters at a time like this. No time to waste weeping, regretting. *Just make sure whatever mess you leave behind is easy for someone else to clean up.*

She pictured Kyle standing by the compact rental car, checking his watch and frowning as he scanned the countryside for her. He'd be muttering something about falling behind schedule and needing to buy a leash, first town they hit.

Another surge, and her breathing space vanished. She sucked water into her lungs and ruthlessly quelled the urge to cough.

This is it. Oh God, Kyle, I'm sorry...

The current surged, swirling and pulling at her as if trying to suck her down a drain. The camera strap held, cutting cruelly into her upper back as she curled her fingers around it and willed them to lock into place, vowing not to let go as she was buffeted without mercy against the cave roof. A small sound purled out of her throat as sharp rocks jabbed every part of her body.

Even those sensations faded away as the cold water numbed her to the bone, and her world narrowed down to the ever-increasing burning in her lungs and her effort to hold firm against the uncontrollable urge to gasp. She clamped one hand over her nose and mouth, knowing it was a futile gesture. She twisted the other hand ferociously in order to permanently tangle it in the strap.

Then, muscle by muscle, she felt her body begin to weaken, relax into the inevitable. Her head buzzed and her ears rang, her brain's alarm bells screaming for oxygen. She could almost hear it as sections of her brain began to shut down. *Don't breathe, don't breathe,* some last vestige of her conscious mind insisted. *Hang on, help will come. It will. It will...*

Gradually, her senses dulled. Her skin began to feel warm

instead of numb and cold. The water seemed to gentle, rocking. She let her free hand drift away from her face. She let her mouth fall open. *Somebody...please...help me...*

Distantly she felt her body jerk once, twice, as salty seawater flowed over her tongue and filled her lungs. No pain. No panic. She listened with detached bemusement as her heartbeat slowed, then stopped.

It's over.

All around her was dark and quiet, save for the distant sound of rushing water. Even that, too, was fading. She opened her eyes and wondered why she didn't feel dead. Though she wasn't exactly sure how she was supposed to feel at this moment, having never done this sort of thing before.

Then, in the distance, she saw a silver orb of light floating toward her.

She'd always heard that when someone died, they saw a light and went through it. Instinctively she reached for it.

Then, to her surprise, a man came out of the light and reached for her.

"Look! There she is!"

Genola hurried to the cliff edge. Toward where Kyle Thorpe leaned precariously into space.

The sea wind tore at her ruana and lashed her hair around her face. Heart in her throat, she unceremoniously grabbed the back of his belt and hauled him back from the edge.

"You'll not be wantin' to join her just now!" she said firmly.

Kyle brushed her hands aside, dropped to his belly and hitched his dark head and broad shoulders over the edge, peering down with his binoculars pressed to his eye sockets.

She fell to her knees beside him, shielding her eyes against the wind as she scanned the damp-blackened rocks a hundred feet below. There! A dot of yellow, the exact color of the jacket Carey had been wearing when she'd slipped out the back door that morning, promising to return after a short stroll along the path that followed the cliffs overlooking the sea. Now the jacket was dirty and flapping in the wind around her still, curled-up form.

"How in blazes did she get down there?" he muttered, and Genola glanced at him, curious. He seemed more angry than worried.

"There's a path, used by sheep, mostly. It would be impassable now."

"First the food poisoning and now this. I swear, that woman is..." He fell silent before completing the sentence. "I'm going to have to go after her," he finished, more than a glimmer of annoyance in his voice as he shoved his binoculars into her hands. He rose to his knees and whipped off his windbreaker.

"You'll do no such thing! Those rocks are no place for you to be climbin' on."

He gestured at the sky, at the boiling wall of storm clouds sweeping in from the Atlantic, already enveloping nearby Great Blaskett Island in a curtain of rain. "The tide is still rising! She'll—"

Genola gripped his arm, digging her fingers in to make him listen. "Run as fast as you can to the house. Go to the kitchen telephone and dial nine-nine-nine. The coastal search and rescue will have the right equipment, and will know what to do."

Kyle drove his hands through his hair as the first fat drops of rain smacked the ground and what was left of the sun disappeared behind the rising storm. "But I can't—"

"You can, and you must! You'll be doing her no good gettin'

yourself killed trying to save her!" She moved to the cliff's edge and looked down again, noticing for the first time a dark shape crouched next to the girl on the ledge. She blinked and put the binoculars to her eyes. The hair stood on the back of her neck the way it always did at...certain times. "Besides, it looks like she's bein' well taken care of."

"What do you mean?" Kyle took the binoculars and peered down at Carey. "Who is that down there with her?"

Genola furrowed her brow. The anger in his voice was unmistakable now. "Does it matter? Keeping her alive, he is."

Kyle looked again, and shook his head. He handed her the binoculars, distracted. "Whatever. We'll sort it out later. I'll go make that phone call."

Genola pushed him on his way. "Get on with you. You can move faster than my old joints. I will watch over Miss Magennis."

And Kyle was gone, tearing up the long, green slope so fast she was sure not a raindrop landed on him.

Hesitant, she crouched and leaned over the cliff, raising the binoculars to her eyes once more.

There he was. No mistaking it. The powerful lenses focused on a man in black who crouched on the ledge with cat-like grace. As she watched, the man moved his body to shield Carey from the rain and wind, pressed his fingers to the side of her neck. The ledge was so narrow Genola wondered how he stayed on it without the aid of climbing gear. A giant wave crashed into the cliff base, washing heavily over the ledge and almost taking them both with it as it receded.

Genola watched the man catch Carey in his arms, lift and move her to a wider spot, then turn so she was shielded from the wet by his impossibly broad shoulders and lithe body. She couldn't be sure from this angle, but it looked like his face was pressed to Carey's, his ribs expanding and contracting, perhaps giving her mouth-to-mouth. The black shirt he wore stretched tight across his muscled back, a hole revealing torn flesh. She blinked as his image flickered and started to fade. He threw his head back, eyes closed and face tense with strain, then his image solidified once more and he bent his head back to his work.

"'Tis an angel." Genola's heart beat faster. A few times in her life, since she was a girl, she had witnessed brief flashes of angels at work, but none of them had ever looked like this one. Those angels had always had snow-white wings. This one—she checked again—definitely had none.

Then, as if he sensed someone watching, he looked up, his vivid green eyes meeting hers. The wind rippled short, dark blond hair across his forehead.

The blond man in the reading. The Knight of Wands...

"Oh, no," Genola muttered, still staring at the scene through the binoculars as the man looked away and again bent his head over Carey's.

"No, indeed. You're no angel. Ye're the devil himself."

Troy had never stayed in a materialized state for this long. The strain tore at him, threatened to separate the layers of his energy field and send them flying off into space like water rings from a dropped stone.

It had taken every atom of his strength to make the three-thousand-mile spatial jump, on top of staying solid long enough to rescue the woman from the flooded cave. He'd intended to bring her all the way to the top of the cliff, leave her there to be found and be on his way about finding John.

But the effort had cost him.

Troy glanced down at the face of the woman in his arms, grit his teeth and held on.

If he lost control of his energy and faltered, she would die.

His superb sense of balance, an asset in life and still now in the afterlife, didn't fail him as he crouched on the narrow rock ledge, braced so the woman's body wouldn't slide off into the roiling sea. Rain slapped them from above, and the wind and waves clawed at them from everywhere else.

Risking precious balance, he used one hand to gently unwind her long, matted black hair from around his arm and away from her face. Her lips were blue and slack, her eyes partially open and dull. He lowered his face to hers, checking for breath. Nothing. He let her head roll to one side and slid his fingers to the pulse point on her neck. If any life throbbed there, he couldn't feel it for the vibrations of wind and storm.

"Oh, no you don't. Don't do this to me, lady..." He tilted her head back and covered her mouth with his.

He blew once, then swayed, dizzy, feeling his grip on his materialized state slipping dangerously with the extra effort it took to breathe for her. He clenched his jaw, tilted his head back and growled deep in his chest, willing his form to stay together, just a little longer. Just until help arrived. He'd seen two people poke their heads over the cliff edge above them, so he knew it wouldn't be long.

"Not yet," he muttered, using the vibration of his voice to send binding messages throughout his energy field, reminding it that no matter what the laws of physics said, he was in charge here. Never mind the fact that before now he'd only managed to stay solid for a few minutes at a time, and only in dire emergencies. The last time he'd done it was for the lives of his sister and Beaudry, and for his effort he'd earned a bullet in his shoulder to keep company with the gaping hole he carried around in his chest.

He lowered his mouth and breathed for her again, turning his head to feel her automatic exhale, this time accompanied by a gush of water.

Yes! Another breath into her lungs. Were her lips slightly warmer? He left his own there for a second or two longer than necessary, testing. A faint green color flickered in front of his eyes, like the brief flash of a hummingbird, there and gone. He tore his mouth away from hers and looked up to see what kind of strange lightning this could be, then he ducked and pressed her body tightly to his as a heavy wave broke over them. The water lifted them both off the ledge, and only by sheer will did he manage to bring them back onto it safely. How much higher was the tide going to rise?

He shook water from his face, pressed the woman's body firmly between himself and the cliff wall and bent his head to hers once again. She had to start breathing on her own soon. He couldn't keep this up.

A movement off to his right snagged his attention. A glowing figure, winged and silent, stood on a nearby ledge, observing, not moving. Her guardian angel, clearly. He spared the being a two-second glare, then lost patience.

"Hey! Aren't you going to do anything?"

The guardian's expression grew thoughtful, then regretful. But it didn't move, either to help or to hinder.

"Thanks a bunch." Troy turned back to the task at hand.

Breeeeeeathe...

Without thinking what he was doing, he willed life into her. Closed his eyes and focused his energy inside her body, targeting her lungs, her barely fluttering heart.

This time, he felt her jaw move under his mouth and her body flex in his arms. The weird, pale green lightning flickered around them again. Her first strong heartbeat resounded like a bell throughout his being, her first voluntary breath sucking in what he'd given her.

Then, before he could lift his mouth from hers, she breathed into him.

Troy nearly lost his balance, and flung out one arm to find a fingertip hold on the rock. Her breath filled his mouth, his chest, and even with his eyes closed he saw the faint green flickers of light strengthen, steady, intensify into a solid glow more brilliant than any Ireland had to offer on its best day. Heat rushed through him, and it took him a moment to register the fact that he felt it at all. As a ghost, normal physical sensations were foreign to him. Now every drop of rain hitting his skin felt like a needle. And his wounds, normally painless, now screamed at him.

He tore his mouth away and stared down at her. Her eyelids trembled, opened, light grey irises expanding as her pupils focused on his face. The same fiery emerald light that flashed round them burned in their depths. Even with their mouths now separated, her strengthening heartbeat rushed around him as if he were a child enveloped in her womb.

What the hell is happening to me?

If he was anywhere else but perched on a narrow ledge, an inch from losing her to the maw of the sea, he would have done a quick about-face and put as much space and time between them as possible. But stay he did, her life force growing stronger and flowing like a river under his hands, into him, through him and back to her. She seemed to be studying him, her mouth moving slightly as if trying to form words. But if she made any sound, it was swallowed by sea and storm. Then her eyes slid closed and her head rolled to nestle against his chest, fitting perfectly under his chin.

He swallowed, trying not to take in any more of the living energy that still enveloped them both. Something about it was as seductive as it was disturbing, and all his instincts screamed to get outside it and look at it from an objective distance before deciding what to do about it, if anything at all.

He took her cold hands, intending to tuck them inside her coat, when he caught sight of the diamond sparkling on her left ring finger.

She belongs to someone. Absurdly, the thought felt like a sucker punch to his gut.

He looked up, and finally, finally, he saw two people rappelling down the cliff, red-and-black jumpsuits making ripping sounds in the wind. A metal litter dangled between them.

"Take her first," he yelled above the crashing tide as the rescuers reached them. Their reply was lost in the noise, but they quickly assessed the situation and expertly relieved him of his burden.

The instant her body separated from his, he felt himself dissolving, the last of his strength leaving as the green light faded. One of the rescuers cried out in alarm, but could do nothing as his grip on the rock slipped, and the icy grey sea closed over his head.

With a supreme effort, Troy managed to pull his depleted energy into a ball and roll a few feet. It was an efficient shape, one he'd used most often in his travels. He hoped he hadn't left any scraps of himself behind among the smooth stones on the beach.

How long had he been lying here? Hard to tell. At least twelve hours, as it was now low tide and nearing dusk. Undoubtedly the media would report the woman's dramatic rescue and his heroic death.

He reached down deep and tried to focus his energy in a beam that would zip him out of here. He'd only driven himself to this point of exhaustion once before, but normally he had enough left to make an escape.

Nothing happened. Just a sense of strain, as if a velvet anchor held him in place.

What the hell...

He needed his energy recharged and he needed it now. Digging down deep, he looked for it...and found it in the shape of a woman's oval face, framed in riotous black curls that tickled the edges of a bright, green aura of energy that seemed to emanate from her heart.

No, not you...

He found himself standing up. Barely, but standing. Immediately he closed his eyes and focused his thoughts back on Cape Hatteras.

He opened them. He still stood alone on the empty Irish beach, staring down at the rocks and the tiny birds that pecked among them for food.

It couldn't be true. Dammit, it couldn't. He shut his eyes tight, gathering himself to make a short hop. Anywhere. Just to the top of the cliff. Hell, three inches to the left. Anything.

A stab of pain hit him at the base of the brain, and with a surprised grunt he fell to his knees. It was as if he were somehow attached to a large rubber band. The harder he strained against it, the quicker it yanked him back down. Worse, even when he stood still, he felt an unmistakable pull, as if there was someplace he had to be—bound and dragged against his will. He shut his eyes and fought an instant of panic. He'd managed to suppress his nearly crippling fear of tight places in order to get through basic training, but sometimes it blindsided him.

How did I let his happen?

If he couldn't move, what was to stop some heavenly cleaner crew from finding John Garrison first and forcing him and Beaudry to switch places again? Troy didn't want to think about the consequences. And the woman—someone in authority might take it upon themselves to undo his good deed.

"It's you. You're that angel I saw before, aren't you?"

Troy struggled to his feet, the pain fading rapidly as he turned to see who had spoken. An older woman stood not ten yards away, her ample figure wrapped tight in a deep purple shawl. The wind twisted its fringed edges around her knees and worked loose several strands of softly greyed brown hair from its bun. A basket overflowing with ribbons of green seaweed hung from one arm. In the other hand she clutched a handful of heather flowers. Curious blue eyes peered at him from her pleasantly weathered face.

Still caught up in his frustration, Troy forgot to be startled by her sudden appearance. He snapped his arms out to his sides. "You see any feathers here?"

She shifted the basket to the other arm. "Indeed I do not. If you've wings, they've been clipped."

"Then… Wait, you can see me?" He furtively checked to see if he'd inadvertently materialized, though he didn't see how that could happen. It took too much effort for it to happen accidentally.

"Not clearly, but I can. I've seen you before." She tilted her head, indicating with her expression she was none too pleased about that fact. "You're after looking for that girl, are ye not?"

He scowled so hard he almost hurt himself. "What girl?" he muttered, deliberately obtuse. Then he gave in to temporary hopelessness and jammed his hands through his hair. "Ah, damn."

The woman took a step closer, her voice softening in compassion. "Now, now, things cannot be as bad as all that."

"Ma'am, you have no idea. If I don't find her, let's just say there may be hell to pay." He looked up at the woman, remembering her previous words. "How do you know who I'm looking for? Do you know her?"

"I do. Your lady was a guest at my house three days ago. The little stone cottage up the way with the thatched roof, it is."

Three days. It had taken him three days to pull himself together. His brain began working overtime on some kind of plan to get him out of here and back on John's trail. The first thing he had to do was find this woman and find out if he was somehow tied to her. If so, his next task was to get himself untied. "Then you can tell me where she is? And her name. Jesus, I held her for hours on that ledge and I don't even know her name. If I can get to her—"

He cut off his words as he saw the woman's eyebrow rise toward the overcast sky. "And what makes you think I'll be tellin' you where to find her?"

Back off, Brannon. You're a little too desperate. "You saw me," he said. *Careful, now.* "You know I can't mean her any harm."

"I see," she said slowly. "You're not meanin' her any harm, but you say there'll be hell to pay if you don't find her. Now I ask you, my fallen angel, how am I to interpret that?" She leaned a little sideways, as if trying to get a glimpse of his back.

Troy sighed and rubbed his eyes with the fingers of one hand. "I told you, I'm not an angel, Mrs...."

"Genola McCarthy."

His mother-taught manners kicked in, and he extended his hand. "Troy Brannon, ma'am."

The woman only regarded him with faint amusement.

"Oh. Hang on a second..." Troy closed his eyes and willed the shift to begin. Nothing. "Give me a minute, here." He still wasn't back to full strength, that had to be it. Something must have happened, though, because Genola had fallen back a few steps, alarm evident in her expression. The woman crossed herself and backed up another step. "Sweet mother of heaven, what happened to you?"

Troy looked down and groaned. In that brief flicker she must have gotten a look at the hole in his chest. He'd grown used to walking around with it. He looked up and raised his hands in a peace gesture. "No, ma'am, you're right. I'm not an angel, nor a demon. I'm just a man. Or, rather, I was a man. Now I'm just trying to hang around on this plane long enough to correct a past mistake and protect some people I love. This—" he gestured ruefully to his chest, "—is how I met my unfortunate end, as they say."

He waited, and presently a little of the alarm faded from her eyes. Hesitantly she stepped forward and held out her hand. He obliged her and did the same. Their fingers touched, his passed through hers. She jerked her hand back, then reached again. To him it felt like nothing more than a breath of air puffed on the skin, but something reminded him of his own mother's gentle caress. He fought a rush of unexpected emotion that swelled around where his heart used to be. He gently disengaged and stepped back, hoping she couldn't get a clear look at his face. *Who is this woman?*

She regarded him for a long moment, then nodded once. "It's too cold and damp out here for my old bones. Ye might as well come with me."

Genola shook her head in amazement as she got up from her kitchen table to fix a fresh pot of tea. "'Tis amazing indeed the places you have been, what you've seen." She sighed deeply as she spooned fresh tea leaves into her old red teapot and poured fresh water from a pot on the Aga stove, the home's only steady source of heat. "As long as you're gadding about causing trouble—don't look at me like that, I *know* ye are—it's too bad you couldn't go back to the beginning of the Troubles and prevent them from beginning in the first place."

"I don't meddle in big events, Genola. Just the little ones."

She eyed him until he looked away with a sheepish expression. "Ah, but as I believe you've learned, little things have a way of turning into big problems. Have you not heard that the breath of air stirred by a butterfly's wing in Canada can cause a raging storm in Ireland?"

Troy opened his mouth and shut it, then grinned that grin that made even her old heart do a little dance. "I'm no more a butterfly than I am an angel."

She raised an eyebrow at him as she seated herself to wait for the water to boil. "No. Not a butterfly. I'd say you're more on the order of the storm."

Troy chuckled and resumed pacing, looking around the room like an interested tourist. Genola wasn't fooled. He was more like a chained animal looking for any way out. His restless energy rattled the dishes on the shelf. She caught him staring at her plate of scones.

"Can you..." She gestured at the plate.

"What? No, sorry to say," he said. "I was just thinking what you told me about your husband. I'm sorry for his death."

She waved her hand and busied herself buttering a scone, careful not to look up until the sting of tears in her eyes had eased. Careful not to look at the vase of heather on the table, which she kept there as a reminder of the handful Seamus used to bring her every day it was in bloom.

She glanced at the wall, which bore a picture of her husband standing proudly next to what was then his brand-new fishing boat. She remembered that day—he had just christened it the *Lady G*. She briefly wondered why she could see and communicate with the ghost of Troy Brannon, but not with that of her beloved husband. Then again, her gift for seeing had never been reliable nor consistent. To this very day, she sometimes thought she heard his familiar whistle floating in the wind. She could never resist going outside to look, just in case. She was always greeted with silence. It was as if the other crowd was playing cruel tricks on her.

That fact she could see Troy, if only dimly, was a complete surprise.

She quickly set those thoughts aside, having learned long ago not to question what could not be answered. "Seamus left this earth forty years ago. On this very day, now that I think about it. A fisherman's wife learns quickly to treasure the years she has with her husband. I have no regrets."

A little silence, and Genola felt him screw down his patience before he asked her yet again. "Do you trust me now, Genola? Will you tell me who and where she is?"

"If she is on this earth at this time, how difficult can it be to find her?"

Troy turned to her, his expression pained. "That's true. But I'm, ah, not sure I have the same powers I had before. I can't just zap myself wherever I want to."

"I see," she said thoughtfully, preparing to pour the tea, having to remind herself she only needed one cup. "Your wings, indeed, have been clipped." She waved a hand at him as his expression darkened. "Yes, yes, I know, ye're no angel. But just think back a moment. How did you find her the first time?"

A confused expression crossed his face. "It was pure chance."

Genola smiled and sipped, mentally rolling her eyes. Men. They were little different, living or not. "Was it, now? Are you sure?"

He frowned and stared into space. Even though his form was dim to her humanity-limited eyes, she could see a dawning deep in his.

"Ah. Something about her called to you, didn't it? I'll give ye a little help. Before the accident, your coming was foretold."

He leaned back, crossed his arms and laughed out loud.

She scowled at him, turned to a kitchen drawer and pulled out her favorite Tarot deck. "These cards have never lied to me," she said firmly, placing the box precisely on the center of the table. "Well," she continued uncertainly, "almost never."

Troy, still laughing, moved to sit on a nearby kitchen chair.

"Are ye tellin' me that you of all creatures don't believe in things ye cannot explain?"

She'd made her point. Troy sobered and stared at the cards.

"What did the cards tell you?"

She shrugged, pulling the cards out of the box and letting her fingers go through the familiar ritual of shuffling. "Only that she was undergoing a time of great change. And a blond man would be part of it."

"That's all?"

"It wasn't a detailed reading. Strange things kept happening, and she would not allow me to read further."

He stared down at the cards in her hand.

"Strange, how?"

She hesitated, then told him. "It was a three-card reading. Past, present and future. Her future kept coming up blank."

"Blank? How can that be?"

"As I said, strange things kept happening." Genola watched his face and suddenly wasn't sure she liked what she saw there.

"It could mean anything," he said offhandedly. "Maybe it means her future is a clean slate."

Genola narrowed her eyes. "It could, indeed. Or..." She leaned forward and watched him closely, squinting to bring his face into better focus. "It could mean she has no future at all."

Troy said nothing. Genola suspected he was purposely blurring his image in order to hide his face from her.

"Could it be you know something about our lady that you're not tellin' me, my fair fallen angel? Is she in that much danger?"

Troy took a silent moment to listen to the sea wind ruffling the thatched roof. "As I said before, I'm only trying to right a wrong and protect those I love. And I meant it—I mean her no harm, Genola."

Genola gave him a hard look, then swept the deck together and began laying out the Celtic Cross pattern.

"I thinks it's time for you to be havin' a reading."

He gave a bark of laughter. "You can't do a reading for a dead man."

She continued to lay out the cards, smacking each one down with a vengeance.

He swallowed. "Can you?"

She finished the pattern and leaned over the table for a better look. "We're about to find out, my lad."

She scanned the layout, felt her heart jump at what she saw, and looked up, perversely enjoying the apprehensive expression on his normally cock-sure face. "You'll have little trouble finding her."

He moved closer to the table and squinted down at the cards. "Why?"

"Her name is Carey Magennis and she *is* in mortal danger. And that's how you found her in the first place, didn't you?"

He crossed his arms, annoyed. "You know where she is. Why don't you just tell me and..."

"And what? How are you going to get there? Walk? As you told me, you can't just transport yourself there in an eye blink." She swept away from the table, snatching her wrap, her purse and her car keys, then planting herself by the back door. The first fingers of dawn ventured through the window. "Get into my car."

"Now that's more like it."

"Oh, no, dear. Prove to me once and for all that you are meant to find her. When I get behind the wheel, you tell me which way to go. If you find her without any help from me, then I'll know for certain sure ye mean her no harm." She yanked open the door.

And came face to face with the milk man.

"Mrs. McCart'y! Where are ye off to in such a great hurry this mornin'?" said the poor man, clearly alarmed.

Genola gathered her startled wits together, conscious of Troy's amused presence behind her. "I'm...off to Tr...er, to see a friend in hospital, Mr. O'Shea." She relieved the man of the proffered two milk bottles and quickly transferred them to the refrigerator.

"Ah, well, I hope 'tis nothing serious, an' you off so early. Anyone I know?" The man poked his head inside the door, and she saw the exact instant his eyes lit on the Tarot cards still spread out on the table. She deftly moved into his line of vision, subtly crowding the man back out the door while she made a motion behind her back at Troy to get a move on. She bustled through the portal, closing it behind her and politely excusing herself past O'Shea.

Troy passed through the closed door, then to her chagrin halted next to O'Shea, who was of course oblivious. Troy, the rascal, looked at her with pure devilment dancing in his eyes, leaned close to O'Shea's ear...

"Don't you dare, ye devil!"

O'Shea jerked as if he'd been poked with a pin. "I beg your pardon, Mrs. McCarthy?"

"Boo!" Troy whispered, which, of course, O'Shea didn't hear

at all. Then he sauntered past Genola on his way to the car, giving her a wink that at once made her want to laugh out loud and box his impudent ears.

"Uh, nothing, Mr. O'Shea. It was a stray cat, 'tis all. Shoo, you. Shoo!" She flapped her arms vaguely in the direction of the fictitious cat, ostensibly lurking somewhere near the corner of the house. When the man turned to look, Genola pretended the cat had gone on its way.

Hurriedly saying her goodbyes, she slid behind the wheel of her ancient Opel hatchback, muttering, "He's thinking I'm a daft woman."

Troy made a noncommittal sound and settled in the passenger seat, lips sealed.

Chapter Three

Tralee General Hospital, Ireland

Everything hurt.

From her toenails to the ends of her hair, everything hurt.

Oh, God, I wish I was still dead.

She opened her eyes to a flurry of activity. Shapes moved in and out of her line of vision, some leaving the room in a big hurry, others hovering around an array of beeping equipment on either side of her narrow, uncomfortable bed. A blurred-beyond-recognition face swam in front of her, someone who raised and kissed her hand, which felt oddly detached. She had the strangest urge to shrink away.

She tried to say something, but winced at the sandpaper tenderness to her chest and throat. *What did I do, swallow the whole ocean?* She shifted on the hard bed, groaning at the myriad aches and pains that small movement awakened. She opted for moving only her eyes to look around the room. Nothing seemed to want to come into focus. Blobs that moved were, she assumed, living people. Blobs that didn't were probably chairs or blinking machines by the bed. The moving blobs were further blurred by what looked like clouds of glowing mist that moved when the blobs moved, sometimes trailing colorful ribbons of light behind. She stared, fascinated, as blues, greens, reds—all the rainbow colors whirled around the room.

Voices, some familiar, some not, faded in and out like bad AM reception on a radio. Kyle's impatient, clipped tones made some of the colorful blobs—nurses?—move faster. A vivid indigo blob that had Genola McCarthy's lilting voice drew her attention for a moment, but she found it impossible to focus on any one thing for long. The lights hurt her eyes.

She caught only snatches of conversation.

...she awake?

...hard to...semi-coma...

...want her on the next flight to the states...

...not possible...private hospital would be best...

Will she live?

Memory returned in jerks and starts, setting off a wracking cough that stabbed pain into her damaged lungs. The face again floated into her vision.

"Sugar? Can you hear me?"

"Where am I?" she managed to whisper. Something jabbed her nose, and she raised her hand to find a cannula hissing moist, cool air. Another tube was taped to the back of her hand.

"In Tralee Hospital, you are." Genola soothed, her indigo color softening to pale lavender. "You gave us all quite a scare."

"Mrs. McCarthy." Carey felt her mouth stretch in a smile. Even the smile hurt. "I should have listened..." Stringing so many words together caused her chest to wheeze painfully.

"You won't be here long." Kyle's voice cut in, emerging from a mass of restless red and orange mist. His hand squeezed hers urgently, and this time she managed to pull away. His colors were making her hurt worse, strange as it seemed. She wanted to turn away from them. "I've arranged for you to be moved to a private hospital where you'll get better treatment." His impatient tone was reflected in the nervous, jerky motion of his colors.

A pale yellow blob, probably hiding a nurse, made a huffing noise and left the room.

Kyle recaptured her hand. She frowned, but was too tired to pull away again. “Do you… Do you remember why you’re here?”

She felt herself drifting toward sleep, her eyelids growing heavy. “Mmm. Drowned. In...a cave.”

Kyle’s stroking touch on her hand stilled. “No, sugar. You were caught on a ledge by the high tide. You and...another person.” His tone remained steady, but the red-orange cloud surrounding him suddenly turned black.

“Actually,” said a mild male voice with a British flavor from somewhere off to her left, “the damage to her lungs is consistent with drowning, Mr. Thorpe.” A hand bearing the end of a stethoscope appeared and pressed it to her chest. She coughed, bringing up salty water that she spit into a basin Kyle helpfully supplied. “That’s right, miss, just keep that up and your lungs will be clear in no time.”

More memories crashed into her brain. Listening to her own heartbeat slow and stop. A strong hand reaching out of the cold darkness, then a flying sensation. A voice urging her to breathe, not to give up. To live. Not Kyle’s voice. A different voice, one that had rolled through her senses like the life-giving waters of a bubbling hot spring.

She coughed again, pain stabbing through her lungs as she tried to sit up. She could swear her entire body sloshed with absorbed seawater.

“Where… What happened to…”

Several pairs of hands eased her back down onto the bed. She didn’t have the breath to fight them. Everywhere the hands touched hurt her bruised and broken skin.

"Who was that man, Carey? What were you doing with him down there?" His hand tightened possessively on hers.

Genola's color turned bright purple.

"What? He...saved me. I drowned, and he pulled me..." Another fit of coughing shook her. The British voice said something about possible pneumonia setting in.

Genola started to murmur something, but Kyle cut her off. "She might as well know it now, Mrs. McCarthy. It won't help to keep it from her." He changed his tone to one meant to soothe, but his next words nearly stopped her heart.

"Sugar, I'm sorry, but the man on the ledge with you...disappeared as soon as he handed you off to the firemen. They said he fell into the ocean. He's probably...most likely he's dead."

Tears sprang up, leaking down the sides of her face. She shook her head wildly back and forth, wiped furiously at her eyes, trying to clear them. "No... He can't be...he..."

She vaguely heard the deep British voice ordering a sedative.

Her gaze settled on Genola's cloud. Impulsively she reached for it, pushing Kyle's angry colors out of the way. She felt her hands enveloped in a warmth that suffused her body with calm. Her peripheral vision picked up a pair of hands injecting something into her IV drip.

"The blond man, Mrs. M....you told me...and it was him..."

"What in the hell is she talking about?" muttered Kyle, simmering off to one side.

"Shhh." The woman hushed her, ignoring Kyle. "'Tis all right, my dear. 'Tis all right."

Carey felt the woman's unspoken assurance begin to clear

the haze of injury and confusion. Forcing herself to slow down her breathing, she let her gaze sweep the room, trying to bring it into focus as the sedative took effect.

She almost missed him.

He crouched in a shadowy far corner of the room, his back against the wall, utterly still. His eyes studied her as a man might study a chess board, contemplating his next move. Odd, she thought, that he was not blurred to her vision like everyone else was. Everything about him was as dark as the shadowy corner he'd folded his body into, from the black boots on his feet to the black shirt stretched over his long arms. The only thing remotely light about him was his hair. Blond hair. The color of a lion's mane. His only movement was a muscle that worked under the taught skin of his lean face. And his eyes. They moved incessantly, missing nothing and no one in the room. Even in the shadows, she knew the exact instant they came to rest on her face.

His green-eyed gaze drilled straight into hers. And narrowed.

She smiled and relaxed, pulling one hand out of Genola's and trying to stretch it toward him. The sedative made spaghetti of her arm, however, and it only flopped crazily in his general direction.

"He's not dead," she slurred, the drug thickening her tongue. "He's right there."

She heard Genola's breath catch. Everything and everyone else in the room blurred and faded, except for the man in the corner.

"Sugar," Kyle said carefully, "there's no one there."

The man looked at Kyle and the side of his mouth quirked. He looked back at her and raised an eyebrow. She found herself grinning at him, silently agreeing that she didn't much care for

Kyle's tone, either.

"Don't be...silly..." She smiled as the dark man with the light hair unfolded himself and rose to his full height, eyes never leaving hers. As if drawn by some irresistible force flowing from her outstretched hand, he moved across the room with an unconscious, athletic grace. As he neared the bed, she noticed something...off. The man looked solid enough to her eyes, but she could have sworn he'd just walked right through a chair.

"Cool," she mumbled. She watched, transfixed, as the man halted beside her bed and leaned down as if he had something to say. Her gaze wandered down to his broad chest. She gasped softly at what she saw there. A gaping wound under his torn shirt, raw, like the pain that lurked behind his narrowed green eyes. Without thought, she raised her unsteady hand toward his chest. But before she could touch him, he flinched away.

"Ohhh... Mrs. M., look...he's hurt. Someone should look at that..." Where was the doctor? The nurses? *This man ought to be in surgery.*

"What is she looking at? Is the drug making her hallucinate?" The tension in Kyle's voice was reflected in the distortion of his colors.

"Perhaps. Perhaps not, Mr. Thorpe," said Genola. "She could be seeing things beyond our ability to see."

"Don't be ridiculous," he snapped. "If she isn't hallucinating then... God, she must be brain damaged or something." He sat heavily in the nearest chair. "I can't believe this. The timing couldn't be worse."

Carey ignored the voices. She saw only the effort it took for the dark-clothed man to back away. He frowned and looked from her to Kyle, then back again. His expression changed, as if he'd come to some realization, or resignation. But then his angular jaw tightened with new resolve, and he once again leaned close.

She fought the drug, fought to keep her eyes open as his lips moved, but she didn't need to see his lips. The words he uttered shivered through her from head to foot.

"Carey Magennis. You have to let me go."

Bon Secours Hospital, Tralee

Carey sipped listlessly at the broth on her tray. Hospital food was, apparently, hospital food, no matter the country. Having been told she was at risk for pneumonia, she did her best to eat. She wouldn't feel completely well until she had North Carolina soil under her feet, and the quicker she built up her strength, the quicker she could go home.

She pushed the tray aside and settled back to gaze out the rain-splattered window. Not much to be seen outside Bon Secours Hospital except grey clouds and a tree branch that whipped in the wind. Kyle had insisted she be moved here as soon as she'd been stabilized, declaring the public hospital at Tralee to be unfit for man or beast. She hadn't agreed, but she was silently glad to go. She'd hoped that once away from there, she'd leave behind the memories of Genola's blond man. But he still flickered at the edges of her peripheral vision when she wasn't otherwise paying attention to something else.

She wondered if this was a common occurrence among people whose lives had been saved because someone else had sacrificed theirs.

The swaying branch outside the window mesmerized her, the white noise of the rain lulling her into half sleep.

"It looks like we're stuck with each other. For a while, anyway. At least until I can figure something out."

She blinked. There he stood, hipshot and arrogant, not five feet away. Slowly, careful not to take her eyes off him lest he disappear again, she levered herself higher on the bed. As much as she'd wanted to put the visions of this man behind her, she found her heart tripping over itself. Dead or alive, he was every inch what she and her women friends classified as "drool worthy".

"How did you get in here?" she croaked, her chest still sore from the inhaled seawater.

"I haven't left your side since Tralee General."

She considered that for a minute while he stood there, appearing as if he had all the time in the world. Underneath, though, she sensed a fine tension running through him. Even in stillness, he somehow seemed in motion.

The memory of him walking though a chair at Tralee General sprang up, along with regret which thudded in her belly. "You're a ghost, aren't you?"

A trace of surprise crossed his face, followed by a kind of admiration. "You aren't scared of me, are you? Because if you are, we've got a big problem."

"Don't be silly," she said, studying the wound in his chest with horrified fascination. "I was raised on the scariest ghost stories in the South ever since I was old enough to stay up past sunset. You aren't missing any body parts, no bones sticking out. So, I'm sorry to say, but for a ghost you really aren't that scary."

He laughed. He actually laughed out loud, throwing back his head, his somber expression lighting up and the dimples at the sides of his mouth deepening into grooves of mirth.

She clapped her hands to her face. "Oh my God, what am I making jokes about? You're the ghost of the man who saved me." Tears blurred her vision. "I'm sorry. I'm so sorry. You saved me, and you died."

To her amazement, he laughed again, and a grin flashed that he quickly wiped off by running a hand down his face. He approached the bed and crouched beside it, resting his arms on the mattress so that his eyes were level with hers.

"You have the basic facts right, but they're a little out of order."

He was close enough to touch. What would a ghost feel like? Tentatively she raised her hand, fingers aiming for his hair. His amused expression faded into wariness, eyes narrowed. He set his jaw but did not move, as if he, too, wanted to find out what would happen.

She passed her fingers through his hair and watched, fascinated, as the close-cropped strands flowed around her fingers. It was warm, and reflected the light streaming in through the window.

An unreadable expression crossed his face, then his gaze flicked to the door. Instantly a blank mask, a warrior's mask, dropped into place. "You've got company."

"You see there, Father, how she stares off into space. The neurosurgeon said it's a classic sign..." Kyle's hushed voice echoed in the stark room. She experienced an odd snapping back to herself, like when someone interrupted her in the middle of a good daydream.

She blinked. The ghost was gone. Sucking in a deep breath, she turned toward Kyle's voice, her eye snagging on the wall clock. An hour had passed since she'd last looked at it. Strange. Her exchange with the ghost couldn't have taken more than two minutes. Had she truly daydreamed the entire encounter? She shook her head, trying to clear it.

"Welcome back, sugar." Kyle smiled at her, coming into the room with a black-robed man at his side. The man wore a white clerical collar and carried a small Bible wrapped with a rosary. A priest? Ah, probably the hospital chaplain come to pay a call. Kyle was his customary buttoned-down self, not one sable hair out of place. No dark circles marred the perfectly tanned skin under his blue eyes, as if he hadn't missed a wink of sleep since he'd taken control of the situation. It was like him...he wasn't a man to sit on the sidelines and let others take the reins.

"I was just telling Father Dowd here what our doctors back home think is going on. And now that you have me, there won't be any more danger of you straying off sheer cliffs in the future."

She sat up straighter in the bed, unaccustomed annoyance at his tone springing up in her chest. "Yes, I do seem to remember you saying something about a leash and collar. Funny, I didn't think bondage was your thing, Kyle."

Kyle blanched, and the priest turned red as the ribbon bookmark dangling from his Bible. Carey's hand flew to her mouth. Where in the world had that come from? Her gaze flickered to the empty spot where, in her daydream, the ghost had been. She thought she heard the echo of a rich masculine laugh, but couldn't be sure. Probably someone down the hall...

"Carey!" Kyle hissed. She tried to convey her apology to him with her eyes, but he looked away, jaw working.

"Father Dowd, I'm so sorry. Forgive me, I'm not quite...myself." Flustered, not knowing what else to do to break the tension, she stuck out her hand. "I'm Carey Magennis, Father. I'm pleased to meet you."

To her relief, the priest's redness appeared to be caused by his attempt to suppress his mirth. He took her hand and squeezed it.

"Your fiancé has been telling me about your plans to marry. How fortunate that tragedy was averted and you can look forward to a lifetime together."

She nodded, wondering why his words made her feel slightly nauseous. She looked at Kyle, who had regained his composure.

"Which I would like to get started right now. That's why I asked the Father to come today," he said, as if finishing the priest's sentence. He swooped in and parked himself on the edge of the bed, slipping an arm around her and taking her left hand in his.

"I've asked Father Dowd to marry us. Right now." He pulled a velvet ring box from his pocket

"Uh..." She stared at the box, stunned, as he levered it open with his thumb. In it, a gleaming gold band rested next to the diamond that had been removed from her hand when she'd been admitted to Tralee General.

"Understand, now," Father Dowd put in hastily, "that this would be an unofficial ceremony, as we do not have the proper paperwork. But, under the circumstances, I think we can make an exception."

Dizzy, Carey looked up and found the doorway crowded with nurses, most of whom were also nuns. Apparently they had all heard of the bold American lad making this grand, romantic gesture. Despite the fact that none of them would probably ever get married, it didn't seem to matter. The gaggle of smiling, starry-eyed women cramming the doorway were as excited as any of the secular world

She looked again at the rings and decided it must be her injuries that were making her stomach knot up instead of what she should be feeling. Happiness. Contentment. Not this flat feeling of...nothing.

"Kyle, we can't do this."

He reared back and regarded her with stunned surprise.

"Why not? We can make it official when we get home."

She fished for a logical reason. "For one thing, we aren't Catholic."

He stroked her arm, patient to a fault. "I just want for us to say the words, that's all. Nothing's legal until we get home and have a real wedding. But...I realize now my original proposal was somewhat rushed and unromantic. I thought this would make up for it. Besides," his voice dropped and his expression grew serious, "I promised your aunt I would take care of you."

Yes. Aunt Loreen. She'd had raised Carey as her own, since her parents' deaths. She patted Kyle's hand and tried, with her raspy voice, to match his patient tone.

"Which is exactly why I wouldn't dream of doing this without her," she reasoned, then held her breath.

A shadowed look passed through his eyes, but was so quickly gone she wasn't sure it had really been there. She pressed on.

"Besides, I've decided I want to be married on the mountain, on my home ground."

"The mountain."

"Yes, the acreage my parents left to me."

"Outside."

She hesitated. "Well...yes, it would have to be, since the cabin isn't large enough to accommodate a crowd."

He gave her a one-armed hug and an indulgent smile. "Well, we'll talk it over when we get home."

It occurred to her suddenly that, in their six-month courtship, he'd said that a lot—"We'll talk it over." It always meant he would not be moved on an issue. Originally, she had liked his decisiveness. Now it just felt like a brick wall.

Kyle ushered the priest and the nuns out of the room with

an apology which the clergyman cheerfully accepted. When they were alone, Kyle returned to his spot on the edge of her bed. She let her head rest against the solid strength of his chest as he took the diamond out of the box and slipped it back on her ring finger.

"Now. That's better." He replaced his arm around her shoulders. "Sugar, I talked to some doctors at UNC-Durham today."

"What for?" A trickle of uneasiness ran down her spine, and she sat up to face him. "What kind of doctors?"

He took a deep breath. "Neurologists. Brain specialists. They—"

"I'm fine, Kyle. I'll be well enough to go home in a day or two."

"Yes, that's true, but this is about... Carey, these doctors tell me—and the specialist here agrees—your symptoms might be pointing to some kind of seizure."

She drew away. "What are you talking about?"

"The way you seem to drift off, stare into space. They could be what's called absence seizures. They also tell me it's treatable. One or two pills a day, but they'll have to run tests first, of course. You'll be fine...just no more wandering off sheer cliffs."

"I didn't fall. I told you."

He waved off her argument. "Either way, It could get you into real trouble if we don't take care of it. This wasn't your usual missed appointment or attention wandering in the middle of a conversation. This was almost your life."

She frowned, looked down and the ring, then out the window, where the grey day still blustered. Maybe...maybe he was right.

Suddenly she longed to be in Genola's calming presence. She wanted, inexplicably, to relive a small part of her ordeal on the cliff, and have the dark-clad man with the lion-colored hair come to her rescue once again. Only this time, not die in the attempt.

Kyle took her silence for acquiescence. "It's for the best, sugar." He reached for her and tucked her securely to his side once more.

She found her right hand drifting toward the spot on the bed where the ghost's arms had rested. She wondered briefly if she had really seen him, or if he was just another trauma- and drug-induced daydream. Maybe Kyle was right.

Her fingers feathered over the crisp sheet where the vision-ghost's elbows had rested.

The white linen was warm to the touch.

Chapter Four

Raleigh, North Carolina, One Month Later

I don't belong here.

Carey observed the errant thought that often nagged at her consciousness these days, then let it go. She closed the book she'd been reading about Civil War-era spies and tucked it back in her tote bag.

She sat on a bench on the periphery of the Moore Square farmer's market, working on the theory that if she just sat still enough, the afternoon's oppressive heat would somehow slip by without noticing her presence.

The tantalizing smells of the market's edible wares blended with the sounds of mingled conversation and the folk music from the stage under the oaks. She closed her eyes and tried to let her imagination transform the still, hot air into a cool ocean breeze. It almost worked, but not quite.

She remembered belatedly that she had forgotten to take her medication that morning. Cold sweat dotted her brow, and she blotted it absently with the back of her hand, scanning the crowded street for something pleasant to look at while she waited for Kyle to meet her for lunch.

She supposed she could have gone into a nearby air-conditioned art gallery to wait, but inside there were far fewer opportunities to people-watch, one of her favorite pastimes. One of the few left to her now that she was on medication. It was for the best, she told herself. Still, she missed her occasional joyrides into the realms of her imagination. She looked around at the graceful spreading oaks, up at the clear sky overhead. And sighed. The world just didn't seem as...colorful a place as it had once been. Another side effect of the meds, she supposed.

Her gaze came to rest on an aged black man shuffling to the slender shade of a lamp post, dressed in clothes looking almost as ancient and unwashed as he. Without fuss, he opened what looked like a small suitcase and extracted a saxophone. Leaving the case open on the pavement, the old man adjusted the mouthpiece and began to play.

The sax was almost as rusty as the old man's musical skills, but Carey couldn't help tapping her foot to the bouncy strains of "Sweet Georgia Brown". Passersby, in Italian suits and designer dresses, would occasionally drop a bill or a few coins into his case, eliciting a nod and a smile from the old man.

No one looked directly at him as they rushed past. She found that somewhat offensive.

Remembering she had some money crumpled up in the pocket of her dress, Carey got to her feet and moved across the sidewalk, unable to resist a few little dance steps in time to the music. Coming out of her twirl right next to the elderly musician, she found her laugh and self-indulgent smile reflected the black pools of his eyes. She saw surprise, a little suspicion, then a spark of pleasure ripple in them. She dropped her bills into his case, forgetting and not particularly caring at the moment what denomination they were. He stopped playing and tipped his dirty baseball cap.

"Thank you, ma'am," came his hoarse, rumbling voice.

She smiled into his eyes, seeing within them unfathomable

suffering she would never, could never know. She wished she could do more for him, buy him a meal or something, but she knew by instinct that he wouldn't accept.

"What would you like to hear, ma'am?" he surprised her by asking, taking off his hat and inclining his head formally.

"I like what you were playing before," she answered, more boldly than she would have imagined herself even a few months ago. "Are you from Georgia?"

"Atlanta born and bred, ma'am," the old man rasped, looking a little taken aback that someone had actually taken the time to talk to him. "I'm hoping to earn the money to go back there someday."

"Then, how about 'Georgia on My Mind'?"

He nodded, still looking a little reticent, and took up the tune. Carey stood where she was, arms folded, and she let her held tilt back as she let herself sway to the music. The old man grinned at her around his mouthpiece as she began to hum along, then softly sing the words.

She swung into verse two, letting her voice soar over the traffic. She'd never had a very good voice, but she found that she didn't care. Here, now, she felt like singing, and gave herself over wholeheartedly to the moment. She looked into the man's eyes again and smiled, determined to somehow make up for the years she had avoided eyes like his. The old man played better than she'd ever heard him play before, and he often paused to add his own basso emphasis as she lost herself in the song...

And then she lost more than herself.

The wailing sounds of the saxophone faded, replaced by the sound of voices murmuring a low, mournful song coming from a long row of backs bent over rows of cotton stretched a half mile to the banks of a river. She saw sweat dripping off faces, raw, bleeding fingers from the sharp pricks of the cotton boles. A young woman directly in front of her had rope burns scored into her dark brown wrists.

"Did you see her wrists? Did you see her back?"

"Weren't no more than she deserved. I caught her reading a book."

Carey turned her head toward the sound of raised voices. A young man, his lithe body clothed in fine fabric and tall, shiny riding boots, stood nose to nose with what must be an overseer, who fingered a long whip coiled in his knobby hands.

"Father will hear about your mistreatment of these people."

"People? I tol' your daddy sending you north to that school would ruin you. He gave me leave to handle his stock as I see fit, get all the work out of 'em I can. She knows the rules, she broke 'em. She's lucky I don't sell her south."

The young man, face flushed, turned toward her, his piercing eyes seeking the young woman out among the cotton rows, who stood and stretched her arms to the sky to ease her tired back muscles...

"Carey?"

Abruptly the music stopped and Carey opened her eyes to find she was standing in the middle of the sidewalk, stock still, her arms lifted to the sky. A small, curious crowd had gathered to watch her impromptu performance.

In the middle of them all, horrified expression frozen on his face, stood Kyle.

She swayed, dizzy, and someone caught her elbow. Another hand, unseen, steadied her at the small of her back. Gasping softly, she turned... No one was there. An unexpected rush of grief swamped her. *What the heck was that?* She tried to shake off the feeling.

Kyle cast an anxious glance around before striding toward

her to take her by the arm and hurry her away from the musician and his rapidly filling saxophone case.

"What do you think you're doing?" he said in his lowest, most patient tone, all the while propelling her swiftly down the sidewalk.

Hearing the old man murmur "God bless you, ma'am" behind her, Carey managed to turn and give him a brief wave and a smile before Kyle led her beyond his sight.

"I was waiting for you." She pulled her arm out of his grasp.

"You know very well what I'm talking about. That little scene with that...street person. What happened to your hand?" Kyle took her hand and turned it in his. His brows drew together. "Did that man do this to you?"

Carey looked down and gasped. Blood welled from a deep cut alongside one fingernail. She pulled her hand out of Kyle's and looked closer. Just visible at one end of the cut was something that looked like a tiny black splinter. "No, of course he didn't," she said, carefully pulling the splinter out with the nails of her other hand.

Kyle peered at it. "Looks like a thorn of some kind."

She held the object between her fingertips and felt sweat break out on her forehead all over again. A chill raced down her spine. If she wasn't mistaken, this was no splinter. It was a prickle from a cotton bole.

Where had it come from?

Blinking, she flicked the prickle away and pressed Kyle's proffered handkerchief to her finger. "It's nothing. Probably a splinter from one of my steamer trunks." She tilted her head to look up at him. "He's just a musician trying to earn a little honest pocket change. He's harmless."

"He was filthy!"

"He's a human being!" A rare flash of temper heated her face. She knew what he was going to say next and resented him for it, resented herself because not so long ago, she might have agreed with him. Or at least not argued about it.

His tone dropped back to low, reasonable patience. "What if someone from my firm had seen you? What would they have thought?"

Her dizziness had passed, but her elbow felt numb, as if she'd struck her funny bone on a hard object. She suddenly felt too tired to have this conversation. "Oh, I don't know, Kyle. That I was having a little bit of fun on a hot day?" She raised her hand and brushed at a stray lock of his dark hair, wondering why that wayward strand didn't affect her like it once had.

He assessed her through his cool blue eyes for a moment. "Did you take your pills today?"

She let her hand drop away. "I... No, I didn't, come to think of it. I must have forgotten."

She watched his expression soften, and she told herself he was only worried about her welfare. Then his gaze came to rest on her attire, and that eyebrow shot up again.

"In a hurry getting dressed this morning?"

Kyle would never come right out and say he didn't like something she was wearing. She glanced down at her billowy orange and pink tie-dyed tank dress and hot pink sandals, which she had indeed thrown on in under sixty seconds.

"I came as soon as I got your message about lunch. I was in the middle of sewing on my new period ball gown."

"Carey, you could have hired someone to do that," Kyle said as his eyes traveled to her hair, faint worry and disapproval sparking in them as he observed her thick, curly locks caught up haphazardly behind her head in a giant claw clasp. After Ireland, she hadn't bothered to go back to the salon for her regular straightening session. She could almost hear him thinking, *She used to take hours with her appearance.*

"True, but I get greater satisfaction doing it myself. It's wonderful therapy." She saw Kyle's face stiffen.

"Oh, I'm sorry, I said the T-word again, didn't I?" Then she clapped a hand over her mouth. Where had that remark come from? "Kyle, I—"

He waved it aside, though the corners of his mouth remained tight. "Just don't forget to take it before tonight, please. I can put up with these little outbursts of yours since your accident, because I know what a strain it has been. But they won't go over well with certain people, as you well know. And please, please, if the subject of conversation turns to something historical, try to control yourself." His words were probably meant to lighten the moment, but the implication was clear. Carey never missed an opportunity to learn, or to teach. Sometimes her inner geek did take over a conversation.

She thought wistfully of her classroom, and of the steamer trunks full of costumes and artifacts she freely used while teaching high school American history. *Correction*, she thought sadly. *Used to teach.* Though she had been confident she would be strong enough to return to the classroom in the fall, the school board hadn't agreed, and asked her to resign. Her principal had fought for her, to no avail.

Kyle draped an arm over her shoulders and they continued at a slower pace. They were well out of sight of his building now, and less likely to run into anyone they knew. Still, he moved her to his other side, where his bigger body blocked her from view of the street. Did he think she wouldn't notice?

"No matter. You'll have plenty of time to change before the Marwoods' charity function tonight."

Carey couldn't hold back a sigh. "Don't worry, Kyle, I won't embarrass you."

Kyle halted and turned her toward him, resting his hands on her shoulders, his expression serious. "It isn't that, Carey. It's just that you've changed. From the beginning we've had certain goals. We agreed we were going to go after those goals together, no matter what it took. Remember?"

"I remember." *You had the goals, Kyle, I just never bothered to argue with you about them.*

"But ever since your accident... You've always had a good heart, Carey, and I love that about you. But now your priorities seem to be...a little skewed."

Carey resisted the urge to shake him. "Skewed? My God, Kyle, I almost died in that cave. No, let me rephrase that. I did die in that cave."

He leaned back from her, as if to avoid her flare of emotion. "Carey, do we have to go over this again? You were not in a cave, you were on a ledge..."

"Don't you think something like that would... If I could just tell you about what happened to me, maybe—" She got a look at his face and her voice trailed off. He'd never wanted to discuss that day, and if she tried to tell him about the man who had died to save her, he shut her out cold.

"Carey, stop. I don't like to think about that day. How close I came to losing you," he said tightly, not looking her in the eye.

"Someone had been there, Kyle," she went on doggedly. "Genola sent copies of the newspaper account of the accident. All the articles mention a man lost while I was rescued."

Kyle regarded her silently for a moment, searching her face, which she could feel was flushed. "Maybe you should go back to the neurologist and have another brain scan. Get your medication adjusted. We need to put this behind us and move on, sugar."

She stepped away from him. "There's nothing wrong with my brain, Kyle, or my priorities. They're still there. Just a little re-ordered, that's all. Is it a crime to let down your hair and have a little fun once in a while? What harm can it do?"

He gave her an odd look, as if she'd sprouted another eye in the middle of her forehead. "Plenty, if the right people get the wrong impression, Carey! I thought you understood this!" He visibly restrained his outburst and took her arms in his hands. "This is what the meds are for, remember? Hasn't it been a big help since you've started taking them?"

She rubbed her eyes and thought of her Aunt Loreen. Aunt Loreen, who had made it her mission in life to raise her niece to do her duty to the family by marrying well. Preferably to a man with the money to make up for her mother's indiscretion and Carey's "poor choice" of a teaching profession—at an inner city school no less, not a respectable private school. Kyle Thorpe had everything Loreen required in a husband for Carey. He was a man from a family with the right social standing, on a steady, sure climb to financial success.

Kyle *was* a good man. It was that accident that had made her lose sight of her goals, she reasoned. To marry, have children and settle into a safe, predictable routine. Kyle would give her that.

"I understand, Kyle."

He took her hand, his face pained. "I know these past weeks have been rough on you, sugar, but the best thing to do is to forget it and get back to a normal life as quickly as possible—"

"I said I understand," she said firmly.

She turned and continued to walk with him toward their chosen restaurant, forcing herself to think about what she was going to wear that night. "I'm going to spend a few weeks this summer interpreting at Guilford Courthouse Battlefield. After I get into the routine there, I'll be able to—"

"Ah, about that job, Carey..."

She halted and swung around to face him. His expression was somewhere between guilt and grim determination. Dread dropped like a lead weight in her chest. "What?"

"They won't be needing you this summer after all."

"Won't be needing me... No one contacted me about... Kyle, what have you done?"

He took her shoulders and resisted her efforts to pull away. "Nothing. I just made a couple of phone calls to find out how strenuous the job was going to be. It's—"

"Kyle!" She managed to work herself out of his grasp and stood staring at him, suddenly unable to feel her feet. He had managed to get her fired from her summer job before she'd even started? The living-history job she had been looking forward to as pure fun, a way to regain her emotional equilibrium?

"—for your own good, Carey. You don't need to waste time and energy running around in an old cotton dress pretending to be someone you're not."

"Who gave you the right—"

"You should be resting. I thought you'd be pleasantly surprised to have the summer to relax, not work. Look at you. You're overreacting. You're all flushed."

She fought to control her breathing. "Overreacting? You cancel my summer plans, which I was really looking forward to, and—"

"Besides, I think we should accelerate our plans for the wedding. I'm thinking August instead of Christmas." He looked at her expectantly, as if anticipating a cry of pleasure.

Instantly she stilled. "I..."

Irritation flashed across his face for a second, to be quickly replaced by patience. "After what happened, I figure, why wait? Life is short enough, right? You'll need this summer to get everything planned. It's going to take all your time, even with your aunt helping."

Carey waved her hands helplessly. "Why did you do this? You should have talked to me about it, not just charged in and taken over."

Kyle's eyes were serious. "Don't you see, Carey? Things are different now. You need someone to take care of you. Your aunt's not going to be around forever."

Carey felt her insides turn strangely quiet and numb, somewhat like the feeling she got when a roller coaster paused at the top of a huge hill. She did her best to ignore the persistent vision of a hand reaching out to her from a silver ball of light.

Beckoning... *Come with me. You'll be safe.*

Troy followed behind Carey and Kyle, jaw clenched and teeth grinding.

I'd sure as hell like to "take care" of you, Kyle, my boy.

Frustration gnawed at his insides. Once she'd started taking those pills that Kyle and his handpicked doctors had pushed on her, she'd been lost to him. Now that he couldn't seem to materialize and take the pills out of her hand, he had no way of reaching her. "Absence seizures", hell. He knew what a misfiring brain's energy felt like, and hers wasn't.

But something had just happened back there on the street. She'd tilted her head back, closed her eyes...and zap. Her life energy had just disappeared from her body, except for a single fragile strand anchored to the base of her brain.

Astounded, he'd reached out to touch the glowing thread of energy, eyes following its trail to where it disappeared into thin air. Before he could figure out what had just happened, she was back, her body swaying off balance toward him. As her aura collided with his, he'd instinctively reached out to steady her, even though he couldn't solidify. Yet she had turned to look for him, as if she'd felt his hands on her skin.

Some part of her knows I'm here. Damn it, I just can't reach that part as long as she takes those drugs.

Troy looked down at his hand and squinted at it, wondering why the hell he couldn't shift.

I do not belong here.

Carey shook off the nagging thought. *Of course I belong here,* she told herself as she maneuvered through a knot of chatting socialites. *I grew up in this world, with these people.* She self-consciously tugged the long sleeves of her dress down over the still-fading bruises from her ordeal in the cave.

I need a drink. She suddenly had a strong hankering for a shot of tequila, which was odd because she rarely, if ever, drank anything stronger than a small glass of white wine.

An arm draped in powder-blue chiffon snaked out of the group and snagged her left hand, halting her progress toward the bar.

"Here you are, my dear! You must show us all your ring." The arm, attached to Mrs. Squire Marwood, pulled her within the center of the perfumed, bejeweled amoeba of women.

Carey obligingly held out her hand and smiled in amusement as said hand disappeared behind a cloud of teased-

and-set heads of hair. After the requisite oohing and aahing, Mrs. Marwood shooed them all back and took both of Carey's hands in hers, blue eyes sparkling with satisfaction.

"Your mother would have been so proud, honey."

Carey met the gaze of the woman who, she was told, had been among her mother's dearest friends, and managed not to let herself tear up. "Thank you, Mrs. Marwood. I like to think so. And that Daddy wouldn't have taken a shotgun to him, either."

The women laughed appreciatively. Carey took in their warm smiles. More highly polished, socially graced women couldn't be found anywhere, but she knew that underneath the expensive clothes and teased hair lay cores of steel and tireless workers for charity and sometimes lost causes. Strong women who dealt daily with life married to powerful men.

"Well," continued Mrs. Marwood, squeezing Carey's hands. "It won't be long before you'll be an old married woman. And you call me Judith. You're one of us now!"

Carey laughed along with the other women, but inside, her heart gave a strange little jerk and began to thump wildly.

"And here's a little surprise for you." Mrs. Marwood beamed at Carey and those surrounding them. "My daughter Paige is going to sponsor you into the Junior League as soon as you are back from your honeymoon!"

I don't belong here.

Carey blinked and found the women staring at her expectantly. She brightened, hoping her dazed state hadn't been too apparent. "Why that's lovely, Judith! Tell Paige I am so pleased and I'll be looking forward to it." Her automatic response was met with murmurs of approval. The women cooed and chattered as she disengaged her hand from Mrs. Marwood's, making polite excuses.

This is what you wanted, she argued with herself as she moved to the bar, rethought her earlier craving and asked for iced tea. The chilled, mint-topped glass in her hand, she wandered toward the ballroom windows, one hand discreetly trying to rearrange one of the hairpins that ruthlessly held her wayward curls in place. She had enough pins, she thought ruefully, to set off an airport alarm, but still she felt a few escaped corkscrew strands tickling the back of her neck.

She spied Kyle across the room, shamelessly using the Marwoods' charity ball to network.

I do not belong here. The thought continued to nag as she looked around the glittering throng, seeing with crystal clarity her life laid out before her.

This is what I wanted. A safe, secure marriage, no surprises. Two kids and a Golden Retriever. *But is it what I want,* she contradicted herself in a flash of insight, *or what is expected of me?*

It didn't matter. It was past time for her to settle down and begin contributing to the Raleigh society gene pool. At least she would still have a career she loved. Teaching was in her blood. Soon she would be ready to look for another job to replace the one she had resigned. Bringing those inner-city children back in touch with their heritage, even if she was white and most of her students were black, was as much of a gift to herself as to them. Maybe more.

She smiled to herself. The principal had been reluctant to hire her until she had invited him to come to a program at the downtown library to watch her work. After hearing her tell a folk tale in fluent Gullah, he had hired her on the spot, white skin or no. She loved the challenge. Perhaps...perhaps she had been too hasty in resigning her position. Kyle had reasoned her into the decision, but maybe she hadn't been in the right frame of mind at the time to think of the consequences.

It's not too late. I'll talk to my principal Monday about reapplying.

The thought cheered her as she gazed at the night-blackened wall of windows at the east end of the ballroom, watching her reflection idly stir the contents of her glass. Beyond that window, she remembered, lay a four-star golf course on ground that was once a Revolutionary War battlefield. A five-acre remnant of the battlefield remained, located at the far end of the property. But between the course and surrounding subdivisions, little was left to identify it as an historical site.

In 1778, this land had been thick with oak and hickory, sassafras and catawba, grape vine and musclewood. She let her eyes drift closed and her head tilt back, imagining bony fingers of winter-bare trees...

...tugging at a woman's clothing as she carried a box of freshly molded musket balls to her husband, encamped with General Greene's regiment. Carey watched the woman adjust a sack holding fresh baked bread and dried meat over her shoulder. Her breath plumed in frigid gasps as a shape loomed out of the darkness, a shape that reached out to grab her arms.

"Thank God ye've come," said the shape in a low, masculine voice.

"As I promised I would. Had you doubts?"

He caught her in his arms and kissed her. "Never, my love." Their embrace was brief. He relieved her of the supplies, moonlight catching on his tied-back auburn hair and shadowing his deep-set eyes. "If I live through tomorrow," he whispered, tears sheening his eyes in the moonlight, "'twill be because of you." With a last kiss on her cheek, he was gone. Back to the ranks before he was missed...

A splash of something cold on Carey's foot brought her back to herself. She blinked, still staring at the window, but it wasn't only her own reflection she saw. Just behind her, over her left shoulder, stood a tall, lean man dressed all in black with short, lion-colored hair and eyes that narrowed as they met hers.

It was him.

His powerful presence bored into her back. As she stared, he leaned close to her ear, his eyes intense, his strong, straight lips moving.

"Carey, don't take the pills tomorrow. We have to talk."

A loud crash. She gasped as icy liquid splattered her feet and ankles. She'd dropped her glass. Her gaze flew back to the window. The man was gone.

The social chatter paused for a few seconds, and Carey stood frozen in the silence, staring at her wild-eyed reflection. It was him. No mistake. Inside her chest, a familiar resonance echoed, as if she'd just breathed in a lungful of static electricity. It crawled under her skin, swirled around her heart and left a strange, yet heady, taste on her tongue.

"No problem, ma'am." Instantly two white-coated busboys appeared with towels and a broom. "We'll clean it right up. Happens all the time. Did you cut yourself?"

She shook her head, which felt cottony, and stepped out of the messy circle of liquid and broken glass. "No, I'm fine, thank you."

"Carey?"

Trembling from head to toe, she sucked in a deep breath and dabbed at the sweat on her forehead with her cocktail napkin as she turned to see her Aunt Loreen beckoning her over, a decidedly aged matron at her side.

Straightening her spine, she turned her back on the window and somehow found herself moving toward the women, though she wasn't sure how because she couldn't feel her feet.

Loreen frowned as she approached. "What's wrong?"

"Nothing, I'm fine," she repeated. "I just dropped my glass. Clumsy of me." She took deep silent breaths to control her trembling. It wouldn't do to cause a scene in the middle of the party. No, indeed. The women in her family were trained to never cause a scene. Ever.

Her steps slowed a little when she noticed Loreen's carefully made-up face. The woman was smiling. Loreen certainly smiled on occasion, but Carey had never seen her smile quite so wide, not even when Kyle had announced their engagement. Carey's eyes narrowed. She loved her aunt, but years of living under Loreen's roof had taught her to be afraid, be very afraid, when Loreen Norton Sinclair smiled like that.

"Congratulations, sweetheart!" chirped Loreen, throwing her arms around Carey in a hug that nearly squashed her breath out. "Oops," she added, extricating one of Carey's hairpins from the teased nest of curls next to her ear.

Continuing to grimace behind her bred-to-the-bone smile, Carey straightened, attempting to tuck the escaped curl back behind a bobby pin and failing.

"What's that on your cheek?" Loreen leaned close again, shrewd eyes zeroed in on a spot on Carey's face. Carey reached up and touched the spot. Her fingers came away wet, as if someone had just spritzed her cheek with mist. Was it iced tea? Furtively she touched her fingertip to her lip, then tasted. Salt. Like tears.

She quickly wiped her fingers and her face with her napkin. "Sorry, I must have been drooling on myself."

Loreen laughed like a tower full of silver bells, but her eyes reflected disapproval of Carey's offhand remark. She motioned to the tall, grey-haired woman at her side, who mirrored Loreen's indulgent smile. "Mrs. Simmons was just telling me the good news."

"What good news?"

"You mean you don't know?" Loreen's face fell. "Oh dear, I've spoiled the surprise, haven't I?"

"Surprise?" Feeling a little idiotic at parroting her aunt's words, Carey managed to keep her tone light, though she felt like she was about to leap out of her skin.

The other woman extended her hand, which Carey automatically shook.

"We haven't met before, but I believe we'll be seeing a lot more of each other come August," the woman said warmly. "My name is Virginia Simmons. I'm the headmistress at Southern Pines. From your impressive resume, and what your fiancé has told me about you, you will be a refreshing addition to the faculty, Miss Magennis."

Carey withdrew her hand as it grew numb, along with her other hand and both feet. "I beg your pardon? What faculty?"

Virginia Simmons looked at Loreen, confused. "Why, Southern Pines Academy, of course. The board approved your contract this afternoon. In fact, I've brought it with me to present it to you myself. Perhaps Mr. Thorpe was planning to surprise her with the news?"

Loreen clapped her hands in delight. "I knew you'd see reason one day, sweetheart. You served your time at that urban wasteland of a school. It's high time you went after something better."

Drowning...drowning...

"I don't recall sending... I never even interviewed..." Carey put a hand to her throat. Was she so far gone that she couldn't even remember interviewing for a job?

Mrs. Simmons' face went blank. "I see," she said, her expression settling into one that said plainly, *Oh, yes, I do see it very well.*

"No, you don't understand..."

"I'll be happy to take care of this for you, Mrs. Simmons. Now excuse us, will you please, ladies? She's just a little overwhelmed by the good news." Kyle's blue silk tie and white shirt moved into her line of vision as he inserted himself between her and the other ladies, plucking the thick envelope from Mrs. Simmons' fingers.

As Carey tried to remember how to breathe, she found herself drawn behind a bank of potted palms. Kyle was saying something to her.

"...meant to tell you before, but I wanted to make sure it was all set."

"All set? What was all set?"

Kyle took her in his arms, which only increased the smothering sensation. If she didn't get outside soon, she was afraid she was going to be sick. Too many surprises for one day.

"Isn't it wonderful, Carey? Southern Pines is one of the finest private schools in the state. You'll be happy there, and your salary will triple. It's right in the neighborhood where we plan to buy a house. And when our children are old enough—"

Carey pulled away and stared up at him through eyes suddenly blurred by tears.

"How—" Her voice choked off, and Kyle smiled tenderly and stroked her cheek, mistaking her wet eyes for tears of happiness.

"I just kept my ear to the ground and when a position came

open, I called in a couple of favors with some people I know on the board," he said, looking pleased with himself. "And the promise of a large contribution to the school endowment fund. It's all arranged. I even took the liberty of having your trunks stored in your new room for the summer. All you have to do is walk in and get started, after you've signed the contract, of course. What's the matter, sugar? Aren't you pleased? It's not a big deal, you know. This is how things like this are done all the time."

Carey put up a hand and found her cheeks wet with overflowing tears. "I...don't know, Kyle. Park Ridge was my home for eight years...my students...I had planned to reapply there when I felt ready." She couldn't hold back a sob.

Kyle looked at her, the warmth in his eyes cooling a little. "They'll have a new teacher next year. They'll adapt." He leaned closer and dropped his voice. "And I think it's best if you don't mention your medication to anyone. If word gets out..."

His implication was clear, but she vehemently shook her head. "That's not true. All I need is a doctor's statement that my symptoms are under control."

He looked at her as if he couldn't believe she could be that naïve. "They only tell you that to be politically correct. You know what the reality will be."

She sat on the edge of a planter to gather her wits. She took a steadying breath and looked up at Kyle again. "Why?"

He crouched before her and took her hands in his, his expression patient and his tone careful, as if speaking to a small child. Carey found the back of her neck bristling as he spoke. "I did it for you, honey. For us. Someone had to take action. If I hadn't done this, you would have been content to go back and spend the rest of your career in a nowhere public school." He reached up and stroked the escaped curl behind her ear. "You are beautiful and a good teacher, Carey, but you're a dreamer. You just need a little direction, a little push. Southern Pines Academy will be the best for you, for our children, for the plans we've made for ourselves. Remember?"

She managed to find a little steel to inject into her spine. Her posture straightened. "I liked the direction I was going. Those children needed me."

"And the children at Southern Pines don't? They deserve a good teacher just as much as those... Well, let's just say your talents should be used on kids who have the potential to match your skills. Besides, what's the difference where you teach as long as you're teaching—and making more money in the bargain?"

She couldn't believe she was hearing this. Carey closed her eyes and rubbed between them, trying to ease a sudden headache. She'd always lived her life in a straight line, looking neither right nor left, rarely straying off the beaten path except for her infamous wandering attention span. She knew Kyle had always said he wanted their children in private school; she hadn't realized until now he had the same plans for her.

She stared at Kyle, the man she was going to marry, as if for the first time. *I do not belong here. I do not belong with you.*

She blinked as this new thought joined with the other one that had been plaguing her. No...no, these thoughts were taking her down a road she was sure she didn't want to go. Or did she? A memory of a ghost's piercing green eyes reared up in her mind.

She was confused...not thinking clearly. She needed air. She pushed herself to her feet. "I have to go."

Kyle stood with her, hands at her elbows. "Are you feeling all right? I know this must have come as kind of a shock. But a good shock, right?"

"I'm sure it's what's best, Kyle." *And if I don't get out of this room in the next thirty seconds I'm going to be sick all over your Italian shoes.* "I'd like to go home. But first let me make my apologies to Mrs. Marwood...and to Mrs. Simmons. I'm sure she must think I'm a chicken wing shy of a picnic."

He shadowed her as she stepped out from the potted palms. "I'll drive you."

"Don't be silly. It won't do to get the gossips talking if we both disappear." Avoiding idle gossip was the one thing Kyle would understand, she thought with unaccustomed bitterness. The new emotion felt sour in her soul. "I'll have the front desk call a cab."

Kyle's face brightened. "Of course. Good thinking. In fact, I'll call for the company limo. You can look this over on your way home." He pulled the thick legal envelope from inside his suit coat and handed it to her. "I'll see you tomorrow then?"

"What's this?"

"Your teaching contract. I'd like to get it back to Mrs. Simmons first thing tomorrow, so I'll swing by later tonight to pick it up."

She watched her own hand close over the envelope then tap it against his silk tie. "Sure, Kyle, I know just what to do with this." She snapped her mouth shut and bit the inside of her cheek. When was the last time she'd used such a sarcastic tone?

He seemed too distracted to notice. He patted her cheek and left her at the door to the smoking room, where a number of men were gathered to imbibe in brandy, cigars and high-powered deals.

She found herself inordinately pleased to see him go.

Troy crossed his arms as he watched Kyle the Rat scurry off to join his herd of suits. With every passing hour time weighed more heavily on his shoulders.

The quicker she dropped this loser and quit those meds, the quicker he could figure out how to get free, and back to the business of finding John Garrison, back to the business of protecting his family. Especially Taylor. The vulnerability he'd sensed in her last time he'd been near her at Cape Hatteras only made his mission more urgent.

He followed Carey—rather, she towed him—out to the limo, and slipped into the back beside her. She immediately raised the privacy screen between herself and the driver and stared straight ahead, eyes glistening. Frowning, he reached out to touch her arm, making contact just as the first of a series of violent sobs shook her body.

Her inner turmoil rolled through him, and he jerked back, fist and body clenched against the urge to materialize and gather her in his arms. Not that he actually could at this point.

It was damned lucky he couldn't. If he gave in to that sweet temptation, he'd never get out of here.

Carey slammed the limo door behind her and ran all the way around to the back of the house, through the rose garden and into her walkout apartment under her aunt's post-antebellum-style mansion.

For once the old lock worked on the first try, and she charged through the darkened apartment, not bothering with lights. The second she crossed the threshold of her bedroom, she went to work removing the trappings of the elegant evening. She kicked off the foot-killing, strappy shoes in opposite directions. She whipped the silky black sheath dress over her head and tossed it over a chair. Then she went to work on the hairpins, stripping them out one by one, leaving a trail as she paced in circles, letting each painful tug remind her to breathe.

She ended up in front of her moon-lit, full-length mirror as she located and rid herself of the last few. When she looked up at her wild-haired, underwear-clad reflection, she saw that the fingers of her right hand were clawed around the engagement ring on her left, ready to rip it off too.

What am I doing?

She turned and walked with deliberate steps to her bed, where she sat on the edge and stared out the east window at the moon, full and filling her eyes, her mind, with its cool, brilliant light.

She closed her eyes and turned away, lying on her side on the bed, listening to her heartbeat slow as a strange calm overtook her.

I don't belong here.

She sat up and pounded her fists into the mattress. "Then where do I belong? Where?" The things she had counted on to define herself—her career, her love of doing living history, even the security of fitting into her world and fulfilling family expectations—had all been yanked out from under her, one by one. True, she had been handed a new job. A good job, from the sound of it.

But it isn't what I want.

What did she want? Ever since her drowning, nothing had been the same, felt the same. She had no words for it, and her attempts to talk about it with Kyle, her future life partner, had been met with a vaguely insulting pat on the head. An admonition to put it all behind her and get on with a normal life. A pill or two to dull memory and keep her mind in the real world.

Or to make me fit into his world?

She pushed herself to her feet and set about putting her clothes away. Dress in hand, she flicked on the light to her walk-in closet and found a reason to smile. Two-thirds of the closet was taken up with some of the period costumes she used in her living-history activities. She'd amassed quite a collection, enough that she had separate wardrobes for in the classroom, and out of it.

She let her gaze wander over the carefully organized closet. Civil War uniforms and women's clothing vied for space with Revolutionary War garb. A Cherokee wedding dress of soft buckskin hung companionably next to the rough-woven cloth of a Lost Colony-era day gown. A long, kilted plaid skirt with a jabot blouse kept company with a red velvet Medieval frock. Her fingers paused on the Cherokee dress, which had belonged to her own mother. Perhaps it had been a gift from Carey's father. She had a dim visual memory of her mother showing her the dress, but its soundtrack was lost in the mists of time.

Carey had envisioned wearing the dress at a sunrise wedding on a mountaintop in the Great Smokies, the one flight of fancy she wanted to make real. Kyle had laughed at the idea.

She hung up her cocktail dress and let her hands feather over her costumes. Creating characters and living in them for the benefit of her students and anyone who saw her perform—then, she was in her element. She could completely lose herself in a character. More than once she had felt as if she were no longer in her own body.

Maybe that was why she hadn't panicked when she had drowned and felt her soul peeling away. In a way, she had done it many times before. Until those miracle drugs, anyway.

But the vivid daydreams she usually had when she'd

missed her dose... She thought back to what had happened earlier at the party, and also that afternoon, with the old, saxophone-playing man. How her daydream had become more real than the street corner she was standing on. What did it mean?

Her wandering hands came into crackling contact with the plastic that covered her own designer, white lace wedding dress. The one Loreen had approved.

Carey turned on her heel and was across the room in three leaps, her hands closing around the bedside phone. She'd had a few sessions with a psychologist after her drowning incident, where they'd talked about post-traumatic stress and panic attacks. But she hadn't gone back after she'd begun taking the medication. After that, her "problem" had been considered "solved". She froze and tried to remember where she'd put the man's phone number. It wouldn't come to her, but another one did, seemingly out of the blue.

I have to get out of here.

Her fingers shook so badly she couldn't punch in the number she wanted. Her heart thudded heavily in her chest and sweat broke out on her bare skin. She pressed a hand to her damp forehead, afraid she was going to faint. She couldn't go anywhere. What was she thinking? She had so much to do. A new school, a completely different class of children, meant she would need an entirely new lesson plan for next year, a scant two months away. Thanks to Kyle and his help. No, his machinations. Her gaze went back to the closet and the froth of white lace pressed flat under heavy clear plastic. The wedding.

A wedding to a man she no longer wanted to spend her life with.

Shaking with the enormity of what she was about to do, she put the phone down. She took a deep breath, then slowly twisted Kyle's engagement ring off her finger. Next she found the thick envelope she'd flung aside when she'd first come in the door. Then she went to her bathroom, took the pill bottles from the cabinet. The anti-anxiety pill. The anti-depressant. And the anti-seizure agent. She placed everything on the center of the white eyelet quilt on her bed. She picked up a pen and paper to leave a note, then reconsidered.

What she contemplated could be considered crazy, but she didn't want anyone to try to talk her out of it. Not this time.

She stared at the small offering on the bed for a long time, a shrine to the future she was about to throw away. Then she picked up the phone and this time dialed the number with a steadier hand. Not the shrink. But a person who she knew would be at least as good for her.

Pick up, Lane. Please, pick up.

"Hello?" Delaney Brannon's voice sounded scratchy, as if she'd been asleep.

"Hey, Lane. It's Carey." She tried to make her voice light and casual. "Got a question for you."

"What's wrong?"

She knew her laugh sounded forced. "Nothing, nothing. I—"

"Don't give me nothing. It's almost midnight and you're too polite to call at this late hour. Unless it's an emergency."

Carey opened her mouth but nothing came out.

"I'm coming over there," said Lane.

"No, no. I just wanted to know if your earlier offer still stands...about my going with you this month as an assistant on your photo shoot. I know you've probably hired someone else by now, and I know I said I had other plans, but...they sort of fell through." She closed her eyes against the imagined sight of Kyle's and her aunt's reactions to what she was about to do.

"It's Kyle, isn't it?"

"It's...a lot of things."

Silence on the other end of the line. She pressed her hand over her mouth, but the words spilled out anyway, unbidden, coming from someplace inside her she hadn't known existed.

"Lane, please. I need to disappear. Just for a while." She held her breath.

"I'm not going to pretend I'm unhappy about this development."

Carey surprised herself with a shaky laugh. "Just don't pull the I-told-you-so card, okay?"

"Deal. I'll be over in a half hour." Lane's cheer was infectious.

Carey gripped the phone tighter. "You can say no. I know this sounds crazy."

"Don't be daft, woman," said Lane in the faux Scottish accent she often lapsed into. "Someone has to help you pack."

Lounging in the closet doorway, Troy Brannon watched appreciatively as the half-naked Carey brushed past him, grabbed a suitcase from under a pile of quilts and hauled it to the bed. Her energy was feeling more than ever like her own. He closed his eyes and let himself wish he could pull her to him and immerse himself in her in every way possible.

He shook himself out of it. Whatever it was she had, it was addictive. That meant she was forbidden fruit—too much of a distraction from his goal. Nothing would make him lose sight of that. Nothing.

Apparently changing her mind, she shoved the suitcase aside and went instead for a backpack and a duffel bag. He watched her pause, then slowly reach down and pick up a pill bottle from the eyelet comforter.

Do it, girl.

For weeks he had watched this woman. He'd had no other choice. His earlier suspicions had been right. He was bound to her like a carrier chained to the dock in Norfolk. The harder he tried to break away, the tighter their invisible bonds became.

She'd seen him in the hospital. Really seen him, not just imagined him through a sedative-induced haze. And this afternoon, and just this evening, he'd felt that familiar jolt that told him she'd felt his presence again, if only for a fleeting second. Some part of her brain could tune in to him.

She didn't need those pills. She was stronger than that. She just didn't know it yet.

More than once he had been sorely tempted to help her along on her path to discovering what a loser this Kyle fellow was. On the outside he seemed the perfect man—handsome, charming and on the way to becoming wildly successful in his career. Troy knew the type. Up to this moment, the man had her completely buffaloed.

Kyle had an agenda. Troy could smell it.

But he'd held himself out of it, telling himself he had only one task to accomplish—find a way to unbind himself from this woman and find John Garrison's lost spirit before someone else did.

Trouble was, once she'd started taking those pills, her brainwave pattern was too altered to sense him anymore. He'd waited, watched, looking for an opening when the meds were low in her system, trying to catch her in the elusive wisp of time between waking and sleeping. Always just missing.

He was a patient man. But he was running out of time.

She turned from the bed, pill bottles in hand and strode toward the bathroom, all long legs and floating mass of dark, curly hair.

That's it...keep going, Carey. You know what you have to do now.

She took a deep breath, opened the pill bottles one by one and dumped them all down the toilet.

Hooyah, baby. Troy punched the air in triumph. Soon she would be back on his wavelength.

When that happened, there'd be no stopping him.

Gráinne Cottage, Ireland

Genola McCarthy shivered in spite of the warmth in her kitchen. Her good thatched roof was tight against the weather, but it didn't quite keep out the wail of the wind as it twisted around the stone corners of the house.

This whole day, and long into this night, a nameless worry had picked away at her until she had retreated to the one room in her house in which she felt completely safe. The kitchen. Here, where she and Seamus had shared everything—worries, food, tea, laughter and five children grown and gone.

As it had all this livelong day, thoughts of Seamus had inexplicably led to thoughts of young Carey Magennis. Genola had lost track of Carey when her intended had whisked her away to another hospital. Something about Kyle Thorpe still didn't sit well with Genola. She couldn't get the memories of how he had behaved that dark day on the cliffs, and later at the hospital. Nothing she could hang her hat on, but something...something.

The ominous Tarot reading that had preceded Carey's

drowning niggled at Genola's subconscious. And the ghost of Troy Brannon, whose power to temporarily overcome the barriers of death had saved her life. Whose potent presence still seemed to linger in this very room, even though he had long since vanished along with Carey.

Genola now wondered if her instinct had been wrong, that the source of the real danger wasn't Troy, after all.

Restless, Genola put a pot on to boil then opened the drawer that held her Tarot cards. She eased into a chair, took the cards out of their box, and held them between her hands, closing her eyes to say a quick prayer of entreaty for wisdom. For protection. Then, fixing a mental picture of Carey's faerie-touched face and black waterfall of curling hair in her mind, she began to shuffle the cards.

She laid them down and spread them with a quick sweep of her hand, letting her palm feel the edges of each one. Quickly, without stopping to consider, she pulled out three cards at random and lay them facedown before her. She took a deep breath, a feeling of dread settling on her shoulders even before she turned over the first one.

The death card.

A small sound squeaked out of her throat. She turned the center card.

The knight of wands. Reversed.

Her brows drew together in a frown. This was new. Same card, but upside down. She turned it right side up and examined it. Then it hit her. The soldier in the picture wasn't Athenian. He was Trojan. And he was defending his city, not attacking it.

I completely misinterpreted the reading.

Heart pounding, she laid the knight down and flipped the last card.

Blank.

Genola let out her breath and sat back in her chair, considering. The blank card no longer shocked her. She looked upon it now as just another message the oracle was trying to send. She tapped it with her forefinger, then the knight of wands. She snorted in disgust. Carey was still in danger, and Troy was mucking about, absorbed in his own problems rather than trying to help the poor woman.

She closed her eyes and willed that fair fallen angel of a ghost to hear her, though three thousand miles of ocean separated them.

"You, my lad, are clearly not doing your job."

Chapter Five

Carey closed the book on Civil War-era spies she'd just finished, snapped off her flashlight and stuck her head out of her sleeping bag for some fresh air. She stared up into pitch darkness at where the tent roof would be if she reached her fingertips up a foot or two. Her muscles ached, as if she'd just run a marathon. Most of Lane's equipment wasn't heavy, but a full day of toting it around, tramping up and down hills, scrambling through brush and boulders, had taken more out of her than she'd anticipated. Perhaps one month wasn't long enough for her body to fully recover from drowning.

It was so late even the crickets had gone to sleep. Barely a sound penetrated her nylon cocoon, save for an occasional breath of cedar-scented breeze that tapped a few tree branches together, or the furtive footfall of some nocturnal creature.

She shifted, savoring the contrast between the toasty interior of her bag, and the chill night air that nipped at the end of her nose. Normally, this was perfect sleeping weather for her. More precisely, any weather was perfect sleeping weather—Carey had never in her life been plagued by insomnia. Until now.

Only two days since she left home in the wee hours of night, two days since she'd flushed the pills down the toilet. She'd been told the drug was short-acting, but perhaps cutting herself off so abruptly hadn't been a good idea. Maybe she was experiencing some kind of withdrawal symptom.

Or maybe she just felt guilty about running away.

No. Guilt is no longer a part of my vocabulary. Period.

In spite of herself, she thought of what Aunt Loreen's reaction must have been to the note she'd left. In the end, Carey had decided to leave one, knowing Loreen would worry and call in every marker she possessed within the various state, county and city law enforcement communities to find her.

And Kyle. When she had her thoughts sorted out, she'd talk to him. Explain that a marriage between them would have been a mistake, in no small part because another man haunted her memories—and sometimes her waking dreams. Not that she would ever tell Kyle about that. To tell him that she couldn't marry him because of an encounter with a ghost... Well, that certainly would qualify her for a one-way ticket to Holly Hill.

On impulse, she reached for her cell phone, turned it on, and in the darkness dialed her voice mail.

"You have...fourteen...unplayed messages."

Kyle's voice. Patient, reasoning. Asking why she hadn't answered her door when he'd come by for the contract. Kyle again. Less patient, reminding her to take her pills, and please call him back as soon as possible. Kyle, angry, asking why in heaven's name did she carry a cell phone if she refused to return calls. By the thirteenth message he was back to his patient tone again, telling her in no uncertain terms to stop acting like a child and come home. She didn't miss the unmistakable note of warning in his voice. She almost didn't listen to the last message, but guilt reared its ugly head and she gritted her teeth.

Aunt Loreen. "Carey, if you get this message, at least call me and let me know you're all right. Whatever it is going on between you and Kyle, we'll work it out, all right? Just call home."

Methodically, Carey deleted all the messages except the last one, disconnected, snapped the phone shut and lay it aside. She stared up into the darkness, eyes stinging.

Blinking hard, she shoved her hair out of her eyes and looked at her watch.

"Damn."

Long hours of darkness stretched before her with little to do but stare at it and grow frustrated trying to make herself sleep. She was probably just trying too hard.

"Was that a swear word I heard emerging from your mouth, Miss Teacher-of-the-Year?" Lane unzipped her own sleeping bag and flicked on her flashlight.

Carey pulled her sleeping bag up to her chin against the night chill. "I'm sorry. I woke you up again, didn't I?"

Lane drew her brows together and pointed a finger at her friend. "Nah-ah-ah. Remember, I told you rule number one on this trip is no apologies."

Carey grinned. "I remember."

Lane's expression softened, as did her whiskey-low voice. "Could you use some company?"

Carey shrugged and looked at her watch again. "It's late, and you need your sleep—"

"It's all right. Thanks to your help, and good luck with the weather, we're already ahead of schedule. We've got time to kill tomorrow. Be right back." And with that, she skinned out of her sleeping bag, unzipped the tent flap and disappeared into the night.

Carey hugged herself and felt her eyes grow wet. "Oh jeez, not again." She dashed angrily at her eyes and breathed deeply to control herself. She'd wanted to come with Lane on her photography tour of Civil War battlefields in an effort to get away, to clear her head. Gather her thoughts into some semblance of order, after having them scrambled beyond recognition in that sea cave in Ireland.

She thought of the man who had saved her, and her persistent visions of him. Some part of her wished that he was more than just something induced by stress, trauma or sedatives. She remembered how she had felt with him near, how his direct gaze challenged her, seemed to challenge everything. Her whole being had felt...brighter, somehow. Like a light was switched on in her soul, only to go out when he disappeared.

If only she could somehow conjure him up one more time. Maybe he could at least tell her why she was still alive, when by all rights she should be dead. Why he had given his life for her.

Lane reappeared, this time with her midnight hair stuffed under a battered Atlanta Braves baseball cap, and carrying one of her cameras she'd retrieved from her truck. She flopped down on her sleeping bag and reached for her boots. "Get dressed, girl. Let's go."

"You're kidding. Where are we going to go at this hour? And it's cold out there!"

"Wimp."

Carey rose to the unmistakable challenge in Lane's voice, and stuck out her chin. "Twerp."

"Weenie."

"Dweeb."

"*History* teacher."

Carey clutched her hands over her heart. "Ouch!" she gasped with laughter.

Lane grinned. "Come on. We're going ghost hunting."

Carey froze in the act of reaching for her boots. "Uh..."

Lane studied her, eyes shrewd. "Poor choice of words?" Her voice softened. "Come on. The walk may help you sleep. If we happen across some ghosts, it'll just be icing on the cake." Then she was gone again, and Carey heard her whistling to herself as she undoubtedly fiddled with her camera.

Carey finished tying her boots in thoughtful silence, then pulled on her jacket and wrangled her rioting hair under a bandanna. Taking a deep breath, she grabbed her flashlight and scooted out into the clear, silent night of Stones River Battlefield. Thanks to Lane's assignment with a prestigious history magazine, they'd gotten special permission to camp right on the battlefields they were touring.

She crab-walked through the tent opening and straightened up in the cool, damp night. The moon had not yet risen, leaving them in an almost-perfect sphere of dark and silence. Except for her flashlight.

"Augh, woman! Turn the light off. You'll be scaring the ghosts away with that thing."

Carey considered the reassuring circle of light on the ground, and wondered at her finger's refusal to disobey her mental order to turn it off. She firmed her jaw. She'd never had issues with the dark before, at least not before the drowning. No point in starting now. Still, she hesitated. "I'd rather not trip and break my neck, thanks," she said dryly.

"Your eyes will adjust in a minute. Try it," Lane prodded, shielding her own eyes from the white circle on the ground.

Carey turned it off. "I hope your liability insurance is paid."

"When I found out you were coming with me, I tripled my coverage."

She snorted. "That didn't even cause a blip on my hilarious meter."

They stood for a minute in companionable silence as they let their eyes adjust. Carey listened to the sound of her own breath going in and out of her lungs, and her heartbeat slowed as her eyes gradually adjusted to the starlight. Tree trunks, boulders, fences and even the distant long slope of a ridge emerged out of the dark. Even the silence wasn't really silent. One by one, her ears picked up the occasional rustle of a faint breeze through the trees, the far-off music of a stream, and the cautious footfall of some nocturnal creature in the leaves.

"It's amazing how many shades of black your eyes can pick out," she observed.

"Yep. Walk behind me. My jacket is pretty light so you should be able to follow me." Lane unceremoniously handed her a portable tripod. "Here, might as well make yourself useful."

"I should have known you just wanted a pack mule along on your little midnight sortie." She sighed dramatically as she slung it over her shoulder and set off down a path in Lane's wake. "I assume you know where you're going?"

"Not really," Lane said cheerfully, the mist cloud of her breath trailing over her shoulder.

"I thought you said you'd been here before!"

"I have, but not in pitch dark. Don't worry, it'll be light in a few hours. We'll figure out where we are then."

"And you're okay with this?"

"Sure, I do it all the time. What's the big deal?"

Carey lapsed into silence. She found she had no trouble following the crunch of Lane's boots on the gravel. The cool night air cleared her mind. She tramped along, unzipping her jacket as her muscles warmed.

What had it been like for the soldiers here, encamped before the battle? It would have been warmer, more humid, she mused. Her mind began to pick and choose stored historical details to build the mental picture. Camp smoke would have hung heavy, thick, hugging the ground due to the moisture in the air. A soldier would have been...

...wiping smoke-induced—or was it homesick?—tears as he squinted in the flickering firelight at the grimy, torn scrap of paper, scratching out a letter to his family. Settling comfortably into the scene her mind's eye created, Carey leaned over his shoulder to get a closer look.

Dear Mama, Tomorrow, they tell me, we are going to fight. I am ready, but I know you will not think less of me when I tell you I am afraid. The Yankees, you see, are dug in on the heights...

The soldier looked up and saw the regimental chaplain approaching, an ever-growing crowd of sober-faced men following in his wake. He carefully folded the letter, stuck it in his pocket and went to join his comrades in prayer, and perhaps a last blessing. The soldier himself wasn't a church-going man, but he wasn't fool enough to not fear God at a time like this. The wind shifted, sending campfire smoke into his face, and he coughed and rubbed his eyes.

Carey heard a twig crack behind her and, curious, turned and followed her mind's eye into the shadows of the surrounding trees. She hadn't gotten far when a tall, angular black shape separated itself from a tree trunk.

"Do you have it?"

Startled, she looked around to see who the blob was talking to. There was no one else she could see. She jumped when the shape gave a low, impatient whistle.

"If you have something for me, now would be a good time to hand it over. I can't stand around here all night."

"Are you...talking to me?" she stuttered.

He didn't answer, but stepped out into a patch of moonlight. He wore a Confederate uniform, but it fit him so badly it struck her that it probably didn't belong to him. His dark hair stuck out from under a kepi, and a few days' growth of beard shadowed his angular jaw.

"Bell!" he hissed.

Another set of footfalls approached from her left. Another voice, low and urgent.

"Ethan, you crazy son of a bitch, what are you doing this close to the camp? I told you I'd meet you in the barn."

"The barn's not safe anymore." He paused and tilted his head in her direction. She froze and halted her breathing, just in case. After a few seconds, he turned away, snatched a piece of dirty paper from Bell's hand and melted into the darkness.

But not before Carey noted, with a hard swallow, that the knife sheath in Ethan's belt was stained with something dark. Blood? Although neither man could apparently see her, she took care to back away quietly and head for the dubious safety of the campfire. Something warned her to skirt the camp and lose herself among the tethered horses. A few of the animals shifted their feet and swished their tails as she passed, but none of them so much as snorted.

She stood among the animals, trembling, uncertain what to do next.

An arm snaked around her chest from behind, simultaneously pulling her backward against a hard, warm wall and pinning her upper arms. A hand clamped over her mouth and she clawed at it, sucking in frantic breaths through her nose.

The horses stamped, one of them snorting loud enough to turn the head of a soldier near the fire.

"Shhh," a masculine voice breathed in her ear. "I'm not going to hurt you, Carey. But it's really, really important that you be still right now."

She obeyed without question. His touch, his voice, were as familiar to her as her own heartbeat. She managed a slight nod, and took a breath as his hand left her mouth. But now she had two arms pressing her back to his front.

Her heart pounded as the soldier by the fire rose to his feet and moved toward them, checking his pistol as he advanced. An involuntary sound squeaked in her throat and strained to get past her compressed lips.

"Back up with me. Slowly," whispered the man at her back.

She gave another jerky nod and let him pull her back into the shadow of the trees. Only when the camp was well out of sight did he let her go.

She pivoted to face him, and caught the tail end of an expression that told her he'd been nearly as scared as she was. His hands remained on her shoulders, surprisingly warm and real for a mere waking fantasy. He held up a finger and remained that way for a full minute until the soldier, satisfied no one was there, returned to his post. Finally he relaxed.

"That was close."

Adrenaline left her limbs with lightning speed, and she grabbed two handfuls of his T-shirt to keep from falling down. He caught her under the elbows to support her, but instead of setting her away from him, he froze in place. She inhaled the scent of warm, male skin and felt energy crackle along her nerve endings, heating, as if a chemical reaction was taking place and creating a whole new substance. She closed her eyes and green sparks showered behind her eyelids.

When she felt her body sag and begin to melt into his, she gasped and straightened away from him. "Who are you and what are you—" *doing here in my fantasy?* She set her hands on his forearms and hooked her fingers there. If this was one of her casual fantasies, why was she aware of heat and a fine sheen of sweat on his skin? Her stomach turned over. "For that matter, what am I still doing here?"

"Those are all good questions. Let's start with the easiest one. My name is Troy. And ever since that day on the cliff, I've been stalking you. But not by choice, trust me."

She stared up at him and wondered if her eyes were as wide as they felt.

"You're real," she said softly, her fingers skimming his arms and skipping up to his face to touch it in wonder. "You're alive."

"No, you were right the first time. This is your fantasy and I'm not... This isn't...uh..." Whatever Troy had been about to say became tangled in the stunned expression that crossed his face. His big, warm hands squeezed her shoulders, then moved up to take hers away. He looked down at them and turned them over, circling his thumbs over the pads at the base of her fingers. Then he studied her face as if looking for answers. "I can feel you."

Remembering the wounds she had seen on him before, she searched out and found the holes in his black T-shirt. The ripped flesh was still there, just as angry and raw as before. Oddly, none of his wounds were bleeding. Her fingers hovered just over the hole in his chest. "Can you feel these? Is there pain here?"

He blinked down at his torso and shook his head. "No. It's hard to explain. I mean, I definitely know the wounds are there but they don't...but still I can feel your skin. I don't get it."

"Maybe it's because this is my daydream." The words shimmered and echoed in her being, fit into every corner of her mind. Truth, she realized, had a way of doing that.

He stroked her cheek. "And in your world, no one ever hurts," he said softly.

His callused thumb passed over her lower lip, and her breath caught. Had Kyle ever made her insides feel hollow and achy like this, with just a touch and simple, direct stare into her eyes?

No. With him she had felt...settled. No, she had a better word for it now. Resigned. She closed her eyes and let the electricity of Troy's touch shoot through her body, an addictive force that made her want to drink him in all at once like a shot of fine tequila.

And then she *was* drinking him in, for his mouth was on hers, exploring, dipping inside, tasting. She slid her arms around his neck, pulled him closer. His life force pumped beneath her palms, against her body as he pressed his hands to the small of her back.

"I wish to hell this was real," he mumbled against her mouth. "You taste like..."

Then he tilted his head back, breaking contact, and set her away from him. He curled his hands into fists at his sides as if to keep himself from reaching for her again.

"I'm sorry, Carey. I never was what you'd call a gentleman, but that was...uncalled for."

That was...amazing. "It's okay," she lied, thinking to herself this was the most not-okay situation she'd ever found herself in.

"Look, nothing has changed. I'm still a ghost—I'm just stuck here with you in your daydream." He shook his head as if still shaking off the effect of their kiss. "In fact, I think we're both stuck here until some outside force snaps your consciousness back to where your body is. I think the experts would call this astral traveling."

"What?" She stepped back and wrapped her arms around her middle, the kiss still burning on her lips. His gaze followed her movement.

"I was a ghost when I first found you. Still am."

She gave an unfunny laugh and tried to regain the equilibrium he'd stolen. "This isn't making any sense."

"I'm not sure how much time we have, so I'll try to sum it up. I died almost two years ago while serving in a special military unit. An explosion. Instead of going...wherever...I ended up staying here on earth. Kind of by accident I discovered I had abilities a bit out of the ordinary for a regular ghost. For one thing, I could zap myself wherever I needed to go by focusing my thoughts." He paused as if he wanted to say something else, then didn't.

She knew her mouth was sagging open wider as he hurried on, but she couldn't help it.

"When I found you, you weren't breathing. I had to do something else I discovered I could do—materialize into some semblance of solid form just long enough to get you rescued. But whatever I did to get you jumpstarted, it stuck us together. Now I'm pretty much anchored wherever you are."

She blinked. "But I'm not really here. This is a daydream." She looked around and her skin prickled. "One I can't seem to wake up from." Breath coming fast, she pulled completely away from him and began turning around in place. "Lane? Lane!"

Abruptly, lights flashed before her eyes. She heard Troy swear, felt him grab one of her flailing hands—hard.

Whump.

She found herself sitting flat on her rump, having plowed into Lane from behind, not noticing she had stopped in the woods at the edge of the battlefield cemetery. Lane, fortunately, had caught herself by wrapping her arms around a sapling.

"Do you mind?" Lane grumped good-naturedly as she righted herself and brushed herself off. She reached for Carey's hand.

Oh thank God.

"Sorry," Carey muttered, accepting the proffered hand and allowing Lane to pull her to her feet. Her heart was still racing. "Uh, my mind must have wandered." *With a vengeance.*

"That's ok. It's part of your charm," said Lane easily, relieving Carey of the tripod which she couldn't quite seem to get her trembling limbs untangled from. Then she paused, leaned closer and sniffed.

"When did you start smoking?"

Carey went still. "I don't. Never have."

"I thought I smelled smoke, and I thought it was coming from you." She sniffed again. "I swear, it *is* coming from you."

Carey lifted her sleeve to her nose and sniffed. Lane was right, her clothing smelled of wood smoke. She rubbed her itchy eyes and found them damp, as if they had been watering from irritation.

It happened again. And it's getting worse.

"What? What happened again? Carey, what's wrong?"

Carey stared at Lane. "Did I say that out loud?"

"Yes, you did. What happened again? What does the smell of smoke have to do with..."

Carey fumbled for her flashlight and flicked it on, aiming it at her own face. "Look at my eyes."

Lane peered. "They're red. Have you been crying?"

"No, Lane, it's from the smoke. And my clothes..." She sniffed at her sleeve again, then swallowed. "I can smell it on me, taste it in my throat. Like I just walked away from a campfire."

Lane retrieved a camera she'd dropped in their collision. "But you weren't. You were walking behind me."

"Maybe... Maybe I wasn't." An idea dawned in Carey's brain, one so preposterous she began to laugh. "Do you think it's possible to be in two places at once?"

Lane's smile was more confused than humorous. "What are you talking about?"

"Remember what my nickname was in college?"

"Yup. 'Unconscious'. You were always either buried in your history books or staring off into space. Sometimes I envied your ability to tune everything else out and travel in your mind to places unknown."

"Now I think I'm doing it with more than just my mind." Pacing in a circle, Carey heard herself babbling but couldn't seem to make herself stop. A mishmash about a cut finger, a Revolutionary war soldier and his woman. A Civil War campfire. Her multiple conversations with the ghost of her dead rescuer, starting all the way back in a Tralee hospital. She left out the part about the way here insides were still quivering in the aftermath of Troy's kiss. That would just be TMI.

Finished, she looked up and found Lane with her hands over her face, groaning. Carey deflated. She'd thought she could tell her old roommate anything.

"You think I'm going insane, don't you?" She flailed her arms helplessly then hugged her middle. "Maybe Kyle is right. Maybe my brain got fried from lack of oxygen. Maybe I do need those drugs after all."

Lane's hand fell away from her face. "No, no. Not at all. I was just thinking that I'm going to have to introduce you to some friends of mine. My cousin, actually." She gathered up her equipment and hooked an arm through Carey's, turning back toward camp. "Come on, I've got a bottle of Irish whiskey with our names on it. We've got a lot to talk about."

"I thought I'd met most of your friends," said Carey, falling in beside her friend.

Lane's grin flashed in the moonlight. "Not the really interesting ones."

Troy rolled to his feet, shaking his head to clear it. He watched Carey and Lane disappear into the darkness, but made no move to follow. Not just yet. He wasn't sure if he could remain upright just now.

He had been following Carey, right on her heels, watching for the instant her focus shifted from the present to a dream state. The transition was incredibly quick; even with his honed reflexes, he'd missed it several times since she'd come off those pills.

He had the ability to inhabit her dreams. He'd picked up the idea from John during their ordeal a few months ago. But the odd thing with Carey was her nighttime dreams had been made impenetrable by the drugs. And on the rare occasion she entered a waking dream, her life force disappeared entirely. In the hospital, the sedatives and her injuries had slowed her down. Now, she could transition from reality to fantasy quicker than he could shapeshift on his best day, going downhill with an angry mob of jihadists on his heels.

He had never encountered anything like it.

Tonight, he'd vowed to stick within a few inches of her—teeth-grinding a task as that was, as her life force still called him like a siren song—and catch her just as she slipped into one of her imaginings. Only then would he be able to communicate with her as he'd done back in Ireland.

He'd learned to watch for the surge, then dip, of energy in her cerebral cortex that signaled her attention was beginning to wander. Tonight his timing had been perfect.

Her neurons fired. He'd reached out to touch her...

Then someone pulled the rug out from under his feet, rolled it up and whacked him upside the head with it. A sound like a phonograph needle scraping over an LP. When his head cleared, he'd found himself in the middle of what looked like a Civil War re-enactment. He knew what one looked like; he and his family had been involved in re-enacting since he'd been a kid. At first he'd wondered why he hadn't noticed the event until that instant. A cavalry officer had paced slowly past, coaxing a limping horse along behind, and a preposterous idea dawned on him as he realized the wound in that horse's shoulder definitely wasn't re-created for show. He'd scanned his surroundings, taking in the dirty uniforms of the men, the tattered tents, the disgusting mess bubbling in a cooking pot. The lack of artificial lighting in the distance.

Then he'd looked across the fire, and there stood Carey, in her twenty-first century clothes, hiding among the dozing horses. Lane was nowhere in sight. He'd had to move fast in order to keep her from accidentally doing something, anything, that might alter the timeline. They might have already done it when the soldier had moved away from the fire to check on the stamping horses.

Thanks to his reflexes, he'd just managed to escape being left behind when her waking dream had abruptly ended. In the next instant, the encampment was gone, and Carey and Lane were on the ground in a heap.

He'd landed flat on his back, watching the world spin and tilt on its axis.

Now, as he watched the women head back to their camp,

Troy rubbed his face and groaned. He now knew exactly where his ability to time-travel had gone.

Carey Magennis had it. When he'd breathed life back into her, she'd apparently taken more than just air. She'd taken a piece of him.

She had no earthly idea what she'd done, or how to handle it.

Genola had been right. Carey Magennis was now in more danger than she could possibly imagine. A cold trickle ran down his spine. Strike that. Whatever could be imagined, good or bad, Carey could imagine it. And make it real.

How to warn her? How to protect her? She was a loose cannon, careening about with no control and no idea that she was in danger. Worse, Troy knew how ephemeral energy was. What if she was gone too long and the fragile thread that connected her spirit to her body deteriorated?

Troy's heart center constricted. If that happened, he'd have another lost soul on his hands.

A Dixie cup of whiskey nestled between her palms, Carey settled herself cross-legged on top of her sleeping bag.

"All right, start from the beginning," said Lane, setting a battery-powered lantern to one side and the Jack Daniels between them.

Carey took a sip from the cup, letting the amber liquid warm her quaking insides and loosen her tongue. "You already know about the accident I had in Ireland."

Lane nodded, folding her legs more comfortably beneath her. "I know that when you came back and told me, it seemed like you laughed it off and put the whole thing behind you. You refused to let anyone make a fuss." She looked down at her cup for a moment, then up at Carey, her dark eyes narrowing. "But it was more than that, wasn't it?"

Carey swallowed. "What I'm going to tell you I haven't told anyone. Well, I tried to tell Kyle, but... Anyway, bear with me because I've worked really hard to put some of this out of my mind. I'm coming to believe that wasn't the best thing to do."

Lane reached out and laid a hand on Carey's where she picked nervously at the rim of the Dixie cup. "You're safe here. I'll be the last person to tell you you're crazy. Trust me."

Carey took a steadying breath. "Okay, here goes. I went out alone for a walk on the cliffs that afternoon, and I found what looked like an easy sheep path to the base of the cliffs. Once down on the beach—Oh God, Lane, it was so beautiful there. Black cliffs towering a hundred or more feet above the ocean, a beach of smooth stones that rattled every time the waves swept in. The waves seemed so far away, a safe distance. I found the mouth of a cave and I figured it wouldn't hurt to explore for a few minutes. Well, you know how I am. I lost track of time and the next thing I knew, the cave was filling with water and I couldn't get out."

"But you did, obviously." Lane refilled their cups.

"This is where things take a strange turn. I didn't get out."

Lane put the bottle down and stared. "But—"

"The tide swept me way back into the cave. The water came up over my head, to the roof. I vividly remember breathing in water, the total darkness. I heard...felt... my heart stop."

Lane gasped softly.

"It was so strange. I knew I was dead. But I didn't feel dead."

Lane carefully set her cup down, long fingers balancing it

delicately on a wrinkle of her sleeping bag. "Then how did you get out? Kyle said they found you clinging to a ledge on the cliff."

"Someone brought me out."

"I've seen the Irish coast, honey. No one can fight that kind of current."

"I know. But what I'm telling you, what I tried to share with Kyle, is that someone appeared out of a light and took my hand. The next thing I remember, I opened my eyes and a man was holding me in his arms, breathing into my lungs. Rain was falling, in buckets it seemed, or maybe it was the waves washing over us, I don't know. I closed my eyes, opened them again, and I was in a hospital bed. And now...I think I'm being haunted by his ghost." She took a deep gulp of whisky, pressed the back of her hand to her mouth and coughed out the burn.

"Easy with that stuff. Who was he?"

"I'm getting to that. They told me that a man was on the ledge with me, but he disappeared soon after the rescuers got there. Everyone assumed he drowned." Carey ducked her chin to control the trembling. Lane hooked her finger under it and tipped her face back up, expression intent.

"No identification of the guy?"

"None."

"Odd that no one outside the incident reported a man missing. Someone must have known him."

Carey shook her head, her shoulders slumped. "No one. Believe me, I scoured the online Irish newspaper archives for any clues. When no one else was around I called everywhere I could think of on the Dingle Peninsula—the B&Bs, the pubs, even the churches—and described him."

Lane's eyebrow went up. "You remember him that clearly?

From just one glance?"

Carey drew a deep breath and plunged. "Actually, I've seen him a total of four—no five—times now. Once on the ledge. Twice he appeared to me when I was in the hospital. Tall. Military-ish. Light hair, green eyes."

Something in Lane's expression twitched.

"I thought my seeing him was drug induced," Carey plowed on. "But I've seen him twice since I've come home. Once at a charity ball when I was musing about how the grounds used to be a battlefield. And again just...just a few minutes ago. We were walking and I started thinking about what it must have been like for the soldiers encamped here. Suddenly I was there in the middle of a camp. You were gone, but he was there and said we were somehow stuck together and wouldn't return until something here woke me up. And this time he told me his name."

Lane threw up a hand. "Wait. Whoa. Back up. What specifically were you doing each time you saw him?"

"Well, I was in a meds-induced daze, or I was..." Carey stuttered to a halt, a formless idea beginning to take shape in her brain. "Daydreaming."

Lane leaned forward. "In an altered state of consciousness. Interesting." She was silent a moment, her gaze unfocused. Then she dived across the tent for her backpack, extracting a small digital camera from an outside pocket.

"What are you doing?"

"Sometimes I capture strange things on my cameras. White smudges, orbs, sometimes clear outlines of people. Ghosts. If this guy is hanging around close to you, maybe I can grab an image of him." Lane turned the camera on and made some adjustments, then reached over and turned off the lantern.

"Hey! I'm already creeped out enough!"

"Get ready for a flash."

Carey rubbed her arms and pondered how she felt about a ghost hanging right over her shoulder. Particularly one like Troy. Could he see her...all the time? The thought generated a tingle throughout her body that had nothing to do with fear.

"Now, call him. Say his name."

She took a deep breath. "Okay." She closed her eyes and tried to concentrate. Concentrate on what? *Oh for heaven's sake, just say the name.* "I want you to show yourself to the camera...Troy."

No flash, but a clattering sound.

"Lane?"

Sounds of fumbling as Lane retrieved the camera. "I...um...Troy. Troy, right? You said—"

"What is it?" Frightened now, Carey felt for the lantern and turned it back on. Lane's face was a mixture of shock and amazement. "What's wrong?"

"Troy what? What's his last name?"

She searched her memory. "I don't... He never told me."

It took a few tries for Lane to catch her breath. With trembling fingers she changed a setting on the camera. "Do me a favor. I've set this thing to record video and sound. Ask him what his last name is."

Carey pulled her sleeves down over her chilly hands and tucked them under her arms. "You're scaring me."

"Just...please. It's important." She held up the camera and pressed the record button.

"Okay. Troy, would you please tell me your last name?" Carey paused awkwardly in the silence. A breath of...something...puffed near her ear. She hunched her shoulder against it as a strange sensation zinged down her spine and her scalp prickled. But she heard nothing.

After a few moments, Lane stopped recording, plugged a set of ear buds into the side of the camera, and handed one to Carey.

Carey stuck it in her left ear with none-too-steady fingers. "Are you going to tell me what's going on?"

Lane blew a calming breath as she pressed buttons to replay the video. "In a minute. Let's just see if I'm right about something."

Carey thought she heard her mutter under her breath, "*Please, God, let me be right.*"

"Here we go. Watch the screen with me and help me listen."

"What exactly am I looking for?"

"We'll know when we see or hear it." Lane pressed the play button.

They bumped heads as they bent over the tiny screen.

"Ow."

"Sorry. Are you sure this will work?" Carey rubbed her temple.

"Well, um, I saw it done on TV..."

Carey watched herself staring into the camera. So that's how she looked when she was scared—like she was starring in her own, messed-up version of *The Blair Witch Project*, minus the snotty nose. It almost made her laugh. She listened to herself ask the question. Watched a curl beside her ear move.

Then, in her left ear, a burst of static that coincided perfectly with distortion in the picture. The voice, almost lost in the eerie whistle of the static, was nonetheless unmistakable.

"I'll take 'Brannon' for one thousand, Alex. Lane, listen carefully. I need you to get Carey—and me—to Taylor. And do me a favor. Whatever you do, don't let her mind wander."

The recording ended. Carey was aware she could probably catch flies with her open mouth, but she couldn't help it. "You know Troy?"

Lane was gazing at the camera in her hands like it was gold. "He's—he was—my cousin. Taylor is his twin sister—the one I said I wanted you to meet."

Carey's mind squealed its tires trying to keep up with this new development. "Why does he want us to go to her?"

The words seemed to spur Lane into action. "Let's get started packing up and I'll fill you in. If you think your daydreaming adventure was strange, wait till you hear the one I'm about to tell you."

Carey rolled off her sleeping bag, following Lane's cue to start stuffing it into its carry sack. "About..." she prompted.

"Well, let's start with one of the oldest ghost stories on the Outer Banks. It's about a Union cavalry soldier named Jared Beaudry..."

Chapter Six

"But I'm terrible at Sudoku." Carey picked up the coffee-stained paperback puzzle book Lane had tossed on top of her duffel bag. Dawn greyed the skies as they finished packing up the last of the campsite.

"Good. Feel free to bitch about it all the way to Hatteras. It'll keep you occupied." Lane grinned at her as she threw the last of their gear into the back of the truck, slammed the tailgate and secured the window. "I'm making one more pass around the campsite to make sure it's clean. I think there's a pen in the glove box."

"I need a pencil," Carey muttered. "One that's ninety percent eraser."

She got into the passenger side and, leaving the door open to the cool morning, began rooting around in the glove box. Footsteps crunched in the gravel on her side of the vehicle.

"Lane, I can't find..."

Something small and shiny sparkled in her peripheral vision, held by a decidedly not-Lane hand.

"You forgot something, sugar."

She jumped so violently she nearly hit her head on the ceiling. "Kyle! What... How did you..."

"Find you?" Despite the height of the truck, he still

managed to block out a good deal of the light streaming in. He had one hand braced on the roof and the other holding out her engagement ring. “It’s not that hard, Carey, when most cell phones nowadays come with GPS. At least the good ones do, and you know I always give you the best.”

The expression on his classically handsome face was neutral, but his eyes glittered with suppressed anger. His subtle body position hemmed her in, and something newly awakened within her bristled against it. “I thought my note was clear. I just needed to be alone for a while.”

He still held out the ring. She ignored it.

“I gave you a chance to respond to my voice mails. You didn’t, and it was time for me to take action. You’ve had your little vacation, sugar. It’s time to come home.” He reached out and snagged her left hand. “I’ve missed you.” He tried to put the ring back on her finger.

She curled her hand into a fist. “I’ve...had a lot on my mind. It wasn’t necessary for you to come running after me, Kyle. I would have—”

His steel-blue eyes turned flinty. “This made it necessary.” He let her go, reached into his pocket and held up an empty pill bottle. “You know the dangers of going off your meds. Someone has to be the responsible one in this relationship, Carey. Obviously it’s going to have to be me from now on.”

She stared at the bottle, the name of the anti-seizure drug jumping out at her in big, bold letters. A spark of anger warred with a suddenly queasy stomach.

“I don’t want to take it anymore.”

“Don’t be stupid. The doctors say you need it.”

“I say I don’t.”

“Are you arguing with me, sugar?” The underlying note of

warning in his smooth tone chilled her. "You've never done that before. Oh, we've had our little moments, but you've always seen reason."

She stuck out her chin. "Well maybe it's about time. And it's about time I tell you I've rethought our marriage plans, as well. I'm turning down Southern Pines Academy and going back to my old school. If they won't take me, I'm moving up to my property in the mountains. I'll teach on the reservation."

He smiled at her. "You're not going to do that."

"And why not?"

He gave her a pitying look. "You're teaching at Southern Pines because you signed the contract. It's done. In fact, I brought you a copy for your records." He pulled it out of his back pocket, shook out the last page and showed it to her. Her own signature mocked her.

What? "Since when did I sign that?"

"The night of the charity ball. I found it on your bed. Signed."

Another paper slipped out of the sheaf onto her lap. "What's this?"

He sighed heavily. "You really don't remember, do you? It's the power of attorney you gave me to dispose of the mountain property. See here? Your aunt witnessed it. Honestly, sugar, you really are starting to worry me."

Am I really that far gone? Shock prevented her from noticing, until too late, that he'd wrapped his fingers around her wrist in a bruising grip.

"You're hurting me, Kyle."

He didn't seem to hear. "Do you see now? You had one of your seizures and don't remember. You need me to take care of you, now more than ever. You're coming home with me before you make a fool of yourself—of both of us." He tried to pull her out of the truck.

She twisted her wrist in a futile attempt to break free. *Drowning...drowning...*

"No!"

His strength made it inevitable she'd lose the tug of war. She yanked anyway, digging at his grip with her other hand. To her shock, his free hand groped for her throat.

"Don't make me do this, Carey." The contrast of his soft, gentle tone with the bruising violence of his grip made her stomach roll.

The panic attack she had been holding down unsheathed its claws and tore at the edges of her vision, turning it grey. She blinked at what looked like a disturbance in the air just to Kyle's left. Like the surface of clear, boiling water, only hanging in mid-air. Then it curled into a ball and smashed into Kyle, jamming his head into the V formed by the truck's body and the open door. It happened so fast he didn't even have time to cry out. He straightened instantly, putting a hand to his bloody head and swaying, his face a blank mask of shock.

Carey reacted. Rearing back, she planted both feet on Kyle's chest and shoved with all her might. This time he managed a surprised grunt as he hit the ground. Carey's fingers scrabbled for the door handle, slammed it shut and hit the lock button. Then she flung herself across the seat and gave the ignition key a violent twist.

Gear shift, Carey. Shift the damned gears, she berated herself. Gears ground until her left foot found the clutch. She punched the accelerator.

Fifty feet down the gravel road, she remembered Lane. It wasn't hard—she was approaching the truck at a dead run from where they'd been camped. Carey slammed on the brakes and hit the unlock button.

Lane dived into the passenger seat, slammed the door. "Go!"

Carey gripped the steering wheel and tried not to give in to panic as she put the pedal to the floor. Within seconds they were careening onto a narrow paved lane that led out to the state highway.

"I saw him but couldn't get to you before you bashed his head," Lane panted, dark pony tail whipping around as she twisted to look behind them. "He's still down. Did you kill him?" The unmistakable note of hope in her voice would have made Carey laugh under any other set of circumstances.

She tried to concentrate over the thunder of her heart pounding in her ears. "I didn't do anything to his head. He slipped and fell or something. I just used my feet to shove him out of the way so I wouldn't run him over."

"Where did he come from? How did he find you?"

Anger flooded Carey's body. And it felt strangely...good. It focused her attention on her driving. "My cell phone. He somehow tracked my cell's signal."

"He can do that? Is that legal?"

"Apparently!"

"I remember seeing a state highway patrol station—"

"No." The word burst out of Carey's mouth before Lane could finish the sentence.

"What do you mean, no?"

Carey barely slowed for the stop sign before swinging the truck onto the two-lane highway leading south from Murfreesboro. "My footprints are probably an inch deep in his chest. I've recently been on psychotropic meds. Who are they going to believe?"

Silence. She glanced sideways and saw Lane staring at her, mouth open.

Checking the mirrors, Carey slowed the truck and pulled to the side of the road. She gripped the wheel of the idling machine, staring straight ahead. "I've been on medication since the drowning. Until a few days ago, that is. They thought I was having something called absence seizures, but I'm not so sure. Looking back, I was never sure. I just...went along because it seemed to scare everyone around me." She forced herself to turn and look at her friend's reaction. "Maybe they're right. I'm scaring me right now." She'd never lashed out physically at another human being in her life. Her limbs shook with reaction.

Lane was silent for a moment, wheels turning behind her dark brown eyes. "Then maybe you'd better let me drive."

Carey pressed her forehead to the top of the steering wheel and started to laugh. And couldn't stop.

Until the truck lurched violently to one side, then the other. Lane dug the fingers of one hand into Carey's thigh and braced the other against the ceiling. The truck settled into stillness once more, motor idling. Both women held their breaths.

"What was that?" Lane whispered.

Carey's heart pounded with a kind of perverse thrill as the only possible explanation dawned. "I think it was Troy. I think it was all Troy, even the head bashing."

Lane threw herself out the passenger side and raced around the front of the truck to fling open Carey's door.

"Scoot over. It's a thirteen-hour drive and I plan to make it in ten. Wait, where's your cell?"

Carey scooted to the passenger side, fumbling in her back pocket as she went. "Right here."

"Give it to me."

As soon as Carey handed it over, Lane dropped it and ground the heel of her boot down on it. Then her hand went to her own jeans pocket and hesitated.

"Crap, I really liked this phone." With a sigh of regret, she sent hers along with Carey's to the great voice mailbox in the sky.

Troy managed to get his raging, F-5 energy under control before it overturned the truck. He'd never felt so impotent in his entire life—or death, for that matter. Kyle was lucky Troy couldn't materialize, or he might have gotten more than a simple gash on the forehead.

How was he going to communicate to Carey and Lane that Kyle had probably already called the authorities to report an assault, and put the highway patrol on the lookout for their truck?

The only thing to do was to try a technique that he'd learned in boot camp. As Lane's famous lead foot engaged the accelerator, he threw out a bubble of static designed to interfere with any nearby electronic surveillance equipment—cameras, cell towers and radar. It was a trick that had come in handy on some of his most dangerous missions.

For now he ignored the fact that it was also the one that had gotten him killed.

He kept an eye on Carey, and every time he felt her mind begin to turn inward, he sent a fresh pulse of static through the radio antenna, enough to startle her with the noise and keep her focused. Lane seemed to sense his urgency, and twisted the volume knob to full blast.

He prayed his energy would allow him to keep it up for the next ten hours.

Chapter Seven

"I don't remember anyone inviting you to move in here." Lily Brannon dropped two paint rollers into the kitchen sink to clean, propped herself against the counter and glowered at her uninvited guest. Her body language said volumes more than the clipped sentence. Arms folded, chin stuck out.

Ross Garrison spared her a glance over the rim of his reading glasses, then returned his attention to the laptop screen in front of him. Honestly, this woman was going to drive him to drink before it was all over. He'd tried to ignore her, but that only seemed to egg her on. He grit his teeth as she advanced to the kitchen table and poked a finger at one of the piles of papers scattered on its surface.

"What's all this?"

"I'd rather you not do that." He tried for mild. "I need these in the order they're stacked."

"That doesn't answer my question."

Holding tight to his patience, he kept his attention glued to the screen. Anything to avoid a confrontation with the curvy little spitfire he just knew was throwing mental harpoons at his head. "Looking for clues that will give these kids some peace."

"On the internet."

It wasn't a question. He didn't know what he'd done to

offend Lily, but she'd had it in for him since he'd hit the doorstep. He'd give her the benefit of the doubt. This time.

"I have special access to a number of online newspaper archives going back to the Revolution. Taylor has enough on her plate right now. And John—Jared..." he corrected himself. He took his glasses off and rubbed the bridge of his nose. "Jared doesn't know what a computer is."

In the next heartbeat, Lily took a step closer, smacked his laptop closed and leaned into his face.

"You're building a case, aren't you?" she hissed.

He looked at her and wondered, not for the first time, if she'd gone around the bend. "No, Lily."

"To send him away."

He removed her hand—carefully—from his laptop and re-opened it. "I'm not going to dignify that—"

"Take him away from Taylor, who clearly isn't good enough for him." Sarcasm dripped from her words.

His last nerve frayed. "Lily, you need to shut up now."

"Hell, why not put her away, too!"

He slammed the laptop closed and came up out of his chair. "I'm looking for my son," he roared. "Can't you understand that?"

"*Yes!*"

They stared at each other. Her anger had vanished. Naked emotion ravaged her fine-boned face.

"Yes, I can," she repeated in a whisper he barely heard over the salt-scented breeze that swirled through the open windows.

Ah, damn. How could he have forgotten she'd lost her son, as well. Permanently. At least Ross had some hope of getting his back. Hell, at least finding out where he'd landed in time, if what they'd told him was true. Lily hadn't even gotten a body back to bury. Ross had his son's face to look at, even if the soul behind John's eyes belonged to Jared Beaudry.

A man for whom John had, literally, taken the road less traveled. And only now was Ross beginning to understand why.

He reached out and tentatively touched her shoulder. Then impulsively pulled her into his arms. She went stiff at first, then gradually relaxed as he smoothed her hair. He hadn't held a woman this way since his wife had passed eight years ago.

He sighed wearily. "This is all foreign territory to me, Lily. You've had...extraordinary children from day one. Give me some time to wrap my brain around this."

Somewhere below his chin, he felt her gulp back tears. "That's not quite true. Both Taylor and Troy hid their gifts from everyone but each other because of... Well, let's just say their father wouldn't have taken it well. They did it to protect me as much as themselves. I feel like if I'd known... If Taylor loses Jared... Ross, I can't lose both my children. I just can't."

"That's not going to happen." The words were out before he could catch himself, and he grimaced. If he understood the situation correctly, he had no business making her a promise like that. But the thought of anyone laying a hand on this woman threw white-hot sparks of disgust and anger in his head.

She drew back and looked at the piles of paper. "But then what's this for if not to work out some way to send Jared back into the hell he came from? And Taylor into a fresh one?"

Ross's voice cracked. "I have to do something, Lily. I feel..." His brain snagged on a word that wasn't normally in his lexicon. "Useless. Every time I see Jared wearing my son's face, it feels like I've lost John all over again. And I can't fix it."

She drew a deep breath and surveyed the organized mess with a bleak expression. "There have to be thousands of archives to sift through."

"Tens of. This pile barely scratches the surface of one of them."

As their tempers cooled, Ross felt the instant she realized they were still standing in each other's arms. Yet she didn't move. And neither did he.

"What are you looking for?" she asked presently, her voice still watery.

"I don't know. Something that doesn't fit. I'll know it when I see it. I hope. It might be half a sentence. Or an obscure detail in a woodcut."

Another short silence. "You're going to need help. I'm a former reference librarian. I have my sources too."

It was as close to an apology from Lily as he'd ever get. He cleared his throat. "Thanks." The front of his favorite Cleveland Indians T-shirt was wet. He didn't care.

"Mom?"

Ross looked toward the breezeway leading into the living area. Taylor, gloved hands full of wallpaper samples, stood with amusement—or was it amazement?—quirking her face. Jared came up behind her, nearly plowing into her with an armload of painting tools.

"Ross? What's wrong?"

"Nothing, now. It's okay, kids. I've got her."

He felt Lily's fingers dig into his back, and he knew his grin had to look six ways to foolish.

"Oh." Taylor's gaze traveled between them two or three times. Then she strolled into the kitchen, waving the wallpaper swatches. "Stephen called. He doesn't like any of these. Says they're too girly for the he-man fishing retreat he had in mind when he bought this place."

Lily disengaged herself and Ross reluctantly let her go, cleared his throat and retreated to re-open his laptop.

"Stephen just enjoys being a pain in my butt," Lily grumped, dabbing her eyes with her sleeve. "Seashells are not girly."

"Pink ones are," Jared put in.

Lily squinted at him. "Who asked you?"

Ross grinned and settled back down to his research. And tried not to think about how much virtual ground he had to cover. All he needed was one lucky break. Just one.

"Shouldn't we knock?" Carey tugged nervously at the hem of her T-shirt and contemplated the dirty jeans she still wore. She couldn't help it. With Lane, grunge was perfectly acceptable. But meeting new people dredged up all the etiquette lessons from her childhood.

Lane paused halfway through the beach house's screen door. "Why? We're all family."

"I'm not."

"Pffft. No one's going to bite you. Here, you first." She backed out of the doorway and held it wide for Carey, scanning up and down the street while trying not to be obvious about it.

"I'm pretty sure we weren't followed. Miracle as that is." No way was she going in there first.

"I'm just going to hang out here a minute to make sure. Go ahead, I'll be along shortly."

The falling dusk dimmed the front room into which she stepped. Ancient, overstuffed furniture in beachy prints looked out of place next to the newly waxed wood flooring and the aroma of fresh paint. No one was in here, but a path of warm light spilled across the floor and led to the kitchen.

She was tired and jittery from lack of sleep, too much caffeine, too little decent food and having to be on guard against letting her mind drift for the past hours. Ten, to be exact. Lane's manic driving had left no room for relaxation, either. How they'd managed it without being pulled over, she'd never understand.

"Hello?" The smell of something baking drew her onward to hover in the kitchen doorway, where otherwise she might have waited for Lane to join her.

A young woman, who was just setting a colander of freshly rinsed lettuce in the sink, turned as she wiped her hands on a towel. "Daira, is that you? You're early..." When she saw Carey she stopped cold, one hand on her rounded belly.

Carey held up her hands in an attempt to ease the woman's startled expression. She knew without a doubt she was looking at Troy's twin sister, Taylor. It wasn't just the light hair and the lean, rangy build. It was the eyes—deep green, beautiful. Haunted.

Carey's babble reflex kicked into full gear. "You must be Taylor. I'm sorry to barge in...our cell phones...um... I'm Carey Magennis, a friend of Lane's. Oh, she's here—she'll be in shortly. We drove in from Tennessee...I hope it's not too much trouble..."

But Taylor didn't appear to be listening. Her gaze was locked on Carey, studying her but not really seeing her.

"And...I think I've brought someone with me to see you," Carey finished.

Taylor closed her eyes and tilted her head, relief softening her angular features. "Troy. He's here." A frown. "He's trying to...but I can't...seem to hear him..." Her brow knit as she concentrated. Then she seemed to realize what she was doing in front of a perfect stranger, and stiffened in dismay.

Carey felt the air around her vibrate, as if someone was shouting and the echoes were bouncing off the walls.

Troy is trying to get through to her.

"I know this is hard to explain," she began hesitantly, "and I will try—later—but for right now, maybe it would help if you held my hand. Lane said you had a gift, but you need to touch something? I'm sorry, I don't quite understand how it works."

Wariness crept into Taylor's eyes and at first she didn't move. "What did you say your name was?"

"Carey. Carey Magennis. I teach history in Raleigh," she added unnecessarily. "I went to school with Lane at Chapel Hill."

"How do you know my brother?"

Carey took a deep breath. "He saved my life."

After a moment, Taylor held out her hand. Carey stepped forward and grasped it.

"Hey, T-Bird.".

He was here. Standing right next to Carey. She felt her eyes go wide, reluctant to blink, as she drank in the site of his worse-for-wear image.

"Hey." Taylor fought the lump in her throat. "Wait just a second, I need to sit down." She towed Carey over to the kitchen table. Once seated, she took Carey's hand in both hers. Carey flushed and looked as if she'd rather be anywhere than listening in on one side of a private conversation. It couldn't be helped.

Troy crouched next to both of them to be at her eye level, one hand on Carey's knee. The contact seemed to strengthen the signal. *"You're gettin' fat,"* he observed with a grin.

She ignored him and cut to the chase. "What happened?

Where have you been?"

"I got a little sidetracked and ran into some problems. It's a long story, but the gist of it is, Carey and I are joined at the subatomic level. Until I can figure out how to break the bond, John's just going to have to stay lost."

Taylor couldn't help but dig at her two-minutes-younger little brother. "Thinking with the wrong head again, bro?"

Carey blushed redder and stared at the ceiling.

"No, smart-ass. Right head, wrong mission."

"How does this 'bond' thing keep you from searching?"

"Before I got hooked into her, I was drilling down through time here, where I last saw John. I was getting ready to move to another place he might have turned up, maybe someplace else Jared had been."

Taylor grimaced. "That's an impossible task. Jared's unit was all over the place."

"If you've got a better idea, don't hold back. I can't move through space and time simultaneously. Believe me, I've tried."

"That doesn't mean John didn't do it, though. He could be anywhere. In any time period."

He sighed. *"You're not telling me anything I don't already know. If I'm going to be hitting places Jared's unit was known to be during the Civil War, I need to talk to him in more detail."* He glanced at Carey.

Taylor didn't miss the trace of worry on his face. She studied them both, trying to see how Troy was anchored. All she could detect was a glowing sheen of bright green energy that seemed to envelope the pair of them.

Carey's eyes were underscored with dark circles, and she appeared to be losing her battle with fatigue. She blinked hard and rubbed at her face.

"Squeeze her hand, Tee. Do it now. Don't let her drift off."

"Why?"

"Are you familiar with astral travel?"

"Astral travel. You're joking."

"I wish I were. It's complicated, but the short version is, when I'm touching her, where her mind wanders, I go with it."

Taylor squeezed, and Carey nodded. "I'm all right." With her free hand, she pulled a pile of Ross's printouts toward her and flipped through them. Taylor almost smiled at Carey's attempt to appear as if listening in on a one-sided conversation between a pregnant woman and a dead man happened every day. She was doing everything except sticking her fingers in her ears and humming a happy tune.

Taylor turned her attention back to Troy. "How did this happen?"

"She was drowning. In fact, by the time I got to her, she had *drowned. I had to materialize and breathe for her, and I think that's what did it. Now I can't go anywhere. Up, down or sideways, unless she does. I'm dead in the water. There's something else—Carey's got an ex who may be out to cause some trouble."*

He gestured to Carey's bruised wrist and throat, and Taylor grimaced. Carey caught her glance and touched her throat self-consciously.

"Nice. Did Lane take pictures of this?"

"Not yet."

Taylor nodded curtly. "I'll take care of it. And we'll be careful."

He looked around, as if suddenly remembering where he was. *"Where's Jared?"*

"He's on the beach fishing with... Oh, Troy..." Taylor's

stomach twisted. "There's something you need to know. John's father is here."

Troy went still for a long time, eyes on her but clearly focused on the memory of the last time he'd seen Ross's son. He seemed to age ten years before her eyes. *"Does he know?"*

She managed a small nod. "He knows. He's doing what he can to help."

Troy's eyes widened in surprise, an emotion he rarely showed. *"That's...just..."* If possible, the shadows in his face deepened and he spent a few seconds staring at nothing, digging his fingers into his brow bone as if he had a sudden headache.

Taylor reached out to touch his face, drew back when she remembered she couldn't actually do so. "Yeah, I know. No pressure."

A trace of a smile ghosted across Troy's mouth, there and gone. *"You'd think he'd be calling the dogs down on us all."*

She chuckled. "He hasn't said as much, but I suspect our family isn't the only one that's a hotbed of weirdness. All the piles of paper on this table are his." She found herself smiling. "He and Mom have had quite the interesting time—"

"Mom's here?"

Instantly any semblance of a mask vanished from Troy's face, leaving a naked emotion she could barely stand to witness. She berated herself for not mentioning it sooner. She might have had some limited contact with Troy's spirit since his death, but their mother had not.

In fact, Lily had never known anything about her children's gifts until Taylor had returned, shell-shocked and broken from that horrific re-enactment on the Outer Banks a few months ago. The one that had brought Jared Beaudry's wandering spirit back to life in a borrowed body, and still plagued her nights with bloody dreams.

"I'll go get them both. Hang tight." Reluctantly she let go of Carey's hand and headed for the back door as fast as her pregnant body would allow. And though she couldn't see him now that she'd lost contact, Taylor paused at the door and added. "I think there's someone who might be able to help. She's coming over shortly for supper."

Troy ducked his head and drew a steadying breath to prepare for seeing his mother again. He had deliberately stayed away since his death, thinking it best not to frighten the people he loved. Carey sighed raggedly, and he found himself running a soothing hand up her arm. She laid one of her hands on his, squeezing.

"I'm sorry...I feel like this is all my fault." Her voice was dreamy, detached.

"Don't. It was worth the risk. We'll figure this..." He forgot what he was about to say when he realized she was talking to him, feeling his hand. That usually only happened when...

Then he saw where her gaze was directed—at a computer printout of an article on a Civil War battle, complete with illustrations.

Antietam.

"Oh, *shit.*"

Chapter Eight

Troy didn't wait for the disorientation to pass. As soon the stench of gunpowder hit his nose, he threw himself backward to the ground, hauling Carey with him and using his body to cushion her from the impact.

If she was screaming, he couldn't hear it over the ear-splitting volleys of gunfire and the unearthly noise humans make when dying violent deaths *en masse.*

He didn't think any of the Minié balls would hurt them, but he wasn't going raise his head and risk finding out. After all, a bullet from a Union officer's pistol had left a mark on his shoulder when he'd put his briefly materialized self between it and Jared Beaudry. Who knew what the kinetic energy of a flying projectile might to do their astral-traveling souls.

Carey rolled off him and flattened herself to the ground, skin grey, eyes wild, hands clamped over her ears. He hauled her up so his face was an inch from hers.

"Stay down!"

A loose horse careened toward them. Troy planted one hand on Carey's head to push it down into the furrow of earth in which they were lying. The animal's white-ringed eye found them and it jumped at the last possible second. Troy risked raising his head to get his bearings.

They were lying in a furrow of what used to be a green,

flourishing cornfield. Now it was filled with blue-coated men who were rapidly losing what little cover they had as Confederate volleys, like flying razor blades, sheared off cornstalks to the ground. All around them men stood, kneeled, lay flat, all in various stages of firing and reloading. If they weren't already dead or writhing on the ground in their own gore.

They had landed in the infamous Antietam cornfield, where three Union regiments had marched straight into the withering fire of Stonewall Jackson's Confederates. And left more than eight thousand of their dead behind in grisly piles. Fully one-third of the casualties on the single bloodiest day of the war had died on these scant few acres of Maryland farmland. *Holy mother of God...*

He swiveled his head, looking for a landmark through the choking smoke. Carey's fingers dug into his shoulder and shook it to get his attention. Her arm shot out, pointing to their left toward a fence that bordered the field. Her lips formed two words: *Hagerstown Pike.*

Instantly his knowledge of the battlefield clicked into place. The fence followed a narrow road that eventually led to a farmhouse and possible shelter. He nodded and, trying to shield her as much as possible, began squirm-crawling toward the fence.

Each hard-won inch of ground they covered was accompanied by the snap and whine of bullets flying overhead, the spray of dirt kicked up by projectiles and running men. Thank God they were relatively close to the fence, but he breathed no sigh of relief when they reached it. He grabbed the seat of her pants and assisted her over the bottom rail, skinning through right behind her.

As she landed she cried out, one hand clutching her thigh.

A soldier a few yards away from her fell to the ground, blood and bone fragments spraying in every direction from a bullet-shattered knee.

Turning away from the sight, Troy hauled her to her feet. "Are you hit?" he shouted.

"I don't know…it just stings like hell!"

"Can you run?"

She nodded. Troy positioned himself between her and the worst of the battle's hairball, shielding her head with one arm as they ran north along the fence line, bent double. The relative safety of the small, white farmhouse loomed ahead. He heard her retching as they jumped over fallen bodies lying along the fence, slipped in the blood-slicked grass. Stray bullets smacked into the wall above their heads as Troy grabbed her arm and swung her around the corner of the house first.

The scene there wasn't any better. Injured and dying men lay in the yard, and Troy's practiced eye picked out a rudimentary triage system in place. Unfortunately the worst of the three categories lay literally at their feet.

Even better, in their energy state, they could see exactly when the souls of the dying left their torn bodies to stagger in aimless circles, many so close he could feel them brush against him. Carey spun and buried her face in his chest. He wrapped his arms around her to block out as much of the sight as he could, resisting the urge to close his eyes against it.

Then he saw something that didn't fit.

Among the milling crowd of newly liberated, confused souls, one of them was stationary. And he looked like he was directing traffic.

He wore a Union-blue uniform and cavalry boots, and his back was to them. Dark hair swept his collar. Troy squinted through the thick gunpowder smoke and reached out mentally to feel for the man's energy pattern. But with so many other souls milling nearby in the chaos, he couldn't get past the interference. Not as long as he was shielding Carey from the worst of it.

His probe must have caught the soldier's attention though, because he glanced over his shoulder, saw Troy and nearly fell over his own feet turning around.

Troy filled his lungs. "John!"

John's eyes were huge in his dirt-streaked face, and his mouth formed Troy's name. Abruptly something out of Troy's line of vision snagged John's attention. He took three running steps in that direction, stopped and looked back at Troy. Troy risked freeing one hand to gesture sharply for John to come to him. John's eyes shifted up the hill, then back.

He shook his head vehemently, and made a wide sweeping motion with his arm. *No. Go back.*

"Why doesn't somebody wake me up?" Carey cried, her terror vibrating against Troy's skin. Cannons thundered from only a few hundred yards away. Her body jerked.

Troy took a breath to shout John's name again.

Carey's nails bit deep into his back. "Wake me up! Wake me—"

Carey came out of her daydream in the middle of an earthquake, screaming her throat raw.

Except it wasn't an earthquake, it was Lane shaking her until her teeth rattled.

She opened her eyes and found herself surrounded by people, only two of whom she recognized. A dark-haired man knelt at her side, holding her legs down. She could still see the ravaged faces of the frightened souls lurching around the farmhouse yard, still feel the slimy sensation of them brushing up against her. She felt sick.

Then the pain hit. She stiffened against it, grasped her thigh and nearly fell out of the chair. Several pairs of hands caught her. She groped for the one that belonged to Taylor.

"Did he make it back with me?"

Taylor gripped her hand and her graze frantically flew around the room. "He's here. He's got a hold of your back belt loop. What happened?"

At the mental image of Troy's hand so near her backside, Carey tried to get out of the chair in earnest.

"Whoa! Wait a second, let's get this bleeding stopped. It's going to need a proper dressing." The man kneeling at her side raised his dark head to look at her with sea-blue eyes that looked much older than the rest of him.

"You're Jared," she managed between gasps.

He raised an eyebrow at Lane. "So much for keeping the family secrets."

Lane shrugged, her arms around Carey's shoulders. "Hey, it's not my fault Troy can't keep his ectoplasmic hands to himself."

Taylor released Carey's hand, fetched a pair of scissors from the kitchen drawer and returned to begin cutting through the fabric just above the blood stain.

Carey looked at the remains of the Antietam article printout crumpled in one hand, then held it out to Taylor. "Reading this was a really, really bad idea."

Taylor took it, laying the scissors on the floor, and straightened the paper enough to read the bold print headline. She blanched. "He wasn't kidding."

"Let me see that." The older man in the room, who looked like he could be Jared's father, plucked the paper from her fingers and examined it.

"What in the hell are you talking about?" A shorter, older version of Taylor stood in the middle of the kitchen, fists planted on her hips.

"Remember, Mom, I told you that Troy had gone in search of John's soul? Well, somehow he got tied up with Carey when he took a side trip to save her life. Now he can't be anywhere but where she is. And let's just say, sometimes she's not all here. When she daydreams, she goes places like *that*." Taylor jerked her chin at the paper while she and Lane worked to widen the hole in the leg of Carey's jeans to get at the injury that lay underneath.

Carey concentrated on breathing through the nasty stinging on her thigh and the lingering mental images of where her wandering attention span had just taken her. *What's next? A trip into the mouth of a volcano next time I watch the National Geographic channel?* Ebbing adrenaline left her limbs shaky and her stomach queasy.

The women peeled back the fabric, and she looked down, prepared to see a bloody mess.

Lane sat back on her heels, relief evident on her face. "The skin's not broken. You're going to have a hell of a bruise, though."

Carey's stomach quailed at the thought that the blood on her jeans might not be her own. Each time she had traveled, she had brought back some small souvenir—a cotton boll thorn, mist on her cheek. And now, blood.

"You mean Troy is here. Now?" Taylor's mother approached with a look on her face that Carey wasn't sure she could deal with at this moment. "Why can't we see him? Didn't you say he could show himself to you if he wanted?"

"It's different now, Mom." The strain in Taylor's voice was equally evident on her face.

The older man in the room seemed to have assessed the situation, and stepped forward to put a hand on the woman's shoulder. "Lily, maybe it's best to wait."

Lily shook him off. "No, I want to talk to my son—"

Suddenly it was all too much. Carey needed air and she needed it now. Kyle showing his true colors, the violence she had just left behind on Antietam battlefield, all unwound like a newsreel in her mind's eye. Five people were either working on her, holding her down or staring at her with such intensity it hurt to look at them.

"Let me up," she gasped.

"Carey, you're hurt. You have to let us—"

Something inside her snapped. "No, I don't *have* to do anything but get out of this house. Now let me go!" She barreled to her feet and everyone made way for her as she hobbled out the back door onto the deck, hopping two steps on her right leg for every step she took on her left. The pain anchored her. She leaned on the railing and drank fresh sea air deep into her lungs. Behind her, voices carried through the open door.

"Give her a minute. She's not bleeding."

"That was stupid of me. She probably thinks I'm a madwoman."

"No, Mom, I'm pretty sure she thinks she's the one going crazy. Trust me, I've been where she is."

"Lane, tell us everything that's happened. Carey can fill in the gaps later, when she's rested."

Rested! Didn't they know she could never rest as long as her brain was this messed up? As long as the tall, brooding ghost of a dead man was stuck to her, probably watching her right now. Maybe even touching her, which opened up a whole new set of problems—and mental images—she just couldn't deal with right this second. Nothing about this situation could be described as restful.

She shivered and fought the urge to run out to the truck, pick up the pill bottle Kyle had dropped on the floor and drive to the nearest Eckerd's to get it refilled.

All she had wanted was her freedom. Now she was stuck on some kind of mad carnival ride that was taking her down a dark tunnel with no way off.

"Are you all right, miss?" A velvety female voice, flavored with a taste of the Western Carolina mountains, drifted out of the evening shadows.

Carey looked up...and into the calm eye of her inner storm. A compact, full-figured woman wearing a red cotton caftan and a head full of tiny, waist-length braids in her black hair, stood at the top of the steps. A pair of flip-flops dangled from her fingers. In the other hand she carried a foil-covered plate. Sand clung to her bare feet, as if she'd just walked up from the beach.

Something about the woman made Carey want to curl up at her feet and sob like a child. She dug her fingers into the wood and stayed where she was.

"Yes," she lied. "Yes, I'm fine."

The woman's gaze swept down to Carey's torn pant leg, the darkening bruise on her skin. "I always knew the Brannon family was a bit overwhelming, but I didn't think they'd try to use a newcomer as crab bait." Amusement sparkled in her amber eyes, but the way she was standing perfectly still signaled alertness.

Carey amazed herself by relaxing into a chuckle. "No, trust

me, they weren't the ones trying to skewer me." The pain in her leg settled into a slow throb, and she tried to ease some weight onto it.

"My name is Daira. I am a recent friend of Taylor and her family."

Even the woman's name sounded soothing. "Carey. I'm an old friend of one of the cousins."

Daira nodded, then dropped her flip-flops onto the deck and approached, holding out an arm.

"Let's say we get you inside and cleaned up, hmm? I hear Lily cooks the best fried flounder in five states, and you look like you could use it."

Some part of her wondering why she instinctively trusted this woman, Carey leaned gratefully on Daira and hobbled back toward the door, where Taylor stood waiting with an ice pack.

Daira Tsutla's heartbeat thundered under her practiced calm. All day she had followed her pendulum's swing across a map of the eastern U.S., watching Troy Brannon's energy signature make its way inexorably toward the Outer Banks. Back to the scene of the crime, as it were. After the crystal had stopped swinging right over this location, she had waited an extra hour to make sure it was there to stay. It wouldn't do to put Quincy and Matthias on high alert for no reason.

Carey's aura was easy to read against the white siding of the house. It pulsated with a nervous, frenetic quiver that signaled her distress. But Daira also detected something that didn't belong there.

It was her job to be able to sense the unique energy pattern of each member of SpIRIT and track them where not even satellites dared to go. Her skills had saved the lives of more than one team member, and she'd never lost anyone. Until Troy Brannon.

Now she could move Troy back to her personal win column, because if she wasn't mistaken, the misplaced energy in Carey's aura belonged to him.

Carey sat cross-legged in the middle of an inflatable mattress in the darkened, upstairs living area, trying not to let the sound of the ocean waves on the other side of the dunes lull her into another waking dream. What she needed, she thought wryly, was someone with a baseball bat to make sure she proceeded directly to full unconsciousness. Do not pass go.

Thus far in this new adventure of hers, it wasn't sleep, it was that halfway-there transition that worried her. But as the lingering side effects of the meds continued to wear off, who knew what would happen next? She didn't even feel safe reading a book anymore.

Downstairs in the various bedrooms, everyone else in the house was finally asleep. Supper had probably been delicious, but she hadn't tasted anything she'd put in her mouth. Everyone seemed to be making too much of an effort to not descend on her all at once, to give her a little breathing room. But the tension had been palpable and she knew tomorrow would be a different story.

Only Daira, who Taylor explained was the professional psychic helping her learn to control her psychometric ability, had seemed perfectly at ease. The woman hadn't batted an eye at Carey's fumbling attempts to describe what had been happening since her drowning, and had promised to try to help sort it all out—tomorrow. There was no point, she'd said, in attempting to proceed when everyone was tired and rattled.

And then there was the situation with Kyle. It seemed everyone wanted a piece of her. In an incredibly short time, her life had gone from a straight, comforting path laid out before her to a twisting mountain road in the dark with no idea which way it was going to curve next.

The only other person awake in the house right now, besides her, was Jared. She had seen the look on his face—and Lily's—after hearing of her run-in with Kyle at Stones River and observing the bruises on her wrist and neck. It didn't surprise her that Jared was now sitting out on the front porch in the dark, and that Ross had stationed himself outside Lily's bedroom door, listening for nightmares. Lane had moved into Taylor's bedroom for the night.

Everyone in this house seemed to have everyone else's back, she mused. It was a deeply comforting feeling she had never before experienced, even in her own aunt's home. And she hadn't even known she'd missed this sense of safety until right this moment.

The occasional creak of a board told her Jared was making a periodic circuit of the house. Old soldiers truly died hard.

Might as well go out and keep him company. She pulled on her sweats, careful of the dressing that held an herbal poultice to her thigh, and limped outside barefoot. The cool dampness on her feet would keep her awake.

Jared looked up from the book he was reading by the bright light of the full moon. He set it aside and got up from his chair as she approached.

"Please don't get up."

He gave her a half smile and remained standing until she had seated herself and helped her pull up another chair to prop her leg on. "Old habits."

"Very old, from what I've been told." She couldn't begin to put into words how weird it felt to talk to a thirty-four-year-old body inhabited by a nineteenth-century soul. One whose courtly manners and air of reserved strength belied the fact his vengeful spirit had sparked one of the oldest and most terrifying ghost legends of the Outer Banks.

She shifted her leg and fished for common ground. She settled on gesturing at his book. "What are you reading?"

"Ah, this. A book about Civil War spies." He offered her the book and she took it, tilting it to see the cover in the moonlight.

"I just finished this. It's good. I was thinking about doing a project on it in my class next year before...before all this happened. I bet you could pick out the errors, though, since you were there."

He shook his head. "No, this was a world I knew little about. But I think my brother may have been involved."

"Really? How so?" Grateful to have something to occupy her mind, she settled deeper in the chair and watched his silhouette as he spoke.

"See, at the time of my...experience on the Outer Banks in 1862, I thought he had been killed. But Taylor had in her possession a copy of a letter written in his hand. There were other clues that he might have survived, but as far as we have been able to find out, he never returned home."

"That's terrible." Carey handed the book back to him. "Younger brother or older?"

"Younger. But if he indeed became a spy, he must not have used his given name, which is making it harder to turn up any information. The last trace of him I have—and not a reliable one at that—is that he might have been a prisoner of war." Jared appeared lost in thought for a moment, then he roused himself. "His name was Ethan."

Carey leaned forward, her interest piqued. "I've heard that name. I had an episode at Stones River similar to the one you saw me have here in the kitchen." She couldn't see Jared's face in the darkness, but he was perfectly still. "I remember a man in the woods. He was meeting someone from a campsite I'd stumbled into. The other guy called him Ethan. Do you think... No, it couldn't be. Ethan had to be a pretty common name back then."

She heard Jared take a breath, as if he'd been holding it while she spoke. "When was this battle?"

"Late 1962. Very late. December thirty-first."

A long pause. "Thank you, Miss Magennis. It gives me some place to start." He seemed to be having trouble holding his voice even. Abruptly he got up and moved toward the steps. "I should have a look around. I'll be back in a few minutes."

"Thanks for looking out for me. It...means a lot."

Jared paused at the top of the steps and shrugged. "You're Lane's friend. That makes you family." And with that, he disappeared into the night.

Carey sat for a long time in the dark, letting those words sink in. Family. Since her parents' deaths, she had considered the children in her classroom to be the closest thing to family. In fact, in the seven short years she'd been teaching, many still came back to visit her classroom. Recently some of her past students had begun trickling back into her life as teaching assistants. It gave her a small taste of what it must feel like to be a proud mother.

Whatever tenuous familial strings that had existed between her and Aunt Loreen had vanished the moment she had seen the signature witnessing the final loss of the one connection to her parents—the power of attorney allowing Kyle to sell it. Ross had noticed the document—and the teaching contract she had allegedly signed—when he'd been helping move some of their luggage indoors. He had immediately taken command of both documents to study them.

Jared's words lifted her heart a little.

Until she thought of how one impulsive act of hers had started this whole cascade of disasters. She shivered and rubbed her arms.

Finally she decided she was tired enough that she could lie down and fall directly to sleep without too much risk of a time-space joyride. Even if she did, at least Jared was nearby to awaken her.

Once snuggled in her sleeping bag, she heaved a sigh and determinedly closed her eyes, wishing she had some way of making absolutely sure she would stay in one place during the night. She thought of Troy's impromptu kiss at Stones River, his solid arms wrapped around her during their Antietam ordeal. She mentally hugged that thought close, hoping it would anchor her. She felt the sinking sensation she normally enjoyed at the moment she fell into a deep sleep, and with relief she relaxed into it.

Crickets chirped. Ocean waves murmured in the night.

A hand swept a stray curl off her cheek and tucked it behind her ear.

"I've got you. You aren't going anywhere tonight."

She felt the warmth of Troy's body only a few inches away from hers, felt his breath on her forehead. She kept her eyes shut tight, afraid opening them would mean she would wake and he'd disappear.

"How did you get here?" She caught her breath as Troy's hand traveled over her shoulder, down her side to rest at her waist.

"The aftereffects of your meds have worn off to the point I can get a foot in the door while you sleep."

Safe. A deep knot of tension she hadn't been aware of suddenly let go in a deep sob. She didn't even question how or why Troy was able to slip into her sleeping mind. She was beyond trying to make sense of anything that had happened to her since she had stepped outside that cottage in Ireland for a walk.

"You should have let me die." The words were out of her mouth before the next sob shook her. Before she even knew she was going to say them. She felt his hand on her arm, felt it tighten and give it one firm shake.

"You are many things, Carey Magennis, but stupid isn't one of them. Open your eyes."

She hunched her shoulders miserably against his voice. She didn't want to hear that tone right now. Patient with an undercurrent of anger.

"Look at me."

Kyle had cured her of taking direct commands from anyone. Her eyes flew open and she rolled away, biting off an unladylike retort that would have told him exactly what he could do with a certain part of his anatomy.

"Oh, no you don't." He caught her around the waist and hauled her back against his chest. Though her body didn't hit his that hard, she heard his rush of breath at the contact, felt the heat of it on the side of her neck. For an instant he hesitated, the arm around her waist tightening. She trembled at the sound of him inhaling a fraction of an inch from her skin.

She almost let herself relax into him. Almost. Then he seemed to shake himself, and he released her.

"A statement like that doesn't get by me unchallenged." He sat up and brought her with him, and they ended up facing each other, knees touching knees. He held onto her arms as if anticipating she would try to get away.

She tried to shrug off his hands and blew at the curls hanging in her eyes. “There’s nothing to challenge. The simple fact is, if I had just stayed on the path that morning in Ireland, none of this would be happening now. You’d be free of me and still hunting for John. You’d be able to communicate more easily with your family. I’d...”

He shrugged in complete agreement, which she didn’t expect. “You’d be married and well on your way to two-point-four kids, a white picket fence...”

“That’s a bad thing?”

“...and a husband who beats the tar out of you for having dinner on the table one minute late. There’s more than one kind of death, sweetheart.”

She lifted her chin, stung. “I wouldn’t have married him.”

“Sure you would have. I know all the signs—I grew up with a front-row seat. Yours were classic. If not him, someone else just like him.”

He really could be a presumptuous, arrogant... “You’re wrong. I would have had choices, Troy. Choices. Now I have none. No matter which way I turn—”

“You always have choices. The one I made that day saved your life. Trust me when I tell you it’s one I almost didn’t make.”

She shoved her wayward hair out of her eyes and stared at him. He had almost let her die?

He sat cross-legged in front of her, a study in restrained power and the absent-minded grace only those blessed with perfect physical confidence possessed. But there was something different about him. The restless energy was subdued, replaced with an inner stillness that was almost as disconcerting. Like a stalking cat waiting for the right moment to make its move.

"I could have ignored the distress signals you were putting out. I wanted to. But I didn't. And it occurs to me, why did I hear you from three thousand miles away, when undoubtedly there were other people, closer, dying at that very moment? Why you?"

His hand came to rest on her bruised thigh, sending soothing heat through the fabric of her sweats—and a different kind of heat straight to the pit of her belly. His gaze bore into hers, studying her like that day she'd first seen him. Like she was a chess board and it was his move.

"Maybe because, like John, you weren't ready to go. Maybe one of these days I'll figure it out, but I do know that nothing happens by accident. If I hadn't made that choice, you're right, you would be dead. I'd still be looking for John. And I'd be the one without choices."

"What are you talking about?"

"Today. At Antietam—"

Fear stabbed through her, and she shook her head frantically. "Don't mention that now. I don't know how my sleeping dreams work yet. We could both end up back there."

He slipped his hands under her hair and held her head still. "No power on this earth will keep me from holding you right here where you are. Right now."

Tears stung her eyes, and she reached up to grab his wrists. "How can you be so sure?"

"I can be one stubborn son of a bitch." His grin was every bit as breathtaking as it was cocky.

She choked out a laugh. "Well, I'm glad one of us has his wits about him."

He tilted his head and studied her face as he caressed her

cheekbones with his thumbs. "Who was the one who took one look around and figured out exactly where we were on the battlefield? It sure wasn't me."

She waved a hand. "You were only a half second behind me in that respect."

"It was a crucial split second. If we hadn't gotten to that farmhouse when we did, I would have missed him."

Carey blinked and shook his hands off. "Him... You saw John?"

"I saw him, and he saw me. Then Lane brought you...us...back here by shaking you awake." His eyes burned with a light that she hadn't seen before. "If you hadn't taken that walk in Ireland, if I hadn't tossed a coin and come to get you, I'd still be looking in all the wrong places."

She let that sink in for a moment. "Are you going to tell his father?"

"Not until I'm sure of what I'm going to do about it. What John wants to do about it."

Her heart skipped several beats, then dropped. "That means..."

He regarded her steadily. As if waiting for her to come to some conclusion herself. It didn't take long.

"The only way to get back to him is... Oh God, no." She began to shake. "I'm not going back there! I can't!" She tried to launch herself to her feet to run. Somewhere. Anywhere her dream would let her.

Then she found herself enclosed in Troy's arms, holding her, his voice in her ear saying something that gradually worked its way through the roaring as he repeated it over and over.

"You don't have to. Carey. Carey, listen. You don't have to

do this right now. It's too dangerous. Do you hear me?"

Every muscle stiff and trembling, she managed to nod. He set her away from him and she searched his face for a lie. It wasn't there.

"We're not making one move in that direction until we figure out one of two things. A, if we can somehow get ourselves unhooked so I can go myself. Or B, teach you how to control where and when you make these jumps so that I'm in the best position to protect you when we land."

"How are we going to do that?" She tried to control the breath pumping in and out of her lungs, tried not to let a sense of hopelessness take over.

"I can do that, with time. And we've got backup. You met her tonight—it's Daira. Now listen closely, because what I'm about to tell you could get you disappeared."

"That sounds like a bad pickup line," she said on a hiccup.

"That's my girl. Your sense of humor is coming back."

She scowled at him. "Not hardly. I don't see anything funny about this." She wiped her nose on her sleeve and tried for calm. "Now who's Daira?"

"She's part of the special ops team I was serving on. Special Infiltration, Recon and Intelligence Team."

Carey blinked. "What's she doing here?"

"I don't know, I haven't had a chance to communicate with her yet. I can only conclude she's in the process of helping Taylor learn to control her gift. Like she taught me."

"And your gift is time-space hopping."

"Well, at the time it wasn't. That developed later...after. My specialty, when I was alive, was camouflage. I could literally blend into any background."

"Like an invisible man."

"Something like that. It's something I wasn't even aware I was doing until SpIRIT recruited me away from the navy."

She couldn't help it; a vision of Troy as a child popped into her mind. "I bet you drove your mother crazy. Not to mention your teachers."

He grinned. "I was always the perfect angel."

"Uh-huh. So, you think Daira can help us." Carey didn't think it was possible to be any more scared than she already was. "Do you have any idea how long it's going to take me to get that accurate? It could be months. Years."

He shrugged a broad shoulder. "We've got time. Now that I have an approximate idea where to start."

"You don't understand." She took hold of his hands to try to bring him back to her version of reality. "I don't have that kind of time. I don't think Kyle is through with me, and the last thing I want is be the cause of someone in your family getting hurt."

He leaned forward and tapped her nose. "Won't happen. And once Daira and I communicate, I hope Kyle tries to get past the perimeter that'll surround this place. I'll enjoy watching Quincy and Matthias visit their own gifts on him."

"Who...?"

"If Daira's here, trust me, they're not far away."

She didn't know what to say to that. Except, "I'm scared. What if..."

He pulled her into his arms, and she dug her fingers into the soft fabric of his worn, black T-shirt, careful to avoid the wounds she had seen there. "Nope. No what-ifs tonight, Carey. If you start dwelling on what might happen, you might make it happen. You don't want that."

She shook her head, mute with fear.

"Listen to my heartbeat. Focus on that."

She turned her head and lay her ear against his upper chest, well clear of the wound below, though he had insisted before that it caused him no pain. She closed her eyes and listened to the steady two-beat. Concentrated on the way one hand stroked her back, and the other sifted through the pillow-induced riot of her hair. The clean heat of his body under her cheek. Then something occurred to her.

"Are ghosts supposed to have heartbeats?"

"Good question. But then again, it's your dream. All I know is, it feels like it's about to jump out of my chest with you up against me like this." He sounded thoroughly distracted as he molded her body closer to his. His lips grazed her ear. "You have really good dreams, Carey. Mind if I stay in it a little longer?"

Fright had nothing to do with the way her own heart pounded now. The way her body throbbed in time with it. Everything else melted away until there was nothing but her and Troy and the night that cocooned them in what felt like the first truly safe place she'd ever known.

A safe place that was Troy's prison. And, it occurred to her, maybe a place from which she could free him. She had innocently stolen his ability from him. What if she could just...give it back?

She lifted her head, ran her fingers into his hair and pulled his face down to hers.

For an instant he froze, as if taken completely by surprise at her boldness. She opened her mouth and teased his lower lip gently with her teeth, some instinct within her warning he would make her stop if he guessed what she was trying to do. She intended—hoped—it would be done before he had a chance to protest. She squeezed her eyes tight and silently demanded whatever higher power existed to fix what she had broken.

Suddenly his arms were hard around her, one pinning her body to his, the other hand buried in the hair at the back of her head. His hot tongue plundered her mouth. He slid a hand under the rounded curve of her bottom and made a low, growling sound in his throat. At the feel of his erection pressed hard against her belly, she lost whatever shred of focus she had left.

Now all she could think about was him, and how desperately she wanted him, his body, how she felt in his arms...to be real. Not just a dream.

Troy tasted her salty tears on her lips. Tasted her fear in her mouth, sensed the crackling energy of her desire. It was a potent mix that acutely reminded him of how long it had been since he'd touched anyone like this. He'd been too preoccupied with his quest to dwell on it before. Now the nearly two years of solitude knifed through him, aimed with painful precision at his cock—with plenty left over to squeeze his heart.

He hooked his fingers under the hem of her oversized T-shirt and peeled it off over her head, then kissed her down onto the mattress. She drank him in like a drowning woman gasping for air, greedy and desperate. He tore his mouth away and buried his face in her throat, reveled in the warm scent of her soft skin. She turned her head to one side, inviting him to find the sensitive spot where her neck met her shoulder. She shuddered when he obliged her with teeth and tongue. His body was already flexing rhythmically, instinct taking over as he worked his hips between her thighs. She arched her back and pushed down on his shoulders.

"Here, please here," she whispered, using her own hands to offer up her breasts to his mouth. He slid down her body and sucked the hard, erect tips, every pull making him hungrier.

Her heels rubbed the backs of his thighs.

He shoved one hand under the small of her back, and she welcomed him, letting him rock his pelvis against hers while he continued to lick and suckle her breasts. The complete abandon with which she opened herself to him simultaneously humbled him and drove him even closer to the edge.

She pulled at his shirt, and he raised up on his knees just long enough to yank it off while she worked at his belt buckle. His mind blanked with nothing but pleasure when her hands found him through his open fly. He actually went dizzy and fell forward, supporting himself on his hands while she continued to drive him crazy, her eyes heavy-lidded as she watched his face. He took it as long as he could, then with a low growl he pulled her sweat pants down her hips.

She bent her knees and raised her feet to help him get them off, then immediately snaked her legs around his hips to pull him down to her.

He buried his face in the side of her sweet neck. And filled her with his cock.

She made no sound, but her nails raked his back and she bowed her body in a curve to take him in deeper, to the hilt.

He realized she was holding her breath.

"Breathe, love," he whispered roughly, fighting to regain the control he'd lost.

One gasp. A long, shuddering exhale. Then another long silence. He raised his head and looked down at her face. Her eyes were closed and her brow furrowed as she worked her hips against his, so lost in the sensations she was forgetting to breathe.

"Again."

Another gasp. And another in quick succession.

He put his head down and rewarded each of her breaths with a deep thrust. She captured his mouth with hers, and quickly Carey's dream became all dueling tongues, sweat-slick skin, mingled breaths and the sounds of their furious, primal coupling in the darkness.

Green lightning flickered behind his eyelids. Some distant part of his mind observed that it was like the first time he had put his mouth on hers, back on the storm-swept cliff in Ireland. Something throbbed in the lower right side of his chest. Faintly at first. Then stronger.

Pain.

Lancing. Intense. It lifted him to his knees with a gasp that hissed through his clenched teeth. Disorientation shoved at him from all sides, and his hand automatically went to the pain. It came away wet.

He looked down at Carey, trying and failing to say something to her around the agony of what felt like a giant's hand squeezing his lungs. She was propped up on one elbow, legs still wrapped around him, the other hand trembling and reaching out to cover the gaping hole that he'd forgotten was there.

The wound in his shoulder exploded in pain. Blood flowed over his hands.

Jesus. Jesus Christ...

"A-ye-gi! A-ye-gi na-quu!"

Carey sat bolt upright, panting. Naked. Alone. Staring at her left hand.

In the darkness it was hard to see, but the warmth, the stickiness—and the scent—was unmistakable.

Her palm was smeared with blood.

Daira barely had time to step out of the way as Carey ran by her, headed for the half bath off the kitchen. She felt her cheeks flaming. In her shifted state, she was invisible to anyone without special detection equipment—which didn't exist outside of SpIRIT. She had slipped into the house, intent on using her pendulum in Carey's aura to ask Troy silent yes and no questions.

Now she pressed herself against the wall, stunned by what she had just seen. She wasn't normally into voyeurism, but once she'd grasped the significance of the scene unfolding before her, no power on earth could have made her turn away from watching her friend Troy make love to Carey Magennis. The tremendous release of energy as they'd come together in Carey's dream had literally lifted Daira's long braids away from her head as if whipped by a hurricane.

The sound of water running in the small half bath spurred her into action. The noise might attract someone's attention. She only had a few seconds to spare.

She moved quickly to the mattress and swept her hand over the sleeping bag. There. She hadn't been prepared for collecting specimens, but she had to risk it. She slipped her knife blade out of the sheath strapped around her calf. In one quick motion, she cut a small sample of fabric.

Within thirty seconds, Daira was well away from the house and texting Quincy on SpIRIT's secure satellite link.

Chapter Nine

Carey scrubbed at the blood on her hand, shaking so badly she splattered pink-tinted water all over the place. She tried to breathe quietly so as not to wake the household, but held her breath so long between silent, open-mouthed gasps she began to feel dizzy. Finally she sank to the floor with her back against the wall. She clamped both water-damp hands over her mouth and squeezed her eyes shut, trying to keep from replaying the scene in her mind's eye.

She had failed.

She needed Taylor, right now, to hold her hand, communicate with Troy and make sure he was all right. But she couldn't go charging downstairs at this hour until she was sure she wouldn't babble incoherently. It wasn't just because of the blood she had scrubbed off. Her body still hummed, hungered for more of what Troy had been giving her right before she'd awakened.

She cast about for some kind of explanation for what had just happened. She reasoned that her wandering consciousness had been hit with a Minié ball during one of her astral jumps through time, and had come away with only a bad bruise on her real body. The blood on her hand was nothing more than a piece of the ghost inhabiting her dream. And ghosts couldn't die, right?

It's okay. It'll be okay. She leaned her head back against the wall and managed to pull in a deep breath. She climbed to her feet and set about cleaning up the mess so no one would have to see it—least of all Lily. Carey did not want to have to explain how it got there.

A flash of silver caught her eye as she wiped the counter with a handful of tissues. Someone, probably Lily, had left it on the bathroom sink—Carey thought she remembered seeing the piece on Lily's wrist earlier. A heavy silver chain with a rectangular plate, like the POW/MIA bracelets that had been popular long ago.

She picked it up to wipe it off and noticed the engraving. Troy M. Brannon. Underneath, a date. A year and some-odd months ago.

Carey realized she was probably looking at the approximate date Troy had died.

For a few seconds she considered another wild idea—somehow going back and changing things so Troy survived that day. It wouldn't take much...maybe as simple as attracting just enough attention to make him step right instead of left at an opportune time. Her heart beat faster with the prospect, then she lay the bracelet down and buried her face in her hands.

If it was possible, Troy would have done it already. There had to be a good reason that he had avoided going back, once he learned he could. Plus, she had just proved to herself that her bright ideas were of no help to Troy. Might, in fact, have made the situation worse.

She finished cleaning up and flushed the evidence. She would talk with Taylor—and Daira—about what had happened. That was all. She was going to have a hard enough time looking Lily in the eye, knowing what she had been doing with the woman's son just before she'd jolted awake.

She paused and stared into the mirror, but not really seeing herself.

Just what had awakened her, anyway? From what little she had figured out about her problem so far, one thing was clear. Once she was gone it took an outside force to bring her back. A physical touch. A sharp voice.

What—or who—had brought her back? She shut her eyes and tried to remember something, anything. It had to have been a voice, but she had been alone when she'd opened her eyes. Or had she?

With quick, jerky movements, she pulled on her T-shirt and sweats—wrong side out and backward—turned off the bathroom light and silently turned the doorknob. She padded into the room and stood still, listening, feeling for a presence.

Nothing, save for the rocking shadow outside the window that told her Jared was still on guard. She moved to a chair by the east window, curled herself into it to wait for the dawn.

She didn't trust herself to fall asleep again. Not after what she'd done to Troy.

She lost track of time, but as the eastern sky began to show an edge of grey, soft footfalls on the stairs reached her ears. A tall, slender figure emerged from the stairwell, and the faint light fell on short, blonde hair. Taylor had come to check on her. Carey sighed quietly. She wasn't sure she was ready for this.

"You okay?"

"No." Carey took a deep breath and plunged. "I...I had a dream, a real one, not a daydream. Troy somehow met me in it and...I don't think he's okay." She hoped Taylor would let her leave it at that as she convulsively thrust out her hand.

Taylor was across the room in three strides to grab it. She went still and silent.

As the minutes stretched, Carey's heart thudded harder with dread. She swung her feet to the floor and sat, back straight, free hand worrying the hem of her shirt. Finally she couldn't stand it. "Tell me you sense him. Tell me he's all right."

Taylor didn't answer.

"Taylor?" She tried to control the shrill note in her voice.

Taylor, without letting go of Carey's hand, turned her head toward the doorway, where Jared stood watching.

"I think we need Daira."

Daira's mental wheels kicked into high gear when the knock came at her door the next morning. In her hands she held the lab results Matthias had just delivered. She hadn't had to say a word when she read them. At her mute nod, Matthias had melted back into the shadows to begin preparations at the base facility hidden under the heart of an unnamed ridge in the Smoky Mountains.

All night she had been wracking her brain trying to figure out how to get Carey to the facility without revealing much, if anything, about SpIRIT

There was simply no way around it. She'd have to be told more than was safe. Probably Taylor as well. And Jared, she admitted with an inward wince, because he was as much a part of this as Carey and Taylor. Daira rubbed her forehead as she approached the door. By the time she opened it, she had herself outwardly composed and calm.

Ah, yes. All three of them were waiting on her doorstep in the pre-dawn darkness.

"There's something wrong," both Carey and Taylor said simultaneously.

Daira assessed the dark circles under the three sets of eyes in front of her and ushered them all to the kitchen table.

Before they had finished settling onto their seats, words were spilling out of Carey so fast Daira had to remind her to stop and take a breath.

"Troy...was in my dream last night. I touched him... He seemed so real..."

Daira struggled to keep her expression neutral.

"He had a chest wound," Carey continued. "He always had it when I'd see him, but this time it was..." She glanced nervously at Taylor. "When I woke up, I had blood all over my hand. And since then, Taylor hasn't—"

"I can barely sense him," Taylor broke in. "I can't hear his voice at all. All I can feel is a faint presence, but it's like a radio signal fading in and out."

Daira didn't let her face so much as twitch. But inwardly the needle on her urgency meter jumped toward the red zone. This didn't sound good at all. Just how much strength had Troy lost in those fleeting seconds? She met Jared's gaze. Jared, whom she understood from working with both him and Taylor, had spent more than a century carrying around wounds so ghastly she couldn't bear thinking about what he must have suffered.

"Give me your hands," she said briskly, holding out hers toward Carey and Taylor. Both women took them without hesitation, and spontaneously joined their hands to form a circle without Daira having to ask. She didn't miss Jared's frown, and how he shifted one hand protectively to the back of Taylor's chair.

She knew they were expecting her to use her psychic ability to sense and possibly communicate with Troy, but she knew that if Taylor couldn't get to him through their strong twin bond, there was no way Daira was going to do it. She had taken their hands to ground them in the face of what she was about to tell them. To keep her own hands from shaking.

"I'm about to tell the three of you something that must never, ever leave this room. If it does, it will put the lives of many good people in danger."

Carey, to her surprise, was already nodding. "I know who you are. Troy told me last night. In the dream."

Daira felt her eyebrows go north. So Troy was conscious of people around him, and recognized her. This was very good news. But they weren't out of the woods yet.

"What are you talking about?" Taylor frowned at the two of them.

Daira schooled her expression and chose her words carefully. "I'm not...exactly who you think I am, Taylor. You didn't happen upon me by chance after you decided to stay here on the Outer Banks and wait for Troy to return."

Taylor's eyes narrowed and she made an attempt to pull her hand away, but Daira went after it and brought it back. She had come to think of Taylor as a friend in the few months they'd been working together. Personal ties were hard to come by in this business, and dangerous to maintain. The thought of losing this one brought on a wholly unexpected stab of pain to her heart.

She plunged on, praying for the right words.

"I've known Troy ever since he was recruited. We were on the same team. I can't go into too many details, but everyone on this team has, shall we say, a unique ability."

"I knew it." Taylor's lips were stiff. "I knew the SEALs would snatch him up as soon as they got a whiff of his gift for camouflage."

Daira coughed. "Is that what he told you? That he had joined the SEAL teams?"

Taylor's brow furrowed, as if searching her memory. "Come to think of it, no. He...never actually said."

"This team is called SpIRIT—Special Infiltration, Recon and Intelligence Team. And Troy's gift isn't just camouflage. Did you know that your brother can literally disappear into his surroundings?"

Taylor blinked. Jared's face was unreadable. His apparent calm unnerved Daira more than she liked to admit.

"He never told me." Her whisper rasped in the thick stillness of the room. "We both knew he had an unusual talent at slipping in and out of places unnoticed, but..."

"He's a shifter," Daira put in. "He wasn't even aware of it himself until he came to us. I taught him how to control his ability. Just like I'm teaching you to control yours."

Now Taylor did rise to her feet. "You mean you've been *recruiting* me? All this time?"

"No. No! God, no. Sit down. Please? I don't want you standing up when you hear the rest of it."

"Hear her out," said Jared, an unexpected ally in her corner. He looked at her as if he was already three moves ahead of her, and simply waiting for her to reveal what he already suspected. Damn, no wonder the man had rattled Taylor the moment they'd met.

Taylor sat, jaw muscles working as she ground her teeth.

"Your connection to Troy is a key factor in the theory I've been working on since the day he disappeared. Why I've been waiting for him to turn up for as long as you have. Now here's the tricky part, the part that could get us all into deep, dark trouble if there are any leaks."

Carey hunched her shoulders and rubbed the back of her neck. Daira knew that neck-prickling feeling well.

"The day Troy disappeared, there was an explosion," she went on. "He was doing recon in his shifted state, and he came upon a couple of insurgents planting a roadside bomb. But he was too late to stop them from arming it." She took a breath and chose her words—and her tone—carefully. "There is...a piece of film..."

Carey made a distressed sound. Taylor closed her eyes and turned her face toward Jared, who scooted his chair next to hers and put his arm around her shoulders. His steady gaze never left Daira's face.

"It was taken from a rooftop security camera," she continued. "I've seen it. In fact I've studied it frame by frame because I noticed something that didn't look right. Troy saw an American convoy approaching from one direction, and a couple of school kids coming from another direction, all converging on where the bomb was hidden." She illustrated with her hands. "He shifted into visibility just long enough to head the children off, but there wasn't time to stop the convoy. I had to slow the film down to catch it." Daira paused and ducked her head briefly, trying not to replay the film in her mind. She had never gotten used to it.

"Catch what?" Carey whispered.

"He only had a second to react. I think he tried another technique I taught him—to use his energy to interfere with the bomb's trigger mechanism. It could be what set the bomb off, and I could see on his face that he knew he'd made a mistake."

Carey closed her eyes and clenched her fists in her lap. Taylor had both hands over her mouth, eyes huge. Heart aching, Daira reached out and took hold of her arm.

"One frame before the bomb exploded—one twenty-fourth

of a second—Troy started to shift. I'm not sure if he's aware he did it. It was probably automatic, like how your eye blinks before you even know a high-speed object is coming toward it."

"What does that mean?" Taylor rasped out the question. Carey's hand crept to her throat.

"It means I think Troy is alive."

In the silence, Carey waited what seemed like an eternity for her next heartbeat. "What?"

Jared, the only one who didn't seem floored by the news, leaned forward. "How?"

"What about the..." Taylor gestured helplessly at the right side of her chest. "How could he survive that?"

Carey didn't know how Daira continued to sound so calm. She herself felt lightheaded.

"Somehow the concussion of the bomb stuck him permanently in a shifted state, which is, in a sense, pure energy. That's how he can get into a person's dreams, if need be, to communicate. Dreams are really nothing but energy simmering in the deepest part of your subconscious. As long as he stays shifted, he doesn't bleed. There may be very little pain, if any."

"There isn't," whispered Carey around a knot in her throat. "He told me he knew it was there, but there wasn't pain like a normal body would have. Except when..." she snapped her mouth shut and felt her cheeks catch fire.

"That's right," said Daira evenly. "When something brings him out of his energy state into solid form. A powerful connection to something...or someone. Taylor, when you told me he deflected a bullet for Jared, it was the first real evidence my theory was right. But I wasn't sure until I saw him last night with Carey."

Carey gasped. "You were there?"

Now it was Daira's turn to blush, even under her brown skin. "It wasn't intentional, I promise you. I only meant to try to communicate with him through your connected aura while you were asleep. Except neither of you were exactly, um, sleeping."

Taylor made a strangled sound. Jared tried not to grin and failed.

Daira plowed on. "Believe me, when he appeared out of thin air—with you—I was as shocked as you were when you woke up."

"Oh…God." Carey thumped her forehead on the table and hid her face in her arms. Incredibly, a laugh bubbled up out of her throat. "Then why did you wake me up?"

Taylor snorted, and Jared rubbed a hand down his face to hide his expression—though his ears were bright red.

"Because if I hadn't," Daira said carefully, "Troy might have bled to death. The blood on your hand and on your sleeping bag proved it. And I saw the way it was pumping out of him before you woke up."

Carey's brief mirth died a quick death. She lifted her head. "What?"

Daira's black eyes held a hollow sadness. "Like I said, in his energy state, he's relatively safe. But in solid form, his wound is mortal."

Silence reigned for a long moment. Taylor spoke first. "You said relatively safe?"

"My guess is, if you're having trouble sensing him, last night's manifestation severely drained his energy. Right now he's probably running on backup batteries, as it were. It may not take much to push him beyond our reach."

"You mean, he dies for real."

Daira's gaze didn't waver. "Maybe."

Taylor had a death grip on Jared's hand. "What are we going to do?"

Daira's manner turned brisk, as if she were relieved to be past the challenge of breaking the news. "I thought I could do this here, on my own, but now it's clear I'm going to have to take Carey to the SpIRIT facility to try to figure out, number one, how we're going to get the two of them unhooked. Second, how to bring Troy out of his shifted form."

"But you said his wound was mortal," whispered Carey.

A brief smile flickered across Daira's features. It was the same cocky, confident grin Troy often wore—probably the same one the whole special ops team possessed.

"He's not going to die. Not on my watch."

"Or on mine," said Jared. "We're coming with you."

Daira got up from the table, as if adjourning a meeting. "That's not possible. It's a top-secret facility and I'm going to have enough trouble getting Carey in there as it is, much less convince my commander no one else knows she's there." Gone was the serene, Zen-like persona Daira had worn so easily. In its place was a woman on a mission.

Taylor rose to her feet and faced Daira, jaw stuck out. "No one's going anywhere until I've talked to my brother." Tears filled her eyes, and she swiped at them impatiently. "It could be my last chance. One our mother may never get, now."

Daira softened. "Of course. There was never any question about that, my friend."

Carey held out both hands toward Taylor, heart in her throat. "I guess that's my cue."

Taylor retreated into her chair, wiped her nose on her sleeve and took Carey's hands.

After a long minute, she sat back with defeat etching lines around her mouth. "If he's trying to talk to me, I can't hear him."

Daira cast about for a solution. "Come into the studio."

Once she had moved everyone into the converted bedroom, she placed the other two women on pillows, knee to knee, hands clasped. Daira sat with them, touching each of their shoulders.

She drew a centering breath, closed her eyes and took a stab at reaching out with her mind for Troy, hoping the three of them together would amplify…something. She tried again. Carey's agitation was like a wall of white noise. This would never work if Carey couldn't stop her mind from racing.

She cracked an eye open and looked at Jared, who sat nearby in a deceptively relaxed pose, jaw working under his short, dark beard. Maybe his old soul would act as an anchor. "Jared, do me a favor and join the circle."

Without fuss, he leaned forward and offered his hands. Both women latched onto them so tightly, surprise briefly widened his eyes.

There. That was better. But not much. She reached out again. All she could sense was a faint presence in one corner of the room. And not a strong one, at that.

Damn.

She opened her eyes and squeezed Carey's shoulder. "Carey, do you trust me?"

Carey's troubled expression told her volumes. "More than I trust myself, if that makes any sense."

"I think it would help if I could get you to relax with some light hypnosis."

Carey paled and shook her head. "I don't... No, bad things happen if I let myself go into an altered state of consciousness."

Daira pressed on, mentally crossing her fingers she wouldn't push too hard. "It'll be very light. You will be fully conscious and in control at all times. I promise." She held her breath.

Carey looked like she was about to refuse.

"Please, Carey, I think it could be the only way to get you relaxed enough to reach Troy. I know you don't mean to, but right now you're fighting it."

Carey shifted. "I don't know. Each one of these episodes gets a little worse. What if... What if one of these times I—we—can't come back?"

Taylor looked as if someone had slapped her, but she bit her lip and said nothing. Jared watched her with a critical eye, on point to call a halt to this whole thing if he thought his pregnant wife-to-be had had enough.

Carey looked for a long time at Taylor's shadowed face, and finally nodded. "Will I be able to stop it once we get started?"

"We'll have a safe word. If I hear you say it, we'll stop." Daira told herself it was true.

Carey bent her head to hide her face, and raked the fingers of both hands through her hair, pulling some of it out of the haphazard ponytail behind her head. When she looked up again her gaze was steady.

"Okay. Let's do it."

A few minutes later, Daira marveled at how easily Carey had submitted to the soothing cadence of her voice. Amazing what a woman would do, properly motivated.

She, Taylor and Carey were arranged on piles of pillows on the floor, Carey lying flat while Daira and Taylor held her hands. Jared let Taylor use his broad chest as a backrest. His own hands rest protectively on both sides of her belly.

"Are you still with me, Carey?"

"Yes," came her absent-minded reply.

Daira planted the first suggestion. "If and when you see Troy anywhere in the room, you won't be upset by what you see. You'll remain calm and detached at all times."

"'kay."

"Remember the word to have me bring you out?"

"Lexington."

"Right. When you say 'Lexington', I'll say 'barbecue' and count backward from three. By the time I reach one, you'll be fully awake and refreshed."

"'kay."

"Good. Now I want you to visualize a beautiful, peaceful place. What's your favorite place?"

The corners of Carey's mouth lifted. "I know exactly where I'd like to be right now. On my mountain."

"Good. Picture it now."

Daira shoved aside the twinge of guilt for what she was about to do. With a deceptively calming monotone and carefully chosen words, she quietly broke her promise not only by taking Carey deeper into an altered state, but sending her to another place in her mind altogether—anywhere but in this room.

There. She felt the exact instant Carey's wall of resistance dissipated. Daira quickly scanned the room and swallowed the gut-wrenching reaction at what she saw in the corner. In her time with SpIRIT, she had seen some pretty horrendous sights, but she had never gotten used to the sight of one of her own team members with injuries that even the most hardened of ER workers would shy away from.

Taylor turned her head to see where Daira was looking, and her breath hissed through her teeth. "Jesus. Troy..."

"Shhh." Jared slipped his arms around Taylor to hold her still, hands cradling her pregnant belly. "Easy. Remember, he's not in very much pain."

"You can see him?"

"Hell, the boy spent some time knocking around inside this body I'm renting. I can see him."

Troy crouched with his back braced against the wall, clutching both hands to the wound in his chest. The one in his shoulder glistened red. He rolled his head to one side to look at them all—and winked.

Daira eyed what looked like liquid energy leaking from between his fingers, and her stomach dropped. "Hey there, hoss." She tried for an easy tone, but it came out strangled with emotion.

"Hey, Choo," he rasped out his nickname for her, the phonetic first syllable of her last name. *"T-bird."* His gaze traveled to Jared, and he just lifted his chin. Jared nodded in return.

It had been so long since Daira had heard his voice, she had to take a second to fight the emotion that grabbed her throat.

"You've been listening?"

"Every...word." He seemed to be having to gather separate bursts of energy for each phrase. Where he was drawing it from, she couldn't say. He even managed a short laugh. *"So...I'm not quite...dead yet?"*

"Well, until now you weren't. Now I'd say you're mostly dead. Are you with me on this?"

Another slight head roll. *"Not yet. Got one more...trip to make."*

Taylor leaned in, mouth set in a straight line. "You found John."

"Yeah...sorry."

"Where?"

"Antietam. But couldn't...get to him. Gotta go back...make sure he's okay."

Daira vehemently shook her head. "Not an option. It'll kill you this time."

"Never...left a man behind...before. Not gonna...start now." He looked at Taylor. *"Don't worry, Tee...Jared's not...going anywhere. I'll make..."* He didn't seem to have the strength to finish the sentence.

Taylor gulped a breath. "We have to stop this. Now. It's draining him even more."

"No...getting stronger...just...taking a while..." His gaze had drifted to Carey, who still lay perfectly still on the pillows, eyes closed. His eyes narrowed and he tried to move away from the wall, but failed. He settled for gesturing at her. *"Look..."*

Daira glanced down at Carey's relaxed face. "What?"

"Can see...she's not...in there."

Daira's thought processes tripped over that one. "You mean...she's—"

"Day trippin'." A frown creased his forehead.

"She did it all by herself?" Taylor turned Carey's hand over in hers, jiggling it a little, getting no response. "I mean, not by accident?"

"Interesting," said Daira thoughtfully.

"Bring her back, Choo," murmured Troy, shifting his shoulders uncomfortably. *"Wherever she is...she's...out there alone..."*

She laid a light hand on Carey's forehead, but paused with a pointed look at Troy. "Not until you promise me you're not going to do something stupid."

That dangerous grin played at the corners of his mouth. *"Can't...make me."*

Daira scowled at him. "You are one stubborn son of a bitch, Troy MacRae Brannon."

"You...taught me...all I know about stubborn."

She rolled her eyes. "All right. Bar—"

"Wait. Something...want you to do first..."

"Barbecue. Three, two, one."

Carey sat straight up, pissed as hell and sending the three people around her scrambling out of her way.

"That bastard!" She launched herself out of the nest of pillows and commenced pacing around the room, the edges of her vision so red she was certain there must be steam pouring out of her ears.

"What? What is it?" Daira helped Jared get Taylor to her feet.

"I visualized my place in the mountains, like you suggested, and I got there just in time to see someone hammering a sold sign on it!" She stopped dead as she realized what she'd just said. "I went there. I consciously thought about it and went there." Her knees went weak and she plunked back down on the pillows. "That's kind of huge, isn't it?"

Daira crouched down in front of her with a tired smile. “It’s ginormous.”

Carey looked from face to drawn face, and slowly pulled one of the dozens of pillows close to her chest. “Was it bad?”

Taylor and Jared looked at each other rather than at her.

“He’s alive,” said Daira gently. “But not as strong as I’d hoped.”

The exhilaration of healthy anger drained away, leaving her numb. Carey nodded. “Okay, then. Let’s get going to wherever…”

“There’s one thing he wants to do. Before we attempt recovery.”

She shut her eyes for a second. “I know what he wants. Go back to Antietam. I already told him I couldn’t do it. But…that’s not quite true anymore, is it? With your help I can probably go anywhere I want.” She tried to draw reassurance from Daira’s firm nod.

“Exactly. We can try to make it as safe for you as possible, Carey. Or—” Daira shrugged. “You can say no. It’s not like Troy can do anything about it. We can head straight for the facility and get this thing under way.”

Choices. Troy had said she had choices. She lifted her chin. “No. I won’t do that to him. Not like someone tried to do to me.”

A bit of new admiration glinted in Daira’s eye. “There’s something I want to try first. Do you feel up to a nap?”

Carey glanced out the window at the brightly shining sun. How long had she been under? It had barely been dawn when they’d arrived. “What do you have in mind?”

Daira headed for a corner curio shelf unit that was groaning with a variety of crystal clusters. “Something that I hope will build up Troy’s energy before we try anything else.”

"Do we need to be here for this?" Jared had one arm around Taylor, studying her drooping eyelids, the way she had one hand supporting her belly as if her entire body were suddenly too heavy to deal with.

"I need Taylor," said Daira, busy selecting the largest chunks of crystal for whatever she was cooking up. "I need her to monitor how Troy is doing and if this thing I'm going to try is even going to work. But it's okay." She interrupted Jared's automatic protest. "She can rest for several hours—I'll make her comfortable right here in the pillows."

Jared subsided, looking doubtful.

"In the meantime," Daira went on, "we're going to need as many brains as possible to research and figure out the safest landing spot for Carey and Troy at Antietam."

Taylor drew herself up taller and nodded. "All right. Now if you'll excuse me, this baby is tap dancing on my bladder. Be right back."

Jared's gaze never wavered from her back as she left the room. "We'll need details."

Carey realized he was talking to her. She swallowed hard and tried to still an inner quaking that threatened to audibly rattle her spine. "The cornfield. We turned up near the fence line, close to Hagerstown Pike, about a hundred yards south of the Miller farmhouse."

Jared grimaced. "Why does it always have to be right in the middle of the worst of it?"

Chapter Ten

"I'll be back when you see me, Bill." Ross disconnected his cell while one of his partners was still talking. He shoved it into his pocket while juggling a couple of bags, one bulging with newly purchased books. The house's first level was empty, but upstairs he heard a rhythmic scraping noise, accompanied by snatches of a female voice venting in the kind of colorful swearing only a well-read woman could achieve.

Ah. Lily, probably engaged in another remodeling battle.

He took the stairs two at a time, a loudly cracking knee reminding him halfway up why he didn't do things like that anymore. Gaining the second level, he dumped the bags on a chair and followed the noise to the half bath. Lily stood on the closed lid of the commode, lush figure shaking in time to strokes along a corner of the wall with a homemade Paper Tiger.

"Whoever—invented—wallpaper—should—be—taken—out—and—shot—at—sunrise. Gah!"

Ross moved in behind her and peered over her shoulder at the progress she was making. Or lack thereof. The citrusy aroma of whatever soap she'd used that morning tickled his nose. And the movement of her mature curves under her loose-fitting T-shirt and shorts stirred feelings in his belly he hadn't allowed himself to indulge in for quite some time. Long enough that it took more than one try to drag his gaze away from the enticing sway of her rear end.

"Problems?"

Instead of jumping a foot in the air, Lily let fly with an elbow—without bothering to look where she was aiming.

"Ow!" He fell back a step, rubbing the center of his chest. "Jesus, woman, a little higher and you could have taken out an eye."

"Would've served you right, sneaking up on me." She scowled at him over her shoulder then resumed scraping.

He propped himself on the edge of the sink and waited for her to look at him again. It didn't take long.

"Can I help you?" She raised an eyebrow.

For the first time he noticed the redness rimming her eyes. Figuring she was in no mood to have him call attention to it, he gestured at the wall.

"There's an easier way to do that."

"What? I've got this wood-block thingie and a squirt bottle of fabric softener. This is what the guy at the hardware store told me to do."

"Mm. Did he tell you to peel the vinyl off first?"

"Uh..." She looked again at the wall, brow furrowed.

He had no trouble reaching past her in the small space. He lifted a corner of the material with a fingernail, and pulled off a strip in a long, clean sheet. Handed it to her. "There. Now squirt the stuff on and let it sit for a few minutes, then scrape it right off."

She stared at it for a few moments, then gave him a sheepish smile. "I think I hate you."

He grinned at her. "You start in that corner and I'll start over here. We'll have it all off in no time."

They worked in companionable silence for a few minutes.

"Where are the kids?"

Lily said nothing for so long he glanced at her, but her back was to him. Only her tight shoulders indicated her distress.

"I saw them headed down the beach toward Daira's before dawn this morning. Lane left not much later with her camera bag and a sandwich... I guess she'll be out all day taking photographs."

There was something she wasn't saying. It hung in the air between them like the ragged strips of wallpaper they were tossing out into a pile in the hallway. She jerked so hard at a section, she lost her balance and would have fallen backward if he hadn't steadied her with a hand on her back.

"Whoa. Easy there."

"They don't—" *Rip*. "—tell me anything. But then again, they grew up hiding things from me, so why should they stop now?" *Rip*.

"Maybe Taylor doesn't have anything concrete to tell you right now." He wadded up a strip and tossed it into the growing pile. "She didn't say anything before she left?"

"Well," said Lily in a voice too steady to be natural. "She left a note saying she hoped they'd be back at some point today."

"There you go. You'll know what she knows when they come home," he reasoned, but a shadow of concern nipped at the edge of his thoughts.

Within twenty minutes, they had the remaining vinyl stripped off and the adhesive soaking with fabric softener. Ross wiped his hands on his jeans.

"Come with me. You can help me with something." Actually he was casting about for anything to distract her until her daughter came home. He grabbed her hand and towed her into the kitchen, snagging his bags along the way. He plunked both on the kitchen table. One bag landed on the hard surface with a glassy clunk.

"What's this?" Lily poked her fingers into the bag and withdrew a bottle. "Scotch?"

He plucked it out of her hand and set it aside. "Wine is for sissies. Especially that stuff you've got in the icebox."

Lily snorted. "I think not. Stephen left it here before he went back to setting up his new practice near Asheville. I wouldn't touch it with a ten-foot pole. Someone needs to teach that boy how to drink properly."

"And you're just the woman to do it, I take it?" It was his turn to raise an eyebrow at her.

She planted one fist on her hip. "You bet your ass I am. Now what have you got for me?"

Ross couldn't explain the warm, fuzzy feeling that bloomed in his chest as he grinned at the roundish little spitfire beside him. He chalked it up to the fact he'd always like a woman who gave as good as she got.

He pulled the stack of books from the bag and extracted the largest. "Remember I told you I was looking for something—anything—that didn't fit?"

"Yeah."

"I was looking through some microfilms of *Harper's Weekly*. It was one of the few publications that regularly printed detailed illustrations along with their news." He began flipping through the book. "This book is a collection of work by some of its regular war correspondents. Do me a favor and tell me if you see the same thing I see."

She leaned in and watched as he slowly flipped through the large, glossy pages of woodcuts. Her hair tickling his shoulder was more distracting than he cared to admit.

"There." She planted a finger on the first of a series of woodcuts depicting the battle of Antietam. "Something changed about this one's style." She reached in front of him to thumb back a few pages, then back to the Antietam series. "But I can't quite put into words what it is."

He nodded. "That's what I thought."

"Who's the artist?" She turned pages back to the front of the book. "J. R. Allen. I'm not familiar with his work. J...R..." She glanced up at him. "You don't suppose...?"

"It could be nothing. A dead end. But I wonder if you'd mind digging into this while I make some calls about these contracts Carey was having some problems with."

"Hold on." She was already headed across the kitchen toward her purse, sitting on the counter. She returned with a pair of reading glasses, which she slipped onto her face as she sat at the table and pulled the book toward her. Then she paused and looked up at him over the rims. "Not. A. Word."

He raised his hands. "Wouldn't dream of it."

With Lily successfully distracted, he settled down at the opposite end of the table with the contract and power of attorney Lane had explained Carey didn't remember signing. Something that her ex, Kyle, thought was worth pursuing her several hundred miles to make sure she knew about in an attempt to force her to return to him. Truthfully, Ross felt relieved that he had something constructive to do other than rooting blindly through old documents for evidence of his missing son, lost somewhere in time.

Knowing Lily's bulldog stubbornness, if there was any shred of evidence hidden in those woodcuts, she'd find it.

Rapid, heavy footsteps sounded on the back porch steps, and both of them looked up just in time to see Jared charge through the door. Alone. Lily was standing up before the screen door rebounded.

It took Jared a few seconds to regain enough breath to talk. "Lily. Ross. We've got work do to."

Lily smacked the book shut. "Where is my daughter?"

"She's with Daira. And Carey and..." His haunted eyes found Lily's. "And with Troy. You aren't going to believe this, but there's a possibility Troy's alive. And that he's found John."

Lily sat down.

Ross stood up. "Tell us everything."

Lane shuffled her bare feet in the ankle-deep water at the low tide line, stopping every few yards to snap photos of random seashells, the dunes, the surf in the long angle of the late-afternoon sun.

After today, she was going to have to get back on the road and finish her assignment. Just as well. Since she'd brought Carey here, she'd felt a little bit like a fifth wheel, and a lot out of the loop. Whatever was going on here, it was probably better if she stayed out of the way.

She shaded her eyes and squinted down the beach. Only about a quarter mile back to the house, and she'd start packing her stuff. The way the sun glinted off Daira's pale turquoise cottage caught her eye, and she lifted her camera to capture the image. A movement at the back door had her pressing the zoom button.

Hm. Daira had a visitor. A visitor with the nicest set of shoulders and the most lickable ass she'd laid eyes on in ages. The sea wind lifted his smoky hair, which was gathered at the nape of his neck with a strip of leather and sported a streak of silver anchored at one temple. As she watched, he gave Daira a quick nod, turned and went down the stairs two or three at a time. She lost sight of him due to the top of a sand dune blocking her view. Just long enough for her to blink a grain of sand out of her eye.

A black canine head with one silver ear appeared at the top of the dune and filled her viewfinder.

What the... A wolf?

She felt her jaw drop as the animal, as if sensing it was being watched, swiveled its head and looked directly at her. Its silver eyes caught the late-afternoon light, seemed to ignite with some unearthly fire.

For a second she forgot how to breathe—but not how to press the shutter button.

By the time it clicked, the viewfinder was empty. Lane lowered the camera and looked around. No trace of the animal remained.

The battlefield assignment could wait a couple days. Right now, she had some research to do about the last time wolves were seen in North Carolina. This could be a scoop worthy of *National Geographic.*

Chapter Eleven

"It would be best if you could sleep."

Carey looked up from her seated position on the floor of Daira's studio, surrounded by twenty-one crystals of varying sizes and colors. Full dark inked the windows black.

What little bravado Carey had pumped up within herself earlier that day had dissipated as she'd tried to do just that—sleep. If only she could silence the increasing volume of the voices in her head blaming her for everything. Most of all Troy's now-weakened condition. If she fell asleep, how could she face him if he slipped into her dream again? She tried to shake it off.

"I know, I'm probably interfering with whatever these rocks are doing, right?"

Daira smiled down kindly at her, one hand resting on the doorframe, her bright blue caftan brushing the tops of her bare feet. "Something like that. They've been programmed to recharge the depleted layers of your aura. Theoretically, because of your connection, it should also help build up Troy's reserves. The best healing takes place during sleep. After a couple hours I will ask Taylor to come in and touch you to see how he's doing." Daira smiled at Taylor, who snored indelicately among the pillows. "She doesn't seem to be having any trouble sleeping."

"Well, she's pregnant. She's allowed." Carey set the pillow

aside before the seam she'd been picking at started to unravel. "I just wish I could be sure I won't go off on a psychic world tour."

Daira tilted her head, setting the beaded ends of a few of her braids swinging. "If it'll help, I can put you under again. We can set the intention that you'll stay right where you are until you wake up naturally on your own. That way there's no pressure. Based on our last session, you should be fine."

Carey nodded, grateful. "Okay. Thanks."

Daira entered the room and positioned herself just outside the circle, legs folded beneath her. "This is a grounding meditation I'm going to chant. It should do the trick. Make yourself comfortable."

Carey obeyed, trying to keep her hands from shaking as she arranged herself on the pillows. Daira leaned in and spent a minute rearranging a few of the crystals, setting a black one near her feet, a clear one at her head.

Carey turned on her side and propped her head on her hand. "Do you mind if I ask you something?"

"You can ask." Daira's half smile was noncommittal.

"Who are your people?"

The smile relaxed, and her black eyes sparkled warmly above her prominent cheekbones and bold nose. "My people are Eastern Band Cherokee."

Something inside Carey eased loose. "That must explain why I felt I could trust you the moment I saw you. My father was part Cherokee, though that's about all I know about his side of the family. I was never told much about him, though I understand his marriage to my mother was quite the scandal. Aunt Loreen can't even bring herself to say his name, come to think of it."

"*Tso-sda-da-lu.*" Daira inclined her head with quiet dignity.

The syllables felt comfortable in her ear, but she shook her head. "I'm sorry, I never learned the language."

"I said, 'then we are sisters'. But I must insist on no further personal questions. In fact, after this is all over it would be best if you simply forget you ever saw me."

Like that could ever happen. Carey settled into the pillows and closed her eyes. "I'm ready."

Daira began a low, rhythmic chant, each syllable sounding like a prayer.

Sleep must have come within seconds, because the chant faded to silence and she heard a slight noise to her left. When she turned her head toward it and opened her eyes, she found Troy only a foot away from her. He lay with her within the crystal circle, which, to her dream-state eyes, glowed and pulsated with energy she could feel tingling along her skin from her head to her toes.

"Pretty cool, huh?" he said, looking around at the array. "Choo really knows how to throw a slumber party."

She sat up and reached for him, trying to get a look at the wound he was hiding behind his hands.

"Don't. I know it looks bad, but I can normally recharge myself from the ambient earth energy around me. This time I'm just a little behind the eight ball."

"This is my doing." She looked for someplace to touch him that wouldn't cause more damage.

"I said don't. Stop blaming yourself for everything, will you? There were two of us going at it in that bed."

She couldn't help it. She snorted. "Going at it?"

"Trust me, I wasn't the only one there wishing it was real. And it's something I definitely want to finish when this is all over. Now that I know I'm going to get out of this alive."

"Well, it's good to have a goal, I guess."

"Fuckin' a, baby."

She moved closer and tentatively stoked his short hair. His cocky grin faded and he closed his eyes, tilting his head into her touch.

"How does it feel?"

"Like I'm in heaven, if you keep doing that."

"No." She cupped his cheek and his lids slid open. "I mean to know you're not a ghost?"

Something stark flashed across his face, and his gaze traveled around the room, rested briefly on the form of his sleeping sister, then back to Carey. "Like I'm closer than ever to everything a man could want—and closer than ever to losing it."

Instantly, discomfort chased the raw emotion from his eyes.

Her heart squeezed and her hand trembled, but she let the comment pass. Right now was no time to force him to talk and waste precious energy he would need for later.

She lay down beside him and searched his face for traces of pain. She saw only bone-deep exhaustion, and blood-like energy that leaked slowly from between his fingers. She had to remind herself he would be all right as long as he stayed shifted.

His eyes, ringed with purple circles, drifted closed. She moved in as close as she could without pressing on his injuries, looping an arm over his shoulders. It was as if their short exchange had weakened him yet again.

"Would you do something for me?"

"Name it, babe."

"Don't go back for John. It'll—"

"Except that."

"—kill you."

"Not with your help, it won't."

She rolled to her back and stared at the ceiling. "You have a lot more confidence in me than I do."

"I'm going to tell you a secret, and if you ever leak it to my Harley-driving posse I'll deny it six ways to hell."

She turned her head to look at him. He was grinning without opening his eyes.

"What?"

"Women are and always will be the stronger of the species."

Uh-huh. "Like flattery's going to get you anywhere." She felt a bit of her old spark returning. "Now that I've had a good look at you, I've changed my mind. You need to get to Daira's recovery team as soon as possible."

No answer. Cold fear tricked down her spine. "Troy?"

"Okay. It's not like I can go anywhere without you."

"Like you said, fucking a, baby." She resolutely pillowed her head on her arm.

His grin widened.

She narrowed her eyes at him. "What now?"

"One of these days...gonna have to teach you to swear without...sounding like a schoolmarm." His eyes remained alarmingly closed.

Unwilling to lose him to sleep just yet, she cast about for something to distract him. "You have a Harley?"

"Uh-huh," he muttered, drifting off. "Two. One is Dark Victory Red, the other..."

His face went slack. She lay facing him, a maddening few inches from his radiating body heat and uneven breath. Afraid to touch him for fear of setting off some trigger that would repeat last night's crisis.

Troy waited until her breathing steadied and deepened into a soft snore that was so cute—a word he'd never felt compelled to use before—he could have listened to it all night.

He opened his eyes and let his gaze slowly trace her softly rounded face, the small pointed chin with the slight dent in the middle. The messy hair, with one fat curl stuck in the corner of her curvy mouth. He resisted the urge to pull it out.

She wasn't going to like what he was about to attempt. If it even worked. But he refused to go anywhere—even back to his own life—without leaving things square with John.

He shifted by degrees until he had her pulled against him, one arm around her body. Practically one pore at a time, he laid his forehead against hers, skin to skin.

And he visualized a hillside above a bloody Maryland cornfield. Near a creek called Antietam.

Taylor stepped quietly into the circle of crystals and, using Daira's proffered arm for balance, knelt down to lightly touch Carey's foot.

"Anything?" Daira whispered.

Taylor looked around the room. Mentally flipped over every pillow on the floor. Panic twisted in her belly.

"He's not here. Daira, he's not... Carey!" She took a solid hold on Carey's foot and shook it. Shook it again, hard.

Carey never moved.

Daira felt the blood drain from her face. She bent over and propped her hands on her knees, letting her head hang down so the dizziness would pass quicker. "That bastard," she muttered, each spit-out word forcing blood back to her head. "He's hijacked her. And damn it, I helped him do it."

Taylor had moved up to Carey's upper half and was grinding her knuckles along Carey's breastbone. Still no response. "How did this happen?"

Daira tried not to think about how many times she'd heard that question in the past few months—and asked it herself. "I put Carey under hypnosis so she could sleep. Unfortunately, I set the intention that she would wake up on her own, without outside influence."

Taylor smacked her forehead. "Great. Now what?"

Daira scrambled to her desk and began punching numbers on the secure phone. "We wait. And have the transport on standby when they get back."

"Can't we just take her now?"

Daira shook her head. "It's not a good idea. I don't know if you can see it or not, but there's a lifeline of energy anchored to her body, which is vital for astral travelers. Moving her might weaken or break it."

Three sharp raps on the back door, and then the sound of several pairs of feet walking through it. Jared, Lily and Ross poked their heads into the studio, all three of them loaded down with books, rolled-up maps and a huge thermos of coffee. They took in Carey's still body, Taylor's vigil at her feet, Daira's exasperated expression—and all of their faces fell.

Mentally, Daira groaned. She had told Matthias they would undoubtedly be coming at some point, and to remind his wolf half to let them pass.

"Thanks for the effort, guys," she said wryly. "But

apparently Troy was three steps ahead of us. My guess is, the both of them are already playing dodge the cannonball."

Yes. They'd landed exactly where he wanted—on the crest of a slope overlooking the Miller cornfield, behind a pile of rocks the farmer had wrestled from the soil. And he braced himself for Carey's reaction.

Thwack. Her open palms impacted his shoulders. "Are you kidding me? Are you *kidding me?*"

"Ow! Do you mind? Bleeding, here. Stay down, we're not quite out of range."

She crouched next to him and looked around, eyes wide with fear. "When we get back home, I'm so kicking your ass. Where are we?"

He grinned to himself. Now this was the woman he had known from the beginning simmered under Carey's mild exterior. "On the slope above the battlefield. The house we were at before is just down there."

She turned away and locked her gaze on him. "I'd rather not look, thanks," she said, her face taking on a decidedly greenish cast. "Why? Why did you do this, Troy? It's insane." She flinched as, somewhere below, a volley of musket fire cracked.

Adrenaline gave him a surge of energy he was well aware was only temporary. "Not yet. If I'm not mistaken, John will be coming up this way shortly." He poked his head briefly over the mound of rock. "Yep. I knew it. There's the reason why."

"What?" Carey followed suit. "Who's that?"

A man sat a few yards below them, partially sheltered by rocks. His back was to them, but they could see a puffing pipe sticking out of the side of his mouth, his elbow moving rapidly as he sketched the battle scene below in bold strokes of charcoal pencil.

"No clue. But I'm pretty sure he's the reason I saw John head up this way."

The words were barely out of his mouth before the man below uttered a surprised grunt and fell backward, staring sightlessly at the sky, pencil still clutched in his fingers. As before when they'd been trapped in the middle of the battle, Carey saw the man's spirit jump out of his body and make a beeline away from the line of fire.

Straight toward her.

Carey screamed and tumbled into a ball behind the rocks, hands clamped over her face as trailing shreds of the man's soul brushed her skin.

"Stay here."

"No!" Carey rolled and lunged for Troy's foot as he scooted out of sight. He was too quick.

Trying to breathe around the pulse racing in her throat, she scrambled around the side of the pile to see what was going on, keeping low. No way was she going to poke her head over the top, now that she'd seen how far a bullet could travel.

Troy crouched by the man's body, examining it closely as he periodically craned his neck to look down the hill toward the house. Abruptly he thrust his arm into the air, signaling someone she couldn't see. She moved a little farther out to get a view down the hill. A man in Union blue was approaching at a dead run, his handsome face contorted in fury.

"What the *hell* are you doing here?"

Troy stood and grabbed the man in a rough bear hug. "Hello yourself, John."

John pushed him away and held him at arm's length, clearly not mollified. "I told you to go back. There's nothing you can do for me here, and I sure as hell am not coming back with you."

Both men stared at each other for several long seconds. John's blue eyes were suddenly wet.

Troy cleared his throat. "You're welcome."

"Yeah." John seemed at a loss for words. He took off his cavalry hat and wiped sweat from his grimy forehead. "Yeah. It's...good to see you."

Troy visibly shoved emotion aside and got back to business. "I know you're not coming back. Neither one of us would do that to Taylor. But I think there's a way to at least give you a life while you're here." He looked down at the body lying literally at their feet.

"I saw him go down. I couldn't get to him before his soul ran off."

"That's what you've been doing all this time? Rounding up the dead?"

John shrugged. "It's a living." He looked past Troy and caught Carey's eye. "We've got a visitor."

Troy looked around and winked at her. "No. That's my ride."

John didn't even ask what that meant. He simply looked her up and down and politely tipped his hat. "Ma'am."

Carey grimaced and gave him a little wave. "Hi. I think I'll stay right where I am, thanks."

John grinned at Troy. "You've been busy."

"Yeah, busy looking for you. Now hurry up, or your ride is going to leave the station without you."

John looked down at the body between their feet. "Uh..."

Troy gestured and they crouched down to look it over.

"See," said Troy, opening the man's shirt. "The ball was nearly spent. It didn't even break the skin, but it must have hit him just hard enough to stop his heart. If you can get in there and we can get it started again, you're golden."

"I don't know, man. Pulling a Beaudry is not what I had in mind."

"This is different. This is abandoned real estate, not a hostile takeover like what happened with you. What have you got to lose?"

Troy's back was to Carey, but she frowned at the uneven way his back expanded and contracted with each breath. The entire side of his shirt was shiny with plasmic energy leaking from his chest wound. She crawled out from her shelter and scrambled toward them, ignoring the way the rough ground scraped her knees and hands.

"Guys... Whatever you're going to do, I think you should hurry—"

The entire scene in front of her eyes flickered.

No.

She cried out and thrust out an arm toward Troy.

He swore and lunged in a twisting fall toward her, arms outstretched.

Their fingers never touched.

Chapter Twelve

In one breath, Carey was inhaling the acrid smell of gunpowder. In the next, clean, moist ocean air. What she could get of it, anyway, with what felt like an iron band around her neck.

Faint grey wisps made the night sky a patchwork of stars and clouds that whirled crazily overhead as she found herself being dragged, her bare feet just brushing the sandy ground. She instantly recognized the trace of expensive aftershave on the sweaty skin of the arm partially blocking her airway.

She dug her fingers into Kyle's arm and tried to pry it away just enough so she could breathe.

"What are you doing?" she managed to squeak out. "Let me...go!"

Thoughts crashed through her brain. *What have you done to Taylor and Daira?* Then, *You forced me to leave Troy behind.* Anger flashed white hot through her body. She kicked and squirmed, but Kyle seemed to possess the strength of three men. Three enraged men.

His voice in her ear, chillingly calm, nearly stopped her heart.

"I don't know who you talked to, little girl, but you've ruined everything. *Everything.* Think you're so clever, think you could just disappear and hire some fucking small-time Yankee lawyer to humiliate me? Stupid bitch."

She wrenched her head to one side and managed half a breath. "I don't know what you're—"

He shook her, and for the first time she felt a hard, sharp edge pressed just under her breast. Oh God...

"The contract. And the power of attorney, you little idiot. A copy of both of them covered in red ink hit my attorney's fax machine yesterday morning. Seems there was some question about its validity, and now everyone from the EPA to the state attorney general's office is asking questions. I've got some very rich, very pissed-off investors gunning for my head, thanks to you."

"How...how did you find me?" she choked out, tears of rage and terror blurring her vision.

"Your quack lawyer was sloppy, dearest. He faxed the documents from the local library. After that it was a simple matter to track you down."

She heard a car door open.

Oh, *hell* no. He was not taking her away from here. She twisted and kicked backward, but her bare heels slipped off target.

"Do you have any idea how far I was leveraged on that real-estate deal? Your property's sale would have secured our future, sugar." His tone had turned smooth and sweet. Carey's stomach churned and she scratched frantically at his skin. He didn't seem to feel it. "It was all for us, for our children. Now you're coming home with me to tell everyone it was all a mistake, and you wanted me to sell it and get it out of your hair. Maybe in a few years, the embarrassment you've caused will be forgotten."

Abruptly he whipped her around to face him, clamping her wrists together in one hand. "But not forgiven. That will take a while longer, I'm afraid. But I'm sure we'll work through it, won't we, sugar?" He yanked her toward him, grinding his mouth down on hers until she tasted blood. A scream clawed at her throat, escaping when she wrenched her head to one side.

Fury pounded through her body, and as she looked at Kyle's face she felt something click into place somewhere inside her. Some kind of connection...a plug inserted and a switch thrown. Power flooded her limbs, and every ounce of her fear and anger focused to a laser point that connected her knee directly to his groin. Then, when he grunted and let go, her balled up fists to his ears. Then her other knee to his nose as she yanked his head down.

Something cracked, and it wasn't just his nose. A popping sensation in her knee joined the satisfying crunch of his cartilage.

Out of nowhere, a black, furry shape flew out of the darkness and attached itself to Kyle's throat, shoving him away from her and pinning him to the ground with swift, silent precision.

Carey stumbled backward, her hand going to a stinging sensation along her rib cage. Daira's voice rang out in the darkness.

"Matthias! No!"

Carey gasped, unable to tear her gaze away as the giant black wolf gave Kyle's neck one hard shake. Kyle's feet kicked, then went still.

"Shit," muttered Daira as she strode into Carey's line of vision. "How did he get past you?"

The wolf turned its head to stare past her, lips lifted in a snarl. Daira followed the direction of his gaze and swore under her breath at the sight of Lane standing stock still at the foot of the dunes, several pieces of broken camera cradled in her hands.

“Get out of here,” Daira snarled right back at the wolf. The animal sprang away and disappeared into the night.

She squatted next to Kyle and put two fingers to his neck. Then she touched something hidden in the hair behind her ear. “Quincy. Clean up on aisle triple-six. This one’s still alive.” Then she rose to her feet and strode purposefully toward Carey, the hem of her flowing dress hitched up between her legs and secured under her belt. She wondered, absurdly, why she had thought of Daira as plump. Her legs were all smooth, solid muscle. And strapped to one thigh was a knife.

Carey’s own legs went numb. Daira reached her and lowered her to a sitting position on the ground, checking her for injuries. “Are you all right? Did he hurt you?”

Carey batted her hands away. “I need Taylor…where is she?”

Daira’s face was tight with suppressed anger. “She’s in the house with the others. She was taking a turn keeping watch over you when Kyle got into the room.”

“Oh my God. Is she all right?”

Daira ducked her head, holding tight to her emotions as she stuck a pen light in her teeth and lifted Carey’s T-shirt to examine the scrape Kyle’s knife had left on her skin. “I don’t know,” she mumbled around the light.

A muted *thup thup thup* drew Carey’s attention toward the dark, abandoned beach. A huge oblong shape with a blur of rotors on top emerged out of a patch of coastal fog and set itself down right behind Daira’s cottage. It was eerie how silent the chopper was. Any farther away, and she would never have heard it.

Could my life get any more surreal? The brief thought flashed through her mind.

"Come on," said Daira. "We can't wait any longer to get you to the facility."

Carey shook her head. "Whatever you're going to do, it's not going to work because I don't think Troy made it back with me."

Daira froze for a second, then passed her hand through the air an inch from Carey's skin, checking her aura for traces of Troy. Carey knew she wouldn't find any. "What happened?"

"When Kyle woke me up, Troy and I were separated. He got left behind at Antietam."

Daira's composure slipped. Almost. She seemed to hold her breath an inordinately long time before she exhaled in a rush of frustration. "When we do get him back," she growled, "I'm going to kill him."

Incredibly, Carey felt her mouth twist in a wry smile. "Well, you'll have to get in line. But first you have to send me back there to haul his sorry butt home."

Both women sobered as they observed Jared exiting the rear of the house, carrying what looked like a rolled-up quilt. The only clue it contained Taylor was the mop of shaggy blonde hair resting on his shoulder.

Chapter Thirteen

Carey felt like more of an outsider than ever, standing with her nose pressed against the window of the state-of-the-future medical treatment room. Inside, Taylor lay surrounded by family. Fighting for her baby's life.

She'd showered, had her various scrapes and bruises attended to, and now she stood alone in a chilly corridor that looked like it had been carved from an old underground mine. Her right knee ached, probably from the force with which she'd kicked Kyle in the crotch. And nose. She tucked that satisfying thought away as she zipped her borrowed sweatshirt up to her chin and jammed her hands into the deep pockets. The sweatpants fit her, but were way too long and dragged on the ground around her stockinged feet.

A sharply whispered conversation down the hall to her right attracted her attention. Daira, now dressed in the same black-and-camo clothing of everyone else she'd seen since arriving here, was arguing with a much taller, knife-edge lean man with salt-and-pepper hair. Just the way he carried himself indicated his superior rank, though Daira did not seem intimidated by his height and attitude. He did not look pleased.

Carey wondered if they realized the cave-like passageway, with its bare rock ceiling, acted like an echo chamber that bounced their conversation right into her ears. She glanced at her surroundings. Wherever they were, it had to be deep underground. On the long flight from Hatteras, she had lost track of time, thanks to the chopper's blacked-out windows.

"You know you're headed straight for a board of review. Bringing five outsiders into this facility, only one of which was authorized?"

Carey assumed the "one of which" meant her.

"It couldn't be helped, Commander Hackett. I couldn't leave Troy's sister behind when it was our screwup that put her baby in danger. There's no other facility existing that deals exclusively with...our kind of people. This is the best place for her."

"And the others?"

"All right, sir," she said slowly, with an edge of sarcasm. "You tell me how I was supposed to keep the father and grandparents of Taylor's baby off that chopper without unnecessary bloodshed. And believe me, it wouldn't have been their blood being spilled. The chopper had already spent thirty-seven seconds too long on the ground—it was either let them on it, or risk full exposure." Her voice dropped. "Besides, none of them knows where they are. We took precautions."

Hackett had no reaction to Daira's insubordinate tone except to cross his arms and draw himself up even taller. "I'm told there is one still on the loose."

She shifted her weight to the other foot. "Matthias is on it."

Lane. Carey hadn't seen her since just after Matthias had taken Kyle down.

"Matthias had better not screw this up."

"He won't, sir. If he isn't here with her within the hour, I'll demote him myself."

"You're damned right you will. Take care of this, Tsutla."

"I take full responsibility, sir."

Hackett began to walk away, then paused without turning around. "You'll inform me when Brannon has been recovered."

Her expression softened. "The moment I know anything, you'll know, sir."

Hackett nodded and disappeared into the shadows down the corridor.

Daira turned toward her, and Carey arranged her face and kept staring into the treatment room as if she hadn't heard a thing.

"Will she be all right?" Carey asked when Daira reached her side and joined her in peering through the window.

"She's stable for now. The contractions have stopped on their own. We'd rather not give her any meds for that—we've discovered they can interfere with the long-term development of the child's gifts." She ducked her head. "And...I shouldn't have told you that, either." She sighed. "This has been a long, long year."

Carey suppressed the urge to put a hand on Daira's arm—she looked too much the hardened warrior in her black T-shirt and dark grey-and-black camo pants. "I'm sure it has. But it's almost over." She pulled her shoulders back a little. "I'm ready whenever you are."

Daira looked at her and grinned. "Let's get this party started, then."

The room reminded Carey strongly of the studio in Daira's beach house—sparsely furnished, lit only with candles, floor covered in huge pillows. The only difference was the sheer number of crystals. Every inch of the round, dome-ceiling room was covered in clear, sparkling quartz. All of them pointing directly at her in the center of the room.

It was little unnerving.

An enormous bald man with coffee-colored skin was finishing up attaching an array of sensors to her head and chest. A silent, redheaded woman with cat-tilted eyes, so tiny that at first Carey though she was a child, efficiently applied a blood-pressure cuff to her left arm and an assortment of monitors to three fingers. Everything, it seemed, was wireless.

Daira spoke into a two-way radio, using some unintelligible techno babble but probably checking to make sure the wireless signals were all working.

"Are you sure this isn't NASA?" Carey attempted to joke through her nerves.

Daira's smile didn't quite hide the worry in her eyes. "Quincy, Saraya, I think we're done here. Thanks."

"Good luck," murmured Saraya.

Quincy's jaw appeared to be clenched too tight to speak. He simply nodded and shut the door behind him as he and Saraya left.

Daira dropped naturally into a cross-legged sitting position in front of Carey. "Okay, here's how it's going to work. You've got a clear idea when and where you're landing."

"Yes." *I hope.*

"We'll be monitoring your brain waves, and I'll be sensing your aura with my hands. As soon as you have a hold of him, we should know and I'll bring you out of hypnosis. Then we'll take a break, and move on to the final stage. That's what all these crystals are for. They're connected to a device that should amplify the energy I sensed the last time I saw...um...when Troy manifested."

"Thank you for putting it so delicately."

Daira tried to smile and failed. "You're welcome."

"Why do I need all this?" Carey indicated the sensors attached to her fingers, the cuff on her arm, which was already taking a reading every couple of minutes.

"Two reasons. One, we just want to monitor your vitals so we can stop if anything gets out of whack. Two...well, we've never tried anything like this before, so we're interested in all the data we can get."

"That's reassuring."

Daira didn't appear to have an answer for that. "Are you ready?"

Mouth going dry, Carey nodded and lay back on the pillows. Daira guided her through a series of deep-breathing exercises, and presently began her hypnotic chant.

Carey visualized the pile of rocks on the hillside above Antietam's bloody cornfield, and let herself sink into the vibrations of Daira's voice.

Cannon fire jolted her eyes open.

As if from a distance, she observed that the sound of it barely phased her anymore. Flipping onto her belly, she scrambled around the rock pile.

And met John's eyes. Except they were peering at her from inside the face of the artist that had formerly been lying dead on the ground.

"It worked," she squeaked.

John ignored the comment. "Take him and get out of here," he rasped. "I don't think he has much time."

Carey realized with shock that he was cradling someone in his arms. It was Troy. A sob collided with a gasp in her throat when she saw his skin's grey pallor. His eyes were open, but dull, unseeing. Terror froze her limbs.

"Now!" barked John.

She nearly jumped out of her skin, and crawled the last few feet in a split second. She held out her arms and John literally dumped him onto her. The dead weight sent her tumbling backward...

...into the pile of pillows in the center of the crystal-encrusted room.

She instantly sat straight up, mouth open, unable to breathe.

Dimly she heard Daira's voice, felt the woman's hands on her shoulders, shaking.

"Breathe, Carey, breathe!" She snatched up her two-way. "Quincy, we're going to need O2. Vitals?"

A deep voice crackled harshly from the radio. "Heart rate is in the red zone. Pressures elevated but dropping. Pulse ox ninety and rising."

Carey heard the door open and shadows gathered around her, holding a mask to her face that fed her sweet, cool air. Her diaphragm finally engaged and she drank it in. She took three breaths and ripped the mask off.

"I think we're too late." She grabbed a handful of Daira's shirt. "He looked like he was...was..."

"No, he's still with us. I can sense his energy in your aura again. Do you hear me, Carey? He's here. But you need to tell me what you saw."

She fought to stay focused. "He...he looked dead. Pale, blood all over him...his eyes...oh God, his eyes looked..." She couldn't finish the thought.

Daira's and Quincy's gazes met and held.

"That's bad, isn't it?"

Daira didn't answer. "Let's take a break and get you calmed down."

"No. Put me back under now. *Now*, Daira. I don't think Troy will make it if we wait."

Again the exchange of glances between the Cherokee woman and the silent black man. Daira blew a steadying breath. "Is everything ready?"

"Everyone's scrubbed in, and the EAD is booted up."

"Choo, we've got a problem." Another voice snapped on the radio. Daira keyed the mike.

"What?"

"The mountain just had a hiccup. The main coils blew."

Quincy threw up his hands, and Daira swore. "How long before it's back up?" she clipped out.

"Two hours minimum."

"What does that mean?" Carey's insides quaked.

"It means we're going to have to do this without amplification." Daira gave in to a rare moment of frustration and threw the radio down. It bounced off the pillows, unharmed. "Or wait until it's back online."

Panic knifed through her. "That's too long. We both know it is."

Daira shoved her hand through her braids, then looked at Carey long and hard. "Do you think you can do it alone?"

No. "Yes." She tore at the sensors on her head, orders pouring out of her mouth as if she were corralling her classroom of rowdy high schoolers. "Get this crap off me. And once I'm under, everyone's got to get out of this room."

"But what if you need—"

"I *need* not to be distracted, or worry about what anyone's going to see." A strange calm settled over her like a protective mantle, and she knew as she stared Daira down, she probably had *do not fuck with me* written on her forehead.

Daira was quiet so long, Carey thought she was going to refuse. Finally she nodded. "You're going to have to trust two of us, Carey. You're heart rate is through the roof. It's going to take both Quincy and I working together to get you under again."

Impatience drove her to give in. It didn't matter what anyone saw. All that mattered was bringing Troy back. "All right. Whatever it takes."

At Daira's pointed gesture with her chin, the room cleared of all personnel except for Quincy. Carey threw herself backward onto the cushions and stared up at the sparkling ceiling, desperate with impatience to get on with it.

She closed her eyes and felt the pillows around her shift as Daira positioned herself at her head, hands on either temple.

"Ground her, Quincy."

She felt the big man's hands wrap around her feet. It was like a circuit had been closed and instantly Carey felt as if she was suspended in mid-air. She had to force herself to focus.

"All right, Carey." Daira's voice floated farther and farther away. "Bring him home."

Chapter Fourteen

She opened her eyes, still lying on her back in the crystal room. But in her altered consciousness, Daira and Quincy were faint, motionless shadows she could barely see.

An alarmingly cold hand immediately wrapped around her left one, and she rolled without hesitation to fling her arms around Troy's too-still body.

"Damn you," she ground out between clenched teeth. "You used up what little you had left to get John into that body, didn't you?"

One corner of his mouth hitched up a fraction of an inch. It was all the response he seemed capable of. That, and one slow blink of his glazed eyes.

A sob burst from her throat. "I can't do this alone, Troy. Not without your strength."

Another blink. His lips moved. *Yes.* His mouth formed an "o" and he blew out a scant breath.

What did he want? She stared at his mouth as he repeated it.

Realization dawned. He was indicating how he had blown his own life energy into her lungs on the cliff in Ireland.

He must have read her expression, for he lifted his chin in a tiny nod, and winked.

"Okay." She forced her roiling emotions into the far corner of her mind. She gently rolled him to his back and slipped one hand behind his head. "Okay. Here goes."

She lowered her face, sealed her mouth over his, and blew. Willing life into him, as he had done for her.

Her only reward was his weak, wheezing cough.

"Come on, Brannon," she muttered. "You're pissin' me off. Fight for it!"

She poured another hard breath into this failing lungs. Another, harder.

His hand slid up her arm, fingers digging in with surprising strength. Behind her closed eyelids, green lights flashed. She sucked in another breath through her nose so as not to break contact, and blew so hard the room began to spin. Troy's body flexed, and his throat vibrated with a tortured groan.

His first strong heartbeat thundered through her entire being like a giant bell.

"Yes! That's it!" Power surged through her body like a speeding freight train, and she wondered distantly if Daira's vaunted amplifier had suddenly kicked on.

An unhealthy gurgle sounded somewhere deep in his chest. She rolled with him so that he was on his side, some distant memory from a first-aid class telling her to make sure his worst wounds were below his heart. She locked her fingers in his hair and kept breathing, even though her own heartbeat began to feel thready and uneven under her breastbone.

Something wet and sticky pooled between their bodies. She squeezed her eyes shut and kept going, her breath beginning to come in short, desperate gasps.

He suddenly planted a hand on her chest and pushed her away. "Stop. You're going to kill yourself." His voice emerged around wheezing as he tried to breathe on this own. His face was a study in pain.

She shook him. “Don’t you give up on me! There are too many people here who’ve put their lives on the line to get you to this point. You’ve got a niece or a nephew just down the hall that’s trying not to be born too soon.”

Troy’s eyes narrowed.

She grasped his chin. “That’s right. Taylor even risked her baby for you. There are too many people with their hearts riding on this for you to give up now. Too many people...” She swallowed a sob. “That love you, damn it. Like...like me.”

He searched her face, something new and bright dawning behind the suffering in his eyes. Presently he nodded.

Then he grimaced. “This is gonna hurt.”

“Wake up, Carey. For God’s sake, wake up and let go of him!”

Carey opened her eyes to chaos. Troy’s body heaved in her arms, his head thrown back and mouth open in silent, fruitless attempts to draw air into his collapsed lungs. Blood was everywhere. All over him...all over her. Dripping from the corners of his mouth.

She screamed and released him. The room seemed full of people in surgical scrubs, rubber gloves and face masks.

“Shrapnel must have nicked an artery,” one of them shouted. “Damn it, we’re going to lose him before we get him out of this room.”

“No we’re not. Get out of my way!” Saraya, the tiny redhead, shouldered her way to Troy’s side.

Without hesitation, she pressed her gloved hand into the

gaping hole in Troy's chest. He made an unearthly sound, and it took the other five people on the team to hold him down. Carey sat frozen in horror, hands clamped over her mouth, unable to tear her gaze away.

Saraya's tilted eyes were unreadable as she worked her arm at different angles until she found what she wanted, blood soaking her sleeve up past the elbow. "I've got it. Move him."

Troy had long since gone limp.

As one unit, the surgical team picked him up and carried him through a wide door that suddenly opened up in the far wall of the room. Glaring lights on multiple stainless-steel surfaces nearly blinded her. Before her eyes adjusted, the door was already sliding shut.

In the utter silence that followed, Carey felt a hand on her back. She looked over her shoulder.

Daira and Quincy sat behind her, both their faces unnaturally pale.

"I felt him start to give up," Daira said, her face drained of expression.

Carey blinked her eyes through double vision as her lungs continued to pump oxygen into her bloodstream. "I'm glad the amplifier kicked in. I almost lost him."

Quincy got up and, without a word, slipped out of the room, his shoulders hunched in an apparent effort not to break down in front of anyone.

Daira shook her head. "No, Carey. It was all you." She looked around the room. "You should have seen this place light up right after you said you loved him." A half laugh, half sob tore out of her. "It was like Christmas."

Suddenly Lily and Ross were through the door and lifting them both to their feet. Carey found herself in the middle of a group hug that seemed to go on for an hour. Her legs turned to water and she went to her knees, arms wrapped around Lily's waist as she allowed herself to melt into the motherly caress, blood-soaked clothing be damned. She felt a big, masculine hand stroking her tangled hair. Had to be Ross.

"Taylor?" she croaked.

Ross's voice rumbled somewhere over her head. "She knew the moment you brought Troy back. Jared is trying to convince her to stay in bed until he's out of surgery."

A laugh barked out of her throat. "Good luck with that." Then she looked up into his face, never letting go of Lily. "Ross, I saw John."

His hand stilled. "Is he..."

She wondered at the numbness that swamped her body and soul, preventing her from delivering the news through tears. "He's all right. He's alive. That is to say, he had a life. Thanks to Troy."

Ross looked away, staring for a very long time up at the ceiling, throat working soundlessly as if he didn't know whether to laugh or cry. It occurred to Carey that he was only now coming to grips with the fact that he had finally, irrevocably, lost his son.

Lily transferred Carey into Daira's hands, then went to Ross as the big man—without a sound, without moving a muscle—went to pieces.

She reached up and cradled his blank face in her hands. "Ross, look at me. We're going to check on our grandchild now."

He stood still as stone, hollow eyes staring into space.

"Ross!" Desperation choked Lily's voice. "Don't you dare do this to me."

He twitched and his gaze found her upturned face, which

blazed with emotion. "Let's go." Satisfied she had pulled him back from the brink, she inserted herself under his left arm and pretended to let him lead her from the room. At the door, she paused and looked over her shoulder.

"I will be back to see my son, Daira. Shortly."

Limbs numb, Carey let Daira lay her down and check her vitals, clearly stalling for time.

"Lily...I don't know how long he'll be in surgery—"

"Shortly," Lily repeated, eyes narrowed. "Don't tell me this place doesn't have a security camera in every corner. I know you people are probably going to try to get me to leave before he's awake for goddamned national-security reasons. If you don't let me see Troy, I'll take this place apart stone by stone."

Daira held up both hands, resigned. "You'll see him, Lily. I promise."

Lily nodded curtly and disappeared with Ross down the hall.

"Right after Hackett eats my liver," Daira muttered.

Carey managed a breathy laugh as she gratefully let Daira replace the oxygen mask on her face.

Too much emotion had been crammed into too short a time. She began to shiver, and an ache settled into every bone in her body. She curled up onto the pillows in a fetal position, letting Daira tuck several layers of warmed blankets around her. She had the feeling if she were forced to endure one more hill on this roller coaster, she would shatter into a million pieces.

A monstrously large, rock-hard pair of arms lifted her from the floor. She looked up into the coffee-colored face of Quincy, who had apparently regained control of himself. The giant cradled her delicately, as if she was precious cargo.

She flung out an arm and Daira grabbed her hand as she followed with the portable oxygen tank. “Daira…I want…”

The Cherokee woman’s face was strained with compassion and regret. “Lily is right about one thing, Carey. You’re all going to have to leave. Soon. It’s not safe for you to stay here.”

Finally, a sob worked its way out of Carey’s chest. She clamped down tight lest she lose it completely. “Tell him…tell Troy…”

Daira’s eyes sparkled with held-back tears. “Tell him yourself. From what I’ve seen, once he’s on his feet—and as bad as he looked, I know he will be—God help anyone who tries to keep him from getting to you. Now rest.”

Daira seemed so certain. Carey hadn’t the energy to feel any more. An unnatural silence settled in her soul as Quincy carried her from the room.

This must be what it was like for Carey. Waking up from the dead.

Troy’s entire body felt like one giant, exposed nerve ending. Normal senses long denied him now battered him from all sides. Beeps, whirs and hisses of machines…sterile smells…a symphony of noise he was having difficulty filtering out. The light blanket that felt like dead weight.

And above it all, the screeching high note of pain.

He knew the drill. Medications that separated normal people from tremendous pain were off the menu for the gifted few like him. The long-term—possibly permanent—affects on his powers weren’t worth the risk.

Or so said those research eggheads who’d never actually had to endure post-op pain without morphine.

Now he was wishing he hadn’t signed away his option to

use them back when he'd been recruited into SpIRIT.

He knew without opening his eyes that he probably resembled a high school science experiment gone wrong. The generator situated somewhere near his feet was silent, but the electricity flowing through the dozens of acupuncture needles peppering his body hummed just under his skin, vibrating his eardrums. The energy, like a flowing river, carried away the worst of it.

Worst being a relative term.

Cold, clammy sweat coated his skin, chilling him to the bone. The sweat had less to do with the pain and more with the straps holding his body immobile. The tube that ran through his mouth and throat, inflating his lungs every few seconds.

Claustrophobia twisted inside him, and he fought the urge to cough up the tube and spit it out.

A pair of cool, smooth hands came from nowhere and worked patiently to uncurl his clenched fist.

"Troy, can you hear me?"

Mom. A new ache joined the cacophony of sensations pummeling him.

"Relax. Let the machine do the work," she said in the same calm, matter-of-fact tone she'd always used when he'd come to her with some boyhood injury. "The less you fight it, the quicker you'll be off it."

He squeezed her hand, then loosened his grip, afraid he'd crush the delicate bones. He wanted to see her face, tried to open his eyes. The dim lighting stabbed clear to the back of his skull and his lids involuntarily slammed shut.

The whisper of moving clothing swished in his ears, and the light glowing behind his closed eyelids dimmed. Cautiously he cracked one open.

Instantly it blurred, and something hot and wet leaked from the corner and ran into his hairline. Lily's face loomed over him.

For once he wished she possessed the nonverbal communication powers he and Taylor had. There were only four words he wanted to say, but the barrier might as well have been the Great Wall of China.

I love you, Mom.

Lily's tired eyes crinkled, and her fatigue-grey face brightened. She bent her head to his anchored hand and carefully kissed his battered knuckles.

"I love you, son. I wish Taylor was in here to help me talk to you."

Taylor. The baby. He automatically tried to reach past the pain to communicate with his sister, but the electrified acupuncture treatment blocked the effort.

"She's fine. The baby is going to be okay." Lily wiped impatiently at her eyes and refocused on him. "It's a girl, by the way."

Troy fixed his one open eye on hers and stared. Deliberately he thought of the one woman he wanted in his arms right this second.

Carey.

Lily let go his hand and fussed with wiping his sweaty forehead with a damp cloth. "They gave Carey something to make her sleep. She's been out...since she brought you back. Did you know she did it all with a cracked kneecap? She must have been running on pure adrenaline. I don't know how you found that young woman, but I owe ev-everything... Without her..." Her lips tightened and she shook her head as if to rid herself of the unwanted thought.

Holy shit.

Lily's gaze nailed him to the pillow. "And by all that's holy, I expect you to do the right thing by her when you see her again. You *are* seeing her again, aren't you?" She took a deep breath and visibly calmed herself. "If Carey Magennis belongs anywhere, it's in this family."

His diaphragm clenched against the painful urge to laugh.

Lily had gifts she didn't even know about. Gifts that had probably saved her life when she'd taken her small children to flee her ex-husband all those years ago. No wonder she'd managed to stay one step ahead of him until the law had put him out of their lives for good.

Oh yeah, Mom. I'm seeing her again. Don't worry about that. If, after everything that had happened, she still wanted to see him. His brow knotted at the thought.

"Good." She seemed completely unaware she was having a conversation with her half-conscious son. Likely she was too exhausted to make the connection.

A dark-haired head floated into his line of vision.

"Ms. Brannon. It's time to go."

Lily set her jaw and ignored Daira. "They say we have to leave this place. But—"

"It can't be helped, Lily." Daira's voice was soft, but firm.

It's all right, Mom. I'll be along soon. I always healed fast, remember?

"I know, I know," Lily muttered, and Troy wasn't sure which of them she was answering. She leaned down and placed a firm, matter-of-fact kiss on his forehead.

Troy squeezed his eyes shut and his throat worked fruitlessly to get a sound past the tube. The machine beeped a warning at him.

She leaned close to get in one last zinger before Daira resorted to a headlock to get her moving.

"When you get out of here, if you show up on my doorstep without Carey, I will be very disappointed in you, son. Got it?"

Troy tried to smile and managed a single wink.

Lily straightened and squared her shoulders. As she turned toward the door, Troy caught sight of Quincy passing by, carrying a blanket with Carey's wild hair spilling from where her head rested on his shoulder.

The breathing machine beeped another warning as Troy pulled against his restraints.

Quincy paused and cast him a comically irritated look. "Settle down, Brannon. She's under our protection now. She's not going anywhere you won't find her."

Fatigue dimmed Troy's consciousness and he had no choice but to let himself sink into it.

Fuckin' a, baby.

Chapter Fifteen

Carey fingered the thick envelope containing the freshly signed contract to start teaching next semester at Quallah High School, on the Eastern Band Cherokee reservation. On impulse, she kissed it and slipped it into the mailbox, closed the door and raised the red metal flag for the mail carrier. The semester had already started, but there would be an opening after Christmas break. She had jumped on it with both feet.

By then, she hoped, the nightmares would be fading. If not, at least she had someone to fall back on. More than one someone. A whole new family that had all but adopted her into their noisy, complicated midst.

Jared and Taylor had turned the renovation of Stephen Powell's beach house completely over to Lily and were spending time in Marietta, Ohio, searching for traces of what had happened to Jared's mother, sister and missing brother, Ethan. Much to Jared's frustration, Taylor still balked at tying the knot, at least until her brother was well enough to be her man of honor.

Ross remained with Lily for now while he healed from grief that had been too-long delayed. Once she was sure both Taylor and Troy were going to be all right, Lily had thrown herself into what she was best at—making his life interesting. In the weeks since their ordeal, Ross had been integral in clearing the legal hurdles that let Carey move into the cabin on her Smoky Mountain property.

Daira dropped by every few days to continue working with her, making sure she wasn't still taking off on spontaneous joyrides of astral travel. But since her auric separation from Troy, it hadn't happened again. Oh, she daydreamed—and nightdreamed—about him constantly, but her soul had stayed right where it belonged. Much to her regret. What she would have given to fly through her dreams to be with him once again.

Patience. Daira said he would show up sooner than I expect.

Not that she expected an appearance anytime soon. With injuries like his, and the fact he'd manage to survive in a shifted state for almost a year and a half, he was probably not only recovering but dealing with life as a lab rat.

Carey grinned. She hadn't known Troy long, but she knew enough about him to know he'd find a way to wiggle out of that situation as fast as possible. In fact, he could be right next to her, watching her right now. Silent. Invisible.

The thought sent a delicious shiver down her spine.

Patience. This one is worth the wait.

She felt in her jeans pocket for the small gift Lily had given her before she'd left the beach house for her new home. A brass button from Troy's own Civil War re-enacting uniform. It was tradition, Lily had said with a sparkle in her eye, for a soldier's woman to carry one.

Carey would have to look that one up to see if it was true, but she liked the idea.

She rested a hand on the mailbox and tilted her head to catch the autumn sun, drinking in the cool, hemlock-scented air.

These days, she often had a sense of being watched, but

not in a creeped-out way. Even if it was only because of what she knew about SpIRIT, knowing Matthias Andros was nearby helped her sleep better at night. Daira had let it slip that Matthias had volunteered to be the first of what would be a long line of watchers, as he felt personally responsible for letting Kyle get close to her in the first place.

The fact that he had somehow failed to track down Lane was probably a factor, as well. He'd either been busted down a few ranks, or he was watching Carey in hopes of catching his quarry.

She grinned to herself. Lane had come and gone more than once, right under the man's nose. Apparently Taylor and Troy weren't the only Brannons with an inherited talent. Lane had discovered hers only when she'd experienced the sheer terror of seeing her family and friends being "kidnapped" in the dead of night by a pack of black-clad, shapeshifting commandos. For now, Carey chose to amuse herself by watching the two of them play cat and mouse.

She shook her head, smiling as she prepared to climb the long slope that led to the cabin on her piece of the Great Smoky Mountains. In the past several weeks, nothing had given her more pleasure than to pull the sold sign out of the ground and chop it up for firewood. Nothing, perhaps, except knowing that Kyle Thorpe would soon be spending a good chunk of the next decade in prison. His mouth-foaming ravings about werewolves practically guaranteed that if prison didn't work out for him, an extended stay in Holly Hill would.

From somewhere down the mountain road, she thought she heard the low, throaty growl of an engine grinding its way up the steep grade.

In spite of herself, she withdrew behind the safety of a thick hickory trunk, brushing at spider webs as she retreated. She waited, heart pounding in her ears and prickles of alarm racing along her skin.

The mail carrier's four wheel drive didn't sound anything like what was coming.

Whatever it was, the engine sounded terrible. Twice she heard it sputter and die, only to come to life again after repeated attempts to restart it. Her mouth quirked in amusement and she stepped out from behind the tree. Anyone intending her harm probably wouldn't be making enough racket to scare away half the fauna on the mountain. Besides, if anything dangerous came near her, Matthias would intervene.

She propped an elbow on the mailbox and waited, curious.

A trickle of a familiar awareness worked its way down her spine and settled low in her abdomen. She closed her eyes to pay attention to it...and noticed flashes of green lightning behind her eyelids.

She straightened away from the mailbox and found herself walking down the road toward the sound of the approaching engine.

With another rev of power, the front wheel of the machine appeared around the curved, rocky edge of the steep roadcut. Then it stalled again. A Harley. Chrome and what could only be described as Dark Victory Red. She couldn't see its rider, but the voice swearing the air blue was unmistakable.

Heart tripping over itself, she broke into a run, ignoring the lingering soreness in her bruised thigh and damaged knee, souvenirs of the events that had changed her life.

She rounded the curve and slid to a halt as their gazes met.

He sat on the machine, head defiantly helmetless. He was much thinner than she remembered. His lion-colored hair longer.

His gaze swept her hungrily from head to toe. "This is what happens when your engine sits in storage too long."

She shifted her weight to one leg and crossed her arms, faking nonchalance while her heart rate accelerated along with the moisture production in her tear ducts. "Need a ride? My car's right up the hill."

He cocked his head, mouth slanted in a devastatingly sexy half smile. "Professional badasses such as myself always give the chick the ride, not the other way around. Climb on."

Attitude? He was giving her attitude? "I am not getting on that thing. You're apt to miss my driveway and end up on a one-way trip down the Tail of the Dragon."

He grinned at her reference to the infamously twisty mountain road that dumped out not far from here. "Just wrap your legs around me and hang on, honey. You'll love it."

She shrugged. "Okay." She'd given in far too easily, but she was beyond waiting any longer to be in his arms. Her belly tight with nerves and need, she strolled toward him, letting her hips lead the way.

What a picture she must make, she thought to herself. Carey Magennis, mild-mannered school teacher, was willingly walking toward what had to be one of the most dangerous men on the planet. Ready to give herself completely to him, body and soul. Feeling safer than she'd ever felt with Kyle, who had oozed perfect-catch on the surface, but had been rotten to the core underneath.

She knew better now. She'd take badass over black-hearted any day.

Troy held out his hand and she slipped hers into it, halting for a few moments to search the shadowed hollows of his too-thin face. Something broke in his expression and he pulled her into his arms, balancing the bike with both feet as she leaned into him, burying her face in the crook of his neck. He smelled of mountain air and clean sweat.

"So...who sprung you from the joint, cowboy?"

An infinitesimal pause, undetectable to anyone who hadn't dealt daily with students. "I heal fast. They let me out this morning."

She snorted. "Try again."

She felt the muscles in his neck move as he grinned. He drew back and his eyes roamed over her face. He tucked a curl behind her ear, letting his fingers trail down her neck as if checking for lingering evidence of the bruises Kyle had given her.

"You're even more beautiful in real life, you know that?"

She ruffled his hair and tried not to let her gaze linger too long on the new lines around his eyes and mouth, etched there by what he had suffered. "Cut the crap, Brannon."

"Let's just say I found out today I can still shift."

She slid one hand under his leather jacket and ran it lightly down his chest, feeling the thick, stiff tape wrapped around his torso.

"Are you okay?"

He buried his nose in her hair and inhaled like a man still getting used to using his five senses again. "I am now. Will be, anyway. There's a rib and part of a lung missing, but all the vital parts are intact."

She shuddered and his arms tightened around her.

"The last time I saw you, someone was up to their elbow in your chest cavity."

He stroked her back. Was there a slight tremor in his hands? "It's over now. It's all good." Apparently that was all he was going to say about it for now. "I've been given a new assignment."

She leaned back and wiped her nose on her sleeve, afraid to blink lest he somehow vanish again. "Oh?"

His eyes, a clearer green than she remembered in her altered state of consciousness, sparkled at her. "Apparently there's someone on the loose in these mountains who knows way too much about a certain special-ops organization. She needs to be watched."

"Really." Amusement stretched the word out about a half a mile.

His gaze dropped to her lips, which tingled with anticipation. "Constantly. Twenty-four-seven."

She laughed. "Yeah. You know those history teachers. Subversives, the lot of 'em—"

His head swooped down and his mouth caught hers, swallowing whatever she'd planned to say next. The kiss didn't last long. He pulled away first, one hand on his ribs as he drew in careful breaths. "Sorry. What lungs are left are a little out of practice."

She realized it couldn't be good for him, holding up the bike on the steep road while she leaned on it—and him. "Can this heap make it up to the cabin?"

"Which heap, me or the Harley?"

"Whichever has the least amount of rust." She climbed on the back as he successfully brought the engine to throbbing life. She buried her face in the warm hollow between his shoulder blades and took comfort in the interplay of his very real muscles as he worked the bike the last hundred yards up the mountain.

As she crossed the threshold of the cabin ahead of him, a

sudden attack of self-consciousness assaulted her. This felt...normal. So far, nothing about her relationship with Troy could be described as normal. Her body had throbbed day and night with eagerness to be in his arms again, but now that he stood before her, she was almost afraid to touch him.

Absurdly, she feared the force of the desire brewing in her belly would be too much for the wounded, whip-thin man in front of her. She fidgeted as she watched his gaze sweep the simple interior of her new home.

"Nice."

"It's a work in progress. At least I've got hot and cold running water now. You've seen your Mom?" *Oh, good, Carey. Way to kill the moment. Get him to talk about his Mom.*

He shook his head and shed his jacket, tossing it over the back of a ladderback chair. "Not yet."

A little jolt of surprise made her blink. He'd come to see her before anyone else? Her babbling gear engaged. "You must be tired. And hungry. Are you hungry? I can...um..."

His gaze finished its circuit of the room and came to rest on her. He certainly looked *hungry*. She forgot the rest of the sentence.

"There's something we started a while back that I'd like to finish, first. If you don't mind." His eyes glittered and turned dark as a night forest as he advanced on her like a big, stalking lion.

Her nipples beaded under her light sweater as his gaze swept over her breasts. "My bed's up in the loft." Why play hard to get, she reasoned, when she really didn't want to?

His surprise and pleasure registered plainly in the wicked smile that lifted the corners of his mouth. He shook his head. "Climbing anything higher than a barstool isn't an option for me right now."

He reached a long arm behind her head and undid the giant claw clasp holding back her hair. It tumbled down around her shoulders.

"I've got one of those," she said huskily. "Right over—"

His head ducked down and she met him halfway, devouring his kiss, letting him back her up step by step until her rear end collided with the edge of the plank dining table.

He tasted like heaven.

He broke the kiss first, breathing hard with his forehead resting against hers. "I couldn't stay away another second." His smart-ass veneer was gone, revealing the expression of a man letting all of himself dangle in front of her, vulnerable. It was a precious sight she suspected no one outside his own family had ever seen.

She ran her hands into his hair, fighting a sob. "I'm glad."

"I hope you didn't think I wasn't coming."

"Not a chance."

He kissed her again, slowly, as if he was afraid of breaking her. Of losing this moment.

She meant to be careful with him, owing to his condition. Good intentions went out the window as the intensity of the kiss, the urgency of his touch, built into a frenzy of need.

Once she had read a romance novel and laughed at the way the hero and heroine's clothing had magically "melted away", but now she totally got it. Her sweater and bra were gone, and her jeans were well on the way to following suit. All, it seemed, with barely a break from his lips. She grasped two handfuls of his T-shirt and tried to be gentle as she peeled it up and over his head, but he was having none of it.

His breath hitched only once when he lifted his arms, but it didn't stop him from flinging the offending garment to one side and yanking her jeans the rest of the way off. Or from propping his hands on either side of her hips and nuzzling his way under her hair, sucking the skin of her neck while she tackled his belt buckle and zipper.

Sliding her fingers under his waistband—noting with a thrill that he wore no boxers—she worked his jeans down just far enough to free his cock. His breath hissed through his teeth as she wrapped one hand around him. He'd never felt this warm in any of their astral encounters.

"Slow," he groaned, holding her wrist when she would have started caressing him. "You don't want me...falling down."

She caught his earlobe in her teeth and did as he asked, again marveling at how quickly and easily her sexual self opened completely to him. Hell, to her. Things had never been like this—she had never been like this—with anyone else.

"What's the matter?" she said playfully. "No gas?"

He filled his hands with her breasts, his thumbs doing things to her nipples that stole her breath and forced the muscles of her back to contract, pushing herself deeper into his touch. She moved her other hand down to his cock, taking time to explore every contour with the sensitive pads of her fingers.

"No transmission fluid," he replied, bending to taste the tip of one of her aching breasts. "It takes time to build...oh, man, keep doing it just like that...time to build blood volume back. Right now you could say I'm robbing Peter to pay Paul. Jesus, who taught you to do that?"

Instantly she stilled, echoes of Kyle's voice coming back to haunt her, accusing her of infidelity the one time she had been the least bit spontaneous in bed.

Troy lifted his head and studied her, his eyes seeing too much. She shook off the memory and reached up to pull his lips down to hers, but he took her shoulders and set her back.

"Youse want I should whack him for youse, gorgeous?" His faux mobster accent tickled her ears, but the steel set of his jaw told her he was far from kidding. The thought that this man would do whatever it took to protect her chased away the rest of the shadows in her soul.

She boldly brought his hands back to her breasts. "Maybe later."

He held them as if fascinated by their weight and texture. "Got a confession to make," he said, still focused on her breasts.

"Uh-oh." She tried to pay attention to his voice as he ran one hand down her thigh to the small, fresh scar on her knee.

"Daira told me about the chipped knee cap. It's kinda my fault." He said this against the sensitive skin just under her ear.

She'd forgive him almost anything if he'd just keep doing that...but...

She pushed on his shoulders so she could see his eyes. "How so?"

Did he have the blood volume for the ruddy stain on his cheekbones?

He blew out a breath and met her gaze. "I asked Daira to plant a suggestion for the next time Kyle tried anything."

She stared at him, stunned. "That was your doing?"

"Uh...yeah. Look, I'm... It wasn't so much me controlling you. It was more of a message from me to him. A little taste of what he can expect if he ever thinks about touching you again."

She tried to keep a lid on the mirth bubbling up out of her belly, if only to prolong the priceless kid-caught-in-the-act look on his face. She leaned in close and looped her arms around his neck.

"Soooo...that's all ya got?"

He blinked.

"There's nothing else you can think up that you'd like me to do? Right now? I heard you military types had no imagination, but—"

Abruptly he dropped to his knees. "Oh my God, Troy, are you all ri... Oh my God. Never mind..."

He'd grasped her hips and pulled her to the very edge of the table. One tug disposed of her delicate, lacy underwear. His hot breath swelled the sensitive flesh between her legs. Then his lips and tongue went to work, doing things to her core that shouldn't be legal. She cried out and fell back, supporting herself with one hand while grasping at his hair with the other. Her feet came off the floor, and she draped her legs over his impossibly broad shoulders.

Sweat broke out on her body as his mouth drove her to heights she'd only dreamed about.

Dimly she observed that it was broad daylight and all her windows were wide open. She didn't care. Likely Matthias had made himself scarce as soon as Troy's Harley hit the foot of the mountain. Cool air goose-bumped her skin as she closed her eyes and licked her lips, tightening her fingers in Troy's hair to hold him steady when he hit a really good spot. Her hips rocked involuntarily against his tongue, and she felt fire ignite deep in her womb.

"Troy...please..."

Amid the haze of mindless pleasure gripping her body, she heard the sound of a packet being ripped open. Heard Troy's muffled groan as he worked the condom over his cock.

He rose to his feet gripped her hips. "I'm not going to last very long this time, darlin'," he rasped, his expression an almost-funny mixture of passion and apology. "Stamina isn't my middle name right now."

"I don't care," she said breathlessly. She wrapped her legs around his waist, filled her hands with his amazing butt and brought him home.

And bit her lip against the involuntary tears that formed behind her tightly clenched eyelids as he filled her to the hilt.

He went perfectly still. "Lord. Wow."

Wow? Troy actually had that ingenuous word in his vocabulary? She almost laughed, but forgot about it when he began to thrust. In and out. Deliciously slow, as if he meant to savor each and every tiny moment. She sought out and found his mouth, and he fed on her like she was his last meal. Or his first one in a long time.

"Bite me," he mumbled against her lips.

"What?" She tried to get him to stop talking by filling his mouth with her tongue.

He turned his face an inch to one side. "Bite my lip. Bite my ear. Do something to distract me before I—"

But she was already writhing against him, deep, rhythmic spasms taking control of her body, the words escaping her lips a good deal more raw than *wow*. He took them all in his mouth as he tipped over the edge with her, shuddered violently in her arms, stole breath from her lungs when his own ran short.

In the sweaty aftermath, he sagged forward and she held him up, taking his solid, satisfying weight willingly against her body. A few more pounds of muscle, she mused, and he'd have them both tumbling to the split-log floor.

Still panting, she turned her head to his ear and whispered a request to bite something of hers that, she noted with satisfaction, almost caused his knees to buckle for real this time.

"I'm not sure that's legal in this state, sweetheart," he said on a deep groan. "Unless we were married."

She leaned back a little and looked at him in wonder. He cocked his head to one side, no trace of amusement on his face.

"You have a really great life ahead of you, Carey. Mind if I stay in it a while?"

Her tears finally spilled over. "Stay as long as you like. I'm not going anywhere."

He grinned and wrapped his arms around her. "Thank God. I didn't want to face Mom if I showed up at the house without you."

She wiped her eyes, marveling at how deftly he managed to keep her off balance. "Tough guy, huh?"

"You *have* met my mother, right?"

She shifted and blushed. "Can we not talk about your mom when we're, um..."

He straightened, devilment dancing in his eyes. "What? This?" He moved his hips and her walls clenched around him. Despite his doubts about his stamina, she felt him begin to harden inside her. "Wondering if my imagination goes any further than the kitchen table?"

He leaned in close and tickled her ear with his lips, causing a shudder to work its way down her body. "Wanna try something?"

She ran her hands over his chest, above the tape, and noted that her fingertips left goose bumps on his skin. "Does it involve getting horizontal?"

"My kind of woman." The shadows under his eyes belied the sexy gravel in his voice.

"Couch." She slid off the table and wedged herself under his arm. Concern flickered through her awareness as he leaned more than a little of his weight on her as they moved across the room toward the piece of furniture in question. She'd bought the huge, overstuffed couch with Troy's height and wide shoulders in mind. Clearly it had been worth the investment.

"Are you sure you didn't leave the facility too soon?"

He gave one short, sharp shake of his head. "I'm good. Just need gravity to re-establish blood flow to the brain. C'mere." With one arm around her waist, he brought her down with him onto the couch. In a moment they were lying face to face, bodies entwined. As she reached across him to pull a blanket off the backrest, he slid a hand along her thigh, curved his fingers behind her knee and brought her leg up over his hip.

"Never mind. It's probably not a good idea right now, anyway. My aim might be a little off."

"Aiming for...?" She snuggled closer, savoring the warm, real contact they'd been long denied. Her body hungered for his again, but she sensed he had something else on his mind. No matter. For once, time was on their side.

"An experiment. In astral travel."

She went still. "I don't any more. Daira said..."

He was watching her with that look in his eye again. "Not against your will. But I bet you can still do it. We already know you have the control."

"You can't, I presume."

"Haven't tried. I figured it would be safer if we tried it together."

At separate points in the last few months, they had held each other's lives in their hands. Instinct told her there was every reason to trust his motives.

She took a deep breath and laid a hand on his stubbled jawline. "What did you have in mind?"

Surprise, then excitement chased across his mobile face.

One corner of his mouth hitched upward.

"Remember Genola?"

Carey raised up on one elbow to look down at him, temporarily distracted from the increasing evidence that his blood flow had, indeed, been re-established to a certain part of his body. "Of course I do. We've been exchanging letters."

Troy tenderly pulled one of her curls out of the corner of her mouth. "We both owe her a debt of gratitude. I think it's time we repaid it."

Chapter Sixteen

"You can open your eyes now. We're here. And *ow*, you can let go too."

Carey obeyed the first request, but ignored the second and continued gripping Troy's hands until she was sure. The air smelled right, of the ocean. The colors of the dark, mist-damp rocks and long, green slopes crisscrossed with neglected, tumble-down stone walls looked right, as well. The Irishness of the landscape was unmistakable.

"You're sure this is it?"

"I knew the exact date, and SpIRIT has records of wind, weather and ocean currents that go back at least four centuries. Remember, I had several weeks at the facility to lay around and do nothing but research." He leaned in close and leered at her. "And think about getting in your pants."

Reminded that in the two weeks they'd been back together he was nowhere near back to full strength, she ignored his attempt to distract her and searched his expression for signs of distress. He was inordinately good at hiding it—except for the nights he'd wake up in a cold sweat of memories. "Even here, where no one remembers these abandoned islands' names?"

He nodded, tucking one of her hands into the pocket of his leather jacket, twining his fingers with hers. "If he's not here, he's on the next one to the southwest. Between my research and Daira's pendulum, we should be dead-on."

She shivered in spite of herself, suddenly not at all sure this caper of theirs was a good idea. "Can we refrain from the 'dead' reference, please?"

He grinned down at her. "You've been through worse. This is a vacation compared to—"

She cut him off before he could remind her of the gory details. "I know, but who knows what shape he's going to be in when we find him? If we find him."

"I bet he'll look better than I did, and that didn't bother you, now did it? Come on, let's go. If there's anything left of the *Lady G*, it'll be on this side."

He moved off down the coastline, and with her hand in his pocket she had no choice but to follow. She had made him vow to never let go of her while they were on this experiment in astral travel. She wanted to take no chances. Or at least as few as possible. Living with Troy had made her braver, but not *that* brave.

Minutes later, she pointed. "Is that it?"

The battered, rusted corpse of what used to be a thirty-foot vessel lay on its side among a jumble of boulders. It looked like it had been there every bit of the forty years since its sinking.

"We'll find out." He picked up his pace, and she resisted the urge to dig in her heels. Then he stopped cold in his tracks. "Look."

"What?" She focused on the wreck. And felt her mouth sag open as the ghost of a stocky, redhaired young man stepped right through the rust-streaked hull and stood regarding them warily.

"Try not to scare him," Troy muttered out of the side of his mouth.

She punched his arm. "Me?"

They approached slowly, Troy showing his free hand in a friendly gesture. "Seamus? Seamus McCarthy?"

The man crossed his brawny arms and peered at them from under the brim of his cap. "An' who would you be?" His rich Irish brogue carried over the sounds of ocean and wind.

He hadn't denied who he was. Carey's heart beat faster and her fear melted away. She stepped forward and held out her hand toward him.

"My name is Carey. And this is Troy. We've come to take you home."

Seamus's mask of caution evaporated, only to be replaced with sadness. He hesitantly touched her fingers, then examined them with surprise.

"You're...like me. *An taibhse.*"

Troy squeezed her hand. They had been afraid Seamus wouldn't realize he was a ghost, that he would think himself shipwrecked and was simply waiting to be rescued.

"Our spirits are here with you," Troy put in before she could answer. "That's what's important."

Seamus nodded and let her fingers slip from his. "Then you are luckier than I. I have tried to cross the water, go home to my wife. I cannot." He stared in the direction of Genola's house. Even in death, he was ever the seaman. He knew by instinct precisely where he was. His haunted gaze took them both in. "I will not go on without her. They've tried to make me, but I have refused. Not until I know she no longer walks this earth."

Carey's heart ached for him. "She does."

Hope edged into his expression. "You'll be knowin' my wife?"

She nodded and smiled encouragingly. "Genola brought us

together." She disengaged her left hand from Troy's—who subtly grabbed a handful of the back of her jacket—and showed Seamus the sparkling emerald on her ring finger.

He grinned and laughed, slapping his thigh. "My Gennie. She always fancied herself the matchmaker."

Troy once again took possession of her hand. "We think we can take you to her. But there's something you have to realize..."

The merriment was gone in a flash, and irritation took its place. "You think I don't know how long I have been here? I know the movements of the sun and moon as well as the back of me own hand." He waved the appendage in question. "I know she is old, grey. I do not care."

He stepped forward, and Troy instinctively moved between him and Carey. She knew he couldn't help it, and she touched his arm in reassurance before moving around him.

"We don't know if this will work. But if you trust us, we're willing to try. For Genola. We owe her that much."

Seamus spread his arms wide. "What have I to lose? Here, the bottom of the sea...even heaven. It doesn't matter—it will be hell without her."

Troy cleared his throat and fidgeted. Carey sensed he was getting antsy about being gone from their physical bodies too long. She was reluctant to rush things with Seamus, but he took the decision out of her hands when he stepped forward, holding his out toward them.

She looked up at Troy, and he nodded. They each took one of Seamus's hands.

"Now I want you to visualize where you want to go. Then just relax, let us do the work and we'll be there in—"

Before she could finish the sentence, she blinked and

found they were standing on the headland just below Genola's house. Seamus opened his eyes, took one look around and with a shout threw his arms around both of them. Only Troy's quick reflexes kept them all from tumbling to the thick, springy grass.

Seamus drew back, gave their shoulders one last shake while he grinned at them wordlessly. Then he turned around, shoved his hands in his pockets and ambled up the hill whistling a cheerful tune.

Carey clung to Troy's arm, still trying to get her bearings. She was quite sure she'd never made a jump that fast, not even when she's been afraid for Troy's life.

Troy regained the power of speech first. Sort of. "Holy... That was...fast."

"Warp speed," she croaked. Then she caught sight of the front door of Genola's house opening. She shook his arm. "Look..."

Genola appeared in the doorway, lifting her hand to shade her eyes from the sun that had suddenly broken through the clouds. Seamus, still whistling, hat tilted at a jaunty angle, lifted a hand in greeting. As if he'd only been gone for a day, not forty years.

Her searching eyes finally found him, and her hand dropped to her chest as if to make sure her heart was still beating. In an instant, four decades seemed to fall away from her careworn face.

Tears gathered in Carey's eyes as Troy looped an arm across her shoulders. She rose on tiptoe to murmur into his ear, "We should go."

He swallowed, clearly fighting not to join her in the waterworks. "Yeah."

In a flash that seemed eons slower than Seamus's speed-of-light trip, Carey found herself exactly where she'd been when they'd set out on their mission. Lying in Troy's arms in their bed.

She sank her fingers into his jacket collar. "We. Are never. Doing this again."

No answer. Just wheels turning behind his green eyes, which sparkled like a kid with a new toy to figure out.

She wiped her eyes and narrowed them at him. "Right?"

He shrugged. "Okay."

She scowled at his too-quick agreement. "I mean it."

"I hear you. Seriously." Clearly bent on distraction, dove for her mouth and moved to roll on top of her.

Something small and hard inside his jacket poked her in the chest.

"Ow, what's that?" Wiggling out from under him, she snaked her hand inside the black leather and, before he could stop her, dipped her fingers into an internal pocket. She hooked a fingertip into the object and pulled it out.

She dangled it between them. The light caught the shine on the heavy gold ring embedded with a smooth, black onyx stone.

He propped his head on one hand and waited for her question, making no move to take the ring from her.

She sat up and faced him with her legs folded beneath her, turning the ring in her hands. Tilted just so, a silver spiral glowed from deep within the stone's ebony depths.

"And this is..." she prompted.

"Everybody on the DL gets one."

"D...The disabled list?"

He took in a deep breath, held it. Then released it slowly. "Apparently there's no place in the field for a man who's missing a piece of a lung."

"So they've cut you loose." She knew she ought to feel relieved he was out of the worst of the danger. Instead, she felt crushed for him.

One side of his mouth kicked up, but he didn't seem quite willing to meet her eyes. "Not at all. I haven't decided if I'm going to accept it."

"That's crazy. You'd leave? Just like that?"

"Darlin', I ain't cut out for a desk job."

Was she actually hearing this? She leaned forward and pushed a finger into his chest. "Those teams in the field need someone on their six who won't give up on them. Someone who's been to the ass end of hell and back."

He smiled at her tenderly. "Those cussing lessons are paying off."

"You should hear the words Choo is teaching me."

He grimaced. "No thanks. They say when Choo curses, every man within a fifty mile radius loses their testicles."

She grinned and held the ring out to him. "Just tell me you'll think it through. See, I have a thing for a guy in uniform. I'm not sure I'm quite ready to see you take it off. Unless it's me doing the taking."

To her relief, he nodded thoughtfully and held out his hand. She placed the ring in his palm and closed his fingers over it.

"I'll need you to think it through, too, Carey."

"Why?" For her, there was nothing to consider. No matter what he decided, she was all in.

"This thing we just did for Genola and Seamus...it could be something useful for SpIRIT. Getting into places with minimal risk."

Lucky for Carey she wasn't eating or drinking anything, or

she would have spewed. “After what we’ve been though? Define *minimal*.”

“But it takes two of us,” he went on. “I need someone at my back, as well—and you’re the only one who can do it.” He was wearing that look on his face again, the one that told her he was waiting for her to make the decision for herself. The one that without words promised her soul, *Come with me. You’ll be safe.*

She couldn’t believe the next words that came out of her mouth. “I won’t give up teaching.”

A light ignited in his eyes at her almost-yes. “No one’s asking you to. We’ll figure it out.”

She took a deep breath and moved to wrap her body around him once again, running her hands over the pounds of rock-solid muscle he’d put on in the two weeks she’d been feeding him up. “Okay. I’ll think about it.”

His expression, a pleasing mix of admiration and respect, warm-fuzzied her heart. “Yeah?”

“Yeah.”

He regarded her silently for a long moment, dangerous grin playing about his mouth. Then he rolled her to her back and kissed her deep into the pillow.

About the Author

Carolan Ivey is a North Carolina native living in Ohio with her husband, two children and two highly opinionated dachshunds. When she isn't writing, she's traveling, herb gardening and exploring her Celtic ancestry through music.

Web site: www.carolanivey.com

Blog: http://carolanivey.blogspot.com

Newsletter mailing list: http://groups.yahoo.com/group/wild-ivey

Myspace: http://myspace.com/carolanivey

Contact: carolanivey@yahoo.com

GREAT CHEAP FUN

Discover eBooks!

THE FASTEST WAY TO GET THE HOTTEST NAMES

Get your favorite authors on your favorite reader, long before they're out in print! Ebooks from Samhain go wherever you go, and work with whatever you carry—Palm, PDF, Mobi, and more.

SAMHAIN PUBLISHING LTD

WWW.SAMHAINPUBLISHING.COM

LaVergne, TN USA
25 October 2009
161971LV00006BB/2/P

9 781605 044125